ONE DEGREE OVER

Colin M. Andrews

Published by New Generation Publishing in 2018

Copyright © Colin M. Andrews 2018

First Edition

The author asserts the moral right under the Copyright, Designs and Patents Act 1988 to be identified as the author of this work.

This is a work of fiction. Names, characters, businesses, places, events, locales, and incidents are either the products of the author's imagination or used in a fictitious manner. Any resemblance to actual persons, living or dead, or actual events is purely coincidental.

All Rights reserved. No part of this publication may be reproduced, stored in a retrieval system or transmitted, in any form or by any means without the prior consent of the author, nor be otherwise circulated in any form of binding or cover other than that in which it is published and without a similar condition being imposed on the subsequent purchaser.

www.newgeneration-publishing.com

 New Generation Publishing

*This book is dedicated to my son, Gareth,
my daughter-in-law, Sandra, and my granddaughter, Iris.*

Chapter 1

Given a clear run free from tractors and flocks of sheep, my journey took about three-quarters of an hour. Even so I'd set out in good time from the house I shared with a friend. We lived a couple of miles from Tencastle, a rural outpost of the University of Wales where we'd both taken our B.Ed. degree.

In the damp September morning the grey sandstone walls of Sir Wilfred Roberts Grammar School, in the small market town of Carrick Major, seemed particularly drab and uninviting. No children, either, to break the foreboding silence and bring life and laughter to the premises. I was considerably more nervous than on my first visit, nearly a year ago. It was totally illogical, I suppose, since I now knew far more about the place. Then my attendance had been required for a fixed, short term, and my responsibilities limited, with allowances made for inexperience. Now I was entering a career as a full-time member of staff, albeit on a temporary contract.

Most of the other teachers had already gathered in the staffroom for the pre-term meeting. Nick Ramsbottom, my Head of Department and mentor from my time on teaching practice, waved an arm in greeting and gestured to a spare seat at the other end of a table. My arrival was acknowledged by a few other familiar faces but I didn't know most of the forty or so other members of staff, having had minimal contact, if any, with them during the previous autumn.

"The prodigal son returns!" John Rhys-Price, the irreverent physical education guru, slapped me on the back as I took the seat in front of him. "How's the dry-stone walling coming along?"

"I'll stick to the day job," I answered briefly. John was not a person to whom one imparted unnecessary information, as he'd soon fabricate a whole story. He'd blown out of all proportion a minor incident in which I had needed to remove a few stones from a wall, even if it was indirectly my fault that the coach full of kids had become stuck in a narrow lane in the first place.

The hubbub of chatter ceased as the Headmaster entered the staffroom, followed by his deputy, Eric Rigby, and senior mistress, Moira Bunn. Dr Melville O. Bedford-Dickson - 'sir', to his face by staff and boys, and 'Moby Dick', behind his back - cut an imposing figure dressed in an immaculate dark suit, bow tie and full academic gown. I couldn't imagine even his wife - I'm sure he was married - addressing him as 'Mel, dear', such was his self-important formal stature. Pompous, one might say.

"Please be seated," he began, superfluously since we were all sitting down anyway and protocol obviously didn't require staff to stand when he entered a room. In his rich, plummy voice that still held a distinctly Welsh inflexion he delivered a few homilies which trusted that we were all fully refreshed after the long summer break, ready to tackle the challenges of the new academic year,

"Says the same thing every year," John muttered in my ear. "Supposed to be a briefing but he doesn't do brief."

As a newcomer, I suppose I should have listened intently to what the Head had to say. However, after twenty minutes or so of a monologue with references to new educational initiatives, alternative funding and whatever, my attention began to wander, studying the faces of my new colleagues and contemplating the view over the town centre rooftops.

Until I heard my name mentioned.

"...welcome Mr Robert Kiddecott who will be replacing Mrs Pagitter while she is... er... ah, indisposed..."

"Why can't he just say she's pregnant, for God's sake," whispered John.

"... remember him from his teaching practice last

year."

I raised my hand in acknowledgement, for those who didn't recognise me.

"We also welcome Miss Milward as our new permanent Head of Music. You will remember that her predecessor, Mr Pintwhistle, was called away unexpectedly last term to attend to a family crisis."

So that's the story he gave, I thought. Tim Pintwhistle had been discovered in flagrante with a nubile sixth-former on a field trip I'd helped with at Easter. For the girl's sake Moira Bunn had covered up the incident but made it abundantly clear that Tim should not show his face in school again.

No-one in my field of vision identified herself as Miss Milward, so I presumed she must be at the back of the room, or not yet present.

Moby droned on for another half an hour at least, bringing us thankfully up to a coffee break.

John buttonholed me as soon as I arose from the chair. "Fancy a pint for lunch?" he asked. "Bull and Dragon, with Mark and Luke, for old time's sake?"

"Possibly," I said non-committedly, "but I've quite a bit to sort out before I head back to Tencastle."

"You still there? I thought you'd get something in Carrick. We've got a spare room, if you're interested."

"I've still got the use of my old digs until Christmas. We'll see what happens then." I didn't really relish a house share with John. His housemate and colleague, Terry 'Luke' Osborne, was okay, much more mild and even-tempered though by no means temperate. He enjoyed a few pints even though he was in charge of religious education. With John you could forget about privacy, since he was worse than a tabloid for spreading salacious gossip.

Nick Ramsbottom rescued me from further debate.

"Glad you were able to join us," he said, in his broad

Yorkshire accent. "Do I gather that you're staying put in Tencastle?"

"For the time being. The cottage I share is still available until the New Year."

"Is your old banger still up to the daily commute?"

"Jessica, you mean? The old girl's still chugging along." My old pink and black Ford Popular had only failed me on one occasion. But for that I might have ended up teaching in Sussex rather than in mid-Wales. "If my appointment here is made permanent, then I'd have to think again, I suppose."

Nick rubbed his stubbly chin. "Well, though I can't say definitely yet, there's a good chance that the job will be yours for as long as you want it. I'm pretty sure Jenny Pagitter will want to be a full time mum."

"Has she had her baby yet?" I asked.

"Any day now. She was due a week ago, but she was determined to hold out for a September birth!"

Draining his coffee, Nick suggested we head over to the science block, one of the most recent additions to the school buildings.

"Right, let's have a look at your timetable." In the small office, Nick's desk was piled high with folders and textbooks. Space was at a premium on the other two tables as well. "I've given you the lion's share of the lower school Chemistry, but you'll also have two CSE exam groups to yourself and a half of a lower-sixth A-level class. If Jenny does return it will mean less examination pressure on her, and also ease you into the job. Believe me, there's a lot to take on board in your first post!"

"Thanks, Nick." I'd been hoping for more examination work but I could appreciate his logic.

"And you'll also have form teacher responsibilities for a class of eleven-year-olds new to the delights of Wilfred Roberts."

"So I'll have a form room base elsewhere?"

"Nay, lad. The Head has decreed that in future our laboratories should also double as form rooms. With an increase in numbers I suppose he's under pressure for space, but I'm not happy about the implications."

I raised the delicate subject of laboratory assistants. I don't normally induce extreme reactions in people, but during my teaching practice one had fallen for me big time and the other I'd seriously pissed off, the feeling being mutual in the latter case.

"Aubrey Turner is still here but he'll show you grudging respect for having the balls to stand up to him."

"Did you get a replacement for Rosetta?"

"We did. Total disaster."

"Why?"

"Young buck thought he knew it all, but hadn't a clue about measuring out accurate quantities of reagents, and sometimes I doubt if he bothered to read the label on the bottles. It's a wonder we didn't have a major incident."

"Rosetta was a bit clumsy though."

"True, but she couldn't help it. This bugger didn't give a toss."

"How long did he last?"

"A few weeks. Last straw was when he started to tell me how to do my job."

"So the post is still vacant?"

"Not now. We made do once he'd left until we were able to get a suitably qualified person. Mrs Maxwell, you'll meet her when she starts tomorrow." Nick gave a wry smile. "She's a little older and more mature. I'm sure you'll be safe from unwanted attention."

Chapter 2

I'd been surprised to get a phone call from Jacob Moses, my erstwhile college housemate, barely a week after we'd said farewell at the graduation ceremony back in July.

"Have you sorted out digs in Carrick?" he'd asked.

"Not yet. Why?"

"Well, I've been in touch with our landlord. He's my cousin twice…"

"Yes, yes," I'd said impatiently, "I know all that."

"It seems he's not coming back from Australia until after Christmas. We can stay on at Ty Melin. If you want to, that is."

Ty Melin was a delightful former mill cottage in the hamlet of Penybont only a few minutes' drive from Tencastle. "That could work quite well," I'd said. "I'm only sure of a job until Christmas." I'd thought of a possible problem. Our other two former housemates had flown the nest. "Would it be just the two of us?"

"I'm working on that. Possibly one more. With us both working, we should be able to afford it though. What do you say?"

With a salary at the bottom of the teacher's pay scale and petrol for the daily round trip I certainly didn't expect to be affluent. I suspected Jake's remuneration as elected President of Tencastle Student's Union would be even more modest. But it would remove, or at least postpone the hassle of finding somewhere to rent in Carrick, and I'd be in a familiar environment.

"I'm up for it."

***

Since I'd arrived the previous evening, I'd seen very little of Jake. He'd had to dash off on his bike for a meeting at the Union. I'd been on the road to Carrick before he surfaced next morning. I purposely headed back to the cottage as soon as I could reasonably get away from the school, eager to catch up on what Jake had been up to over the summer. And no doubt he'd be keen for an update on my relationship with Dilys Morgan, the blind date he'd set up for me at the graduation ball.

"Anyone at home?" I called as I entered the cottage. No reply. "Jake, are you there?" I tried again and as I went into the lounge I realised I was addressing his backside. His head was peering up the chimney.

"What?" He flapped a hand at me. "Pass me that broom, will you?"

I looked round and saw a broomstick with a small hearth brush taped to one end. "This?"

"Yeah." He grabbed it, thrust it up the chimney and waggled it around. "It's ... Oh, shit!"

A huge pile of soot fell into the fireplace and a black cloud enveloped everything in the vicinity - including Jake. His shirt was now the same hue as his skin. Jake had probably inherited his long straight black hair from his mother, but his ebony skin was a legacy of the father he never knew.

"Er, why did you do that?" I asked.

"Heard a rustling. I thought perhaps a bird had got stuck in the chimney. I was trying to frighten it."

"Probably succeeded. Blackbird was it?"

"I dunno..." He coughed, and the penny dropped. "Oh, very funny!"

He stomped off to have a shower. I did my best with the vacuum cleaner to clear up the mess before he returned, hopefully in slightly better humour.

"What have you been up to over the summer?" I asked when we'd both got a glass of beer in hand.

"Oh, this and that, you know." Jake took a generous

swallow of amber nectar before elaborating. "I've tamed the dragon."

I raised an eyebrow. "I thought they were extinct in this part of Wales."

Jake missed the sarcasm. "Barbara Bowen-Martin, you remember?"

As if I could forget. A political animal, she'd got her come-uppance against Jake over an ill-considered objection to the blacked-up faces of our embryonic group of morris dancers in Tencastle. In a damaging display of mutual pig-headedness she'd also locked horns with the previous Union President.

"How..." I began, but Jake needed little encouragement to enlighten me.

"Well, it seemed pretty obvious to me that normal relationships between 'town and gown' needed to be restored. I couldn't see the first move coming from Madam Big-Mouth so I wrote to her. Stroked her ego a bit by recognising her important position in the town, and indicated my willingness to work together in resolving our differences."

Jake was good at turning bullshit into charm when necessary. "So did she bite?"

"Yes, though in very guarded terms. She wanted to involve a whole army of advisors."

"So what did you do?"

"I suggested an informal meeting, one-to-one, on neutral territory."

"And she agreed?"

"Eventually. I conceded that a follow-up in a more formal setting might be necessary."

"So where did you have your tête-a-tête?"

"Afternoon tea at the Rivers Hotel. Suitably up-market and not a place where she'd be likely to throw a wobbly."

"I bet it took more than cucumber sandwiches to stop her breathing fire and brimstone. After all, you once made her look very foolish in public."

"With Carpiog Morris, you mean? It's unlikely she would have made the connection with my name, but I was prepared for the penny to drop when she realised I was black. Before she had time to react, though, I was shaking her hand and welcoming her support for ethnic minorities..."

"Hypocrite!"

"... and apologised for the distress I must have caused her through standing up for my friends."

"Bloody hell, Jake, you'll be telling me next you kissed her arse! How did she take it?"

"Stoically, I guess. She could hardly have walked out on me without losing face." Jake drained his glass. "Fancy another one?"

When Jake returned from the kitchen with two more bottles of Brain's Best - not usually seen so deep into mid-Wales - I pressed him to continue.

"Well, we had a surprisingly productive discussion. She accepted my point that the college and the students make a considerable contribution to trade and employment in the town. I offered my support in principle for some of her social projects."

"Such as?"

"You don't really want to know. Pretty nebulous and probably unworkable in practice but what the hell?" Jake contemplated his glass of beer in silence for a few seconds. "Anyhow, enough of my ramblings! Tell me how you're getting on with Dilly."

I'd known Dilys Morgan since my first year in college but through a series of misunderstandings on both our parts, she and I hadn't really hit it off until the night of the Graduation Ball. It had been even more galling that there had remained so little time at college before we were obliged to go our separate ways. Dilly had declined my invitation to stay at my parents' farm in Devon during the summer. Her father, a professor of something, she'd told me, was taking the whole family with him on his extended lecture tour of America during the summer vacation. This also scuppered my hopes of a few days' holiday beside the sea at her home in Aberystwyth.

Just the one unforgettable evening was the sum of our relationship to date, apart from a brief encounter at the graduation ceremony where we were both in the restrictive company of our parents and siblings.

"Ring me when you're back in Wales," she'd said, with a modest farewell peck on the cheek.

I had hurriedly scribbled her number down on the receipt for the obligatory graduation photograph, and even transcribed it to my pocket diary that same evening, lest the piece of paper should have gone astray.

When Jake was out of earshot tackling a mountain of accumulated washing-up in the kitchen, I dialled the number in hopeful anticipation, and, I confess, with a little apprehension.

"Yes?" rasped a voice at the other end of the line.

"Is that the Morgan residence?" I enquired tentatively.

"Yes. What do you want?" The curt response was punctuated with a hacking cough.

"Could I speak to Dilys, please?"

"Phyllis? There's no Phyllis here!" he barked.

"It's Dilys… Dilly," I said patiently.

"You'll have to speak up, young man. What did you say your name was? Billy?"

I closed my eyes and took a deep breath. In the background I heard a female voice say, "What's up, Gramps, who is it?" followed by the reply, "Dunno, says his name's Billy." Christ, she hadn't told me she'd got a senile old grandfather. No reason to, I suppose.

"Hello, hello, can I help you?" a soft voice with lilting Welsh accent enquired. It didn't sound quite like Dilly though. However…

"It's Rob here. Is that you, Dilly?" I said hopefully.

"N...no." She sounded puzzled. Like me.

"Could I speak to Dilly?"

"Well," she chuckled, "you could do, but you won't get much of a reply."

"I don't understand."

"The only Dilly here is our cat. I think you must have got the wrong number."

"But that is the Morgan family, isn't it? Professor Morgan's house?"

"Morgan, yes. It's a common enough name round here. But my dad's a bus driver."

"Oh... er... oh," I was lost for words.

"I'm sorry, but I really think you have misdialled."

"Okay, er... thanks! I'm sorry to have troubled you." I felt like slamming the phone down but it wasn't the poor girl's fault.

Bugger and damnation!

I was still muttering bloody hells and other choice epithets when Jake came back from the kitchen.

"All sorted?" he asked, seeing from my demeanour that it damn well wasn't.

"No!" I replied sharply.

"All over then is it?"

"I had the wrong number!"

"You're joking!" One glance told him I wasn't. "You pillock!" he added.

"I don't need reminding, thank you!"

"Okay, Rob, calm down! Here, let's have a look at the number."

I handed him my diary.

"You could have got a couple of numbers the wrong way round," he suggested. "Or, is this number a two or a seven?"

I took a cursory look at it. "God knows."

"Why not try some other combinations?"

"Have you any idea how many possible variations you can get with those numbers, even without substituting the twos and sevens?" I said sarcastically.

"I'm only trying to be helpful," said Jake.

We both sat in silence for the best part of five minutes, which was probably just as well, since I was far from being in the mood for conversation. Jake then stood and paced the room, hand on chin.

"You've obviously not got her address," said Jake, to which I nodded, "but did she tell you where she was going to teach? You could write to her there."

My cloud of despondency disappeared like magic. "Jake, you're a genius!" I leapt up and clapped my hands on his shoulder. "Machynllech! She's teaching in a primary in Machynllech!"

"Steady on, for a moment I thought you were going to kiss me!" His brow furrowed. "Suppose there's more than one primary in Mack... wherever?"

"I don't think it's that big. Shouldn't be difficult to find out." I breathed a sigh of relief. "I owe you a pint, Jake!"

Chapter 3

I arrived early on Wednesday, the first proper day of term, feeling much more confident than I had the previous day at the staff meeting. In the staffroom I found my newly-labelled pigeon-hole already stuffed half-full of brochures, leaflets and other miscellaneous bumf. Among invitations to join every one of the teaching unions, details of pension rights and a thick treatise on the latest initiatives from the Government to address falling standards in education, only a voucher for a half-price pasty at the town's bakery attracted my immediate attention. The rest I might peruse later. Or not.

I didn't need to use my new set of keys, since the Science Block was already open. I caught a glimpse of head technician Aubrey Turner pottering around in the ground floor prep room. Upstairs, two banks of metal lockers now stood in the corridor outside laboratories C1 and C2, the latter of which was to be my base. The lockers, in lieu of pupils' desks in the labs, were clearly lockable but anyone with a bent paper clip could gain access in seconds. I doubt if Moby Dick had considered the likelihood of severe congestion in the corridors when decreeing that laboratories should also be form bases. Some ground rules would need to be established, I thought.

Nick emerged from C1. "Morning, Rob, just showing our new technician round. Come and meet her."

I followed Nick into his lab and caught sight of a bob of blonde hair. She turned as Nick made to introduce her.

My jaw dropped. I couldn't believe my eyes! "San… Sandra?" I said hoarsely.

A wide-eyed look of surprise quickly replaced the welcoming smile on her face. "Robert? Rob Kiddecott?"

Totally taken aback by our reactions Nick's eyes darted

between the two of us, unsure of what to do, and settled for a lame, "You know each other?"

I nodded. "Yes, Nick we do." I didn't add that the last time I'd seen her she'd been lying naked on her bed.

Sandra recovered her composure. "We met when Rob was on his first teaching practice." She didn't mention that she'd tried to seduce me. "That was before I got married."

Nick looked quizzically at us both, and said as he left the room, "Well I'm sure you've got a lot to talk about then."

We watched him depart in silence. Sandra slowly turned to me and her serious expression collapsed in a fit of giggles, relieving the tension. "Rob, I had no idea you were working here."

"I'm covering maternity leave for this term," I said guardedly, still not quite sure of my ground. "I got the impression from Nick that Mrs Maxwell, the new technician, would be an older woman."

"Well, I am. Three years older." She gave a wistful smile. "Look, can we meet for a coffee later, say after school?"

I hesitated.

"Don't worry, Rob, your virtue will be quite safe. I'm a respectable married woman now."

I raised an eyebrow, then nodded acceptance. After all, we'd be working together for the next three months at least.

My registration group - all new intake youngsters, keen and fresh-faced (well, mostly, since a few were in need of a good scrub behind the ears and one poor lad had acute acne) - were in my charge all morning. I was surprised how quickly the time passed in the issuing of notebooks, timetable and library tickets, allocation of lockers, and in welcoming them to their new environment. I tried to make the code of conduct for their use of the laboratory as a form base sound as positive as possible rather than a long list of prohibitions. Time would tell whether they got the message.

I still felt pretty shattered when I collapsed into an arm-chair in the staffroom to eat my packed lunch. I'd intended to have a hot meal in the canteen but Jake had encouraged me to take a couple of his leftover fish cakes. He'd acquired a new cook book but hadn't yet had the wit to scale down the quantities to serve two people instead of six, muttering something about 'economy of scale'. Looking at the solid, cold mass I wished he'd exercised a little more economy with the fish scales that glistened like specks of mother-of-pearl amongst the mashed potato. I'd jibbed at taking a pot of his special peppery sauce.

Nick wandered over and took the seat next to me. "I hope you're not going to cause me to lose another lab technician," he said. A little too loudly, I felt, as John Rhys-Price was well within earshot, and his antennae would be quivering to pick up the slightest hint of scandal.

With difficulty I swallowed the first mouthful of goo before replying. "Unlikely."

That evidently wasn't enough to satisfy Nick's curiosity. He waited for me to elaborate.

"She had a kid at the primary school where I did my first teaching practice. She was also a governor."

"And?"

"She'd heard I played the guitar. She invited me to a musical evening with friends at her house. There was a misunderstanding."

"That's all? A misunderstanding?"

"That's all." At least all I intended to tell him. I'm pretty sure he thought I'd behaved inappropriately before in some way with Sandra but I didn't feel it was my business to sully her reputation.

"Hmm." He put a lot of meaning into that short expression. He clearly didn't believe me.

"We didn't sleep together, if that's what you're thinking." A near miss though.

Fortunately Nick didn't probe any further and left me to my lunch, which I decided to probe no further.

***

Only about ten per cent of the children at Sir Wilfred Roberts Grammar School actually lived in Carrick Major. The rest were ferried in from outlying villages and isolated hamlets up to twenty miles distant. By four o'clock the school premises were virtually deserted, apart from a handful of students who were auditioning for a drama production.

I'd agreed to meet Sandra in the bakery café in the town square after all the buses had departed. One elderly couple were its only other customers, about half-an-hour before closing time.

"So how long have you been living in Carrick?"

"We moved to a village a few miles away about six months ago. That was soon after we got married. Bill, that's my new husband, he's manager of the estate agents in town. That's how we met."

"That's quite a way from Abergynwyn." Where I'd met her.

"Oh, he was working out of Tencastle then. He was surveying the house, you know, where I lived."

"So you were thinking of selling up and moving anyway?"

"The house wasn't mine. It belonged to Terry, my former partner. We'd already separated. He wanted me out." She grimaced. "Got a new love of his own I guess."

"Your daughter, Fanny. Terry was her father?"

"That's right. Bastard!"

She'd called me that too.

She looked up at me, a worried expression on her face.

"I really didn't expect to see you again, Rob. I'm not sure it's a good idea us having to work together. I'm thinking that I ought to hand my notice in."

"Sandra, please don't do that!" I said, perhaps a little sharply. I'd face one hell of an inquisition from Nick if I caused him to lose another technician. "Really," I continued, a lot more gently, instinctively putting my hand on hers, "That's all behind us now. We've all moved on. Anyway, I'm only on a term's contract. I'll probably be gone by the New Year."

"I'm so sorry!" She was close to tears. "I behaved so badly. I was so lonely and I thought you found me attractive."

"I did. I do. Sandra, you are a very attractive woman. But it didn't seem right for a young student to have an affair with the mother of a kid at the school."

She looked up again, the familiar smile beginning to appear. She brushed a truss of long blonde hair from her face. "I understand, Rob. And I'm glad now that you didn't take advantage of me." Serious again. "Can we still be friends?"

"I hope so. And colleagues."

We both stood. She kissed me on the cheek. "Thank you. Thank you so much."

Chapter 4

Jake and I didn't see a lot of each other during the week, since I had to leave the house early in the morning, usually before he had surfaced, and he was rarely at home in the evening. Despite the fact that, unlike the schools, the college term was not due to begin officially until the third week in September, Jake's duties in the Students' Union already seemed to be keeping him well occupied. For my part, the onus of lesson preparation and the onset of marking the kids' work kept me pretty busy in the evenings. By the time these tasks had been completed I often felt too shattered to drive into Tencastle for a pint at the Castle Inn, our favourite undergraduate watering hole.

After my first full week of teaching I was more than ready for a lie-in on Saturday morning. Not so Jake, whose crooning of the latest folk song in his repertoire accompanied noisy washing-up. The only consolation was that he couldn't play his banjo at the same time.

I staggered downstairs. "For Christ's sake, Jake, do you have to be so darn cheerful in the morning?" I grumbled. "Spare a thought for the working classes!"

He thought for a couple of seconds. "But you're not working today."

"That's the point. I intended to rise at my leisure, until you started your serenade."

"Sorry!" And then added, "But it's too nice a day to stay in bed. Anyway, we have got work to do."

"We have?"

"Clear all our clutter out of the spare room."

I looked at Jake with suspicion. "And who are we expecting?"

"Benji's coming back."

"What!" Benji, our resident scatter-brained in-house

artist during our first year at Ty Melin, had left us in the lurch the following September. He'd taken off, brushes and all, to the Indian subcontinent to find the meaning of life. Or something. "You're not serious?"

From his expression, Jake obviously was.

"I could live without having to pick my way through paint pots and canvases again," I said.

"You won't have to."

"How come?"

"He's found Jesus." Jake made it sound as if the Messiah had been stuffed in the back of his sock drawer.

"So I suppose he's going to do a Michaelangelo and plaster the ceiling with naked cherubs?"

"No, no, he's given up all that. He's a changed character."

"You've spoken to him then?"

"Only on the phone."

Resignedly, I mused whether a bible would be preferable to a brush in Benji's hands. "When is he arriving?"

"Next Friday evening. I told him that you'd be happy to give him a lift from the station. You don't mind, do you?"

I opened my mouth to utter a suitable retort. And stayed silent. I'd long learnt that any argument with Jake's plans was totally futile.

The clutter clearing took all of ten minutes. Unless Benji had radically changed his habits, it would take him even less time to create total chaos in the room.

The telephone interrupted my thoughts about whether to use the sunny day to look up some old friends in Tencastle or attack the garden. It had become quite overgrown following two months of neglect over the summer. And the greenhouse my father had insisted on buying for me now nurtured nothing but a couple of desiccated indeterminate plants and an assorted collection of mud-encrusted flower pots.

"For you," Jake called. I couldn't fathom why he was grinning like a Cheshire cat.

"Hello?"

"Rob, is that you?"

"Dilly?" My spirits bounded.

"Yes, it's me. Oh, Rob, I was so pleased to get your letter. I thought you'd forgotten about me. You said you were going to ring."

"I did try, but I'd got the wrong number, as I explained. I hope it was okay writing to you at the school."

"Well, the Head's a bit old-fashioned and waffled on about keeping social and professional interests separate, but he excused the lapse on this occasion."

"I'd better get your phone number down correctly this time, then. And your address." To be certain, I read the numbers back to her. "It's wonderful to hear from you, really it is. I'm not sure what I would have done if you hadn't phoned or written. Probably walked the streets of Machynllech looking for you."

"Would you really?" she chuckled. "That's so sweet."

"Can we arrange to meet up soon? You would be very welcome to come and stay for a weekend." And for the sake of propriety I added, "We've got a spare room."

No sooner were the words out of my mouth than I realised we wouldn't have a spare room much longer.

"I'd like that."

Oh well, sofa so good.

"There is a problem though for a weekend," she said hesitantly. "I don't have a car, and the train would take hours. That's even if there any trains back on a Sunday evening."

"Yes, I see." Aberystwyth as the crow flies wasn't a great distance, but the rail connection via Shrewsbury was tortuous. Not that the roads were particularly straightforward. "No buses?" I said hopefully.

"You must be joking!"

"Um." I didn't relish the frustrations of conducting romance at a distance. Then I had an inspiration.

"You could..." We both spoke the same words together. And laughed.

"You first," I said.

"Well, if your old banger is still going, you could come to Aber for a weekend. If you don't mind meeting my parents."

"That's a definite possibility. Thanks." I was pretty sure I wouldn't be sharing her room there.

"And your idea?"

"Half term. Do you get the whole week off, like me?"

"Yes, I do. Why?"

"If you could get part way by train or bus, some place where I could meet you, we could then head back to Tencastle, and get you back the same way, avoiding Sunday timetables."

"That sounds brilliant. Or, even better, why don't we combine the two. I come down for the weekend, then you take me back to Aberystwyth. I'd only have to do the train journey one way."

"But it'll be weeks before I see you!"

"I'm happy to wait."

The prospect of a whole week with Dilly was certainly worth waiting for, though the several weeks beforehand would seem like a lifetime.

"Are you heading for town today?" said Jake later that morning.

"Probably." I'd decided the gardening could wait. "Why?"

"One or two things I need to do. If we were still here at Penybont beyond Christmas I'd seriously consider getting a car myself."

"I thought you enjoyed cycling."

"Not so much fun when I have to do it every day." He'd often taken advantage of a lift when we were both at college.

"You want me to drop you off at the Union?"

"Aren't you going there too?" Jake sounded surprised.

"Possibly, but I thought I might look up some old friends." Although all my contemporaries, apart from Jake, had moved on to various teaching posts around the country, there were still one or two people I'd known well through Carpiog Morris who were still to complete their final year. In particular, one diminutive bundle of energy and enthusiasm who'd got engaged to Huw Parry-Evans, our Welsh bagpipe player.

"Thought I'd call on Min and Huw."

"You intending to stay overnight?"

"No. Why?" I said, puzzled.

"Well they're both with Huw's parents in Pembrokeshire this term. Min's on her final teaching practice in Haverfordwest and Huw's doing the odd bit of supply work in between helping on his father's farm. They won't be back until after Christmas."

***

The following Friday after school I drove back into Tencastle rather than take the more direct route to the cottage. With the imminent arrival of Benji it seemed prudent to get well stocked up with provisions from the supermarket. Material considerations like food were never high on his list of priorities. I would also have plenty of time for bangers and mash and a leisurely pint at the Castle.

I looked at my watch. Ten minutes since the train had arrived and departed. And at least five minutes since the last passenger had passed through the gate. There were no more trains in either direction until the next morning.

"Bloody Benji!" I muttered. "Flaming typical!"

I wandered back to Jessica, and sat inside, considering

what to do. I could phone the cottage on the off-chance that Jake was there and the even less likely possibility that Benji had rung and left a message.

Someone tapped on the passenger window. A clean-shaven young man dressed in a grey suit peered inside. His sleek black hair was tied into a pony tail.

It was easier to get out than try to lower the window. "Can I help you?" I said.

"Well, I hope so, Rob," he said. "I recognised Jessica."

"Benji?" I couldn't believe my eyes – or my ears.

"The same. I spotted your car. Jessica hasn't changed."

"Which is more than I can say about you!" No shock wave of black unkempt hair with beard to match, nor scruffy jeans and manner of speech to complement his former image of an avant-garde artist.

"I've been reborn."

As if that explained everything. "Right. Um, er, well, welcome back to Tencastle!" I took his proffered hand. And puzzled, I said, "How come I didn't see you come off the Shrewsbury train?"

"That's because I was coming from Swansea. Didn't Jake say?"

I shook my head.

"You weren't here, so I've been up in the town for the last hour."

"So you've already eaten?"

"No, but it's my fasting day."

I wondered if he was still a vegetarian.

As we headed off towards the cottage I had so many questions that I wanted to ask, about what he'd been doing over the past year and his change of life-style. I settled for something mundane, certain that we'd get chapter and verse of his reincarnation, in due course. "What are your plans back here in Tencastle?"

"I've re-enrolled for Religious Studies at college. Take the message to the young children of Wales."

Christ, I hoped Benji wasn't going to be a holy fanatic like Joseph Carpenter, who'd been at the same school as me on first teaching practice. A self-righteous pain in the arse until I'd got him to see the light, so to speak.

"And I'm keen to set up a country retreat for bible study and meditation. Ty Melin would be ideal."

While we already led a semi-monastic existence at the cottage I couldn't see Jake being keen on supplications at supper. Nor me for that matter. Anyway there was a practical objection. "We've only got the place until Christmas."

"Ah, yes. Shame" He fell silent for a short while. Then, apropos of nothing, asked, "Is the garden shed still there?"

"A few garden tools in it. Why, you're not thinking of converting it to a chapel, are you?"

"No, a stable."

One never used to take the pre-Christian Benji seriously. "A stable?" I conjured up images of the nativity at Bethlehem.

"Transport," he said, and added by way of explanation, "I learned to ride in India."

"You wouldn't get an elephant through the door," I said.

"A horse. Ride into college each day, you know."

Novel, I gave him that. "And you'd park it where? I can't see the college authorities letting you tie it up to the cycle racks or letting it graze on the lawns."

"Dunno yet."

Arrival at the cottage forestalled any further exploration of equestrian excursions.

Chapter 5

Nick had noticed that the relationship between Sandra and myself had become much more easy-going since the morning of our first encounter.

"Sorted yourself out with yon fair lass, then?" he said.

I took the chair next to him in the staffroom ready for the head's morning briefing. "No problems, Nick. It was just so unexpected. After we'd parted company in, er, rather unusual circumstances I never thought we'd meet again. Least of all here!"

"Well, she had relevant experience and good references. But you'd know that already, I guess?"

"Not at all. I only knew her as a single mum."

"She'd worked as a technician in a path lab at Swansea Hospital."

I wondered how she'd ended up with a kid, living in the back of beyond. I'd never really thought about it before but she must be in her early thirties at least even though she could easily pass for an attractive young woman almost ten years younger.

Like the new music teacher, Janet Milward, sitting just across from me. Shoulder-length straight auburn hair that almost glistened in the light, a delicately moulded oval freckled face with a slightly turned-up snub nose, deep brown eyes and petite mouth, with no need of lipstick. She could certainly turn a few heads and, indeed, John Rhys-Price had already been sniffing around, trying out his charms, apparently without success. She caught my eye and smiled. I acknowledged with a quiet, "Hi" and a wave of my hand.

I'd been listening, more or less, to Moby Dick's morning bulletin, which usually had a high content of self-promotion for the innumerable committees and official bodies on which he sat. It's a wonder he was ever in school. The mention of Tencastle caught my attention.

"... from Tencastle on their final teaching practice. Next week Miss Williams will be joining the humanities department and Miss Dickens will be teaching English."

I had a vague feeling that the names should have registered with me.

***

With Sandra working at the school, I knew there was a strong possibility that her daughter would be in one of the classes I taught.

"Hello, Mr Kiddecott," the precocious child had said cheerily, breezing in with the rest of the new-intake science group for their very first lesson with me.

I'd gone through the register, asking each pupil to respond, so that I might get a head start to putting faces to the names, and, hopefully, commit them to memory. When I'd got to Myfanwy Hughes, she had called out, rather sharply, "I'm Fanny. Don't you remember me?"

As if I could forget. She'd grown taller and, no longer completely flat-chested, evidently had already entered puberty. Under her mop of blonde curly hair, she was beginning to look more like her mother. "Yes, Miss Hughes," I'd said formally. "And you should remember to put your hand up if you wish to speak." And then to soften the rebuke, "Okay, Fanny?"

Her glower had changed to a beaming grin. "Yes, Mr Kiddecott. Sorry, I'll be a good girl for you."

It seemed a rather strange comment, but I had thought no more of it. Fanny had indeed been as good as gold during the lesson, though several times during the practical work I had noticed her chatting with her neighbour and indicating me with a flick of her eyes.

On Friday of the second full week I was a little irritated to be summoned over the Tannoy system to the head's office at the end of morning school. I wasn't worried, though. I presumed Moby Dick wanted to see how I was getting on after a fortnight in the job. He could have just as easily left a polite request in my pigeon hole.

It was evident from the moment I entered that a social chat was not on the agenda. A macho-looking bloke in a suit occupied the chair beside the head's desk. I was not invited to sit down.

Dr Melville O. Bedford-Dickson shuffled some papers and regarded me beneath hooded eyebrows. "Mr. Kiddecott," he began with a voice full of gravitas, "I have received some very serious allegations, about," he coughed, "about your inappropriate behaviour."

What the hell? I hadn't taken his dedicated parking space, for God's sake!

"So serious, in fact, that I have no alternative but to suspend you with immediate effect whilst further investigations take place."

"What!" I felt like I'd been kicked in the stomach. My head was reeling. Where the hell had this come from?

"Detective Sergeant Colville will want to speak with you," Moby Dick said in a tone clearly indicating that, for his part, the interview was over.

Colville? I'd seen that name somewhere recently. My shock had given way to anger and I gathered my wits. "Dr Bedford-Dickson, I believe I have the right to know of what I am accused before you so summarily dismiss me!" I tried to keep my voice under control.

The Principal, unused to being challenged, turned to the detective to reply.

"Suspected grooming of a minor."

"That's ridiculous!"

"Is it?" The detective growled, "I'd expect you to say that."

"And on what evidence do you base this accusation?"

"I'm afraid I am not at liberty to divulge our sources,"

he said smugly.

"And I suppose you are not at liberty to say where this grooming is supposed to have taken place, or how?"

"That's correct." Fortunately he then added, "Enticing little girls with sweets. Ring any bells?"

It certainly did, but not quite the way he was expecting, as my brain registered a connection. "Did you say your name was Colville?"

"Detective Sergeant Colville to you," said Moby Dick.

I ignored him. "Do you by any chance have a daughter just started at this school?"

"Mr. Kiddecott, I really think that is none of your business..." Moby began.

"Hear me out," I snapped. "Sergeant?"

"Yes, as a matter of fact I do. And therefore a personal interest in protecting her from paedophiles."

"Does she have a friend, Fanny Hughes?"

The sergeant's eyes briefly registered recognition, before he regained his inscrutable expression. "You know the girl?"

"Of course, she is in one of the classes I teach."

Colville snorted in frustration, "Before you came to this school, I mean."

"Yes. And I gave her sweets." I was actually beginning to enjoy the exchange.

His eyebrows shot up uncontrollably. "What? You confirm that the allegations are true?"

"No. I admit to giving her an acid drop sweet. Along with all the other children in the class as part of a science lesson on my first teaching practice."

Dr Bedford-Dickson's frown was now directed at the policeman. His smugness had disappeared.

I continued, "The regular class teacher was present throughout, and, if you still don't believe me, you can ask Fanny's mother. Mrs Maxwell, formerly Miss Hughes, works here as a lab technician."

Another thought occurred to me. "Tell me, Sergeant Colville, are you here as part of a formal police investigation, or just using your official title to cover your own private action..."

"Mr Kiddecott! That's quite enough!" Moby Dick banged his fist on the desk.

"... based on nothing more than your daughter's tittle-tattle?"

From his resigned shrug, I could see that I'd hit the mark.

He rose to go. "I think, Headmaster, that my business here is concluded."

Mine wasn't. I was still angry about my treatment, and he wasn't even offering an apology. "I..."

Moby interrupted. "Mr Kiddecott, I think we should draw a line under the matter."

"Yes, we should indeed!" I replied hotly. "If there are no repercussions on my teaching career at this school and no further word of these spurious allegations, I personally have no wish to take the matter further." I paused, choosing my parting words carefully. "While I can appreciate Detective Sergeant Colville's concerns about possible child abuse, I believe that more discreet enquiries would have been appropriate before jumping to conclusions."

I turned and made my exit, leaving Moby open-mouthed. I stood outside the Head's door and breathed deeply several times.

"Been in Moby's bad books?"

John Rhys-Price was the last person I'd have wanted to see in the corridor at that moment. "Piss off!"

"Ooh, touchy, aren't we? Not been having it off with another lab girl, have you?"

I grabbed his jacket and spun him around, oblivious to the fact that he had a considerable advantage over me in height and muscle. "Not with one, not with another, not that it's any of your damn business!"

It probably worked to my advantage that he'd never seen me anything other than easy-going and friendly. He straightened his jacket and looked at me warily. "Okay, okay."

I immediately regretted my outburst. "I'm sorry, John," I said more calmly, "But I'd really prefer it if you did mind your own business."

By the end of the afternoon I was still inwardly seething at the lunchtime events, which could so easily have had dire consequences for my teaching career, had I not realised that Fanny's casual chatter to her friend had been so wildly misinterpreted.

The succession of ponderous hay-wagons which impeded my journey back to the cottage did nothing to improve my mood. Nor did the great pile of horse dung right where I usually parked Jessica.

"Benji!" I yelled.

No Benji, but Jake appeared from the back garden. "What's up?"

"Is Benji here?"

"No, he's gone for a ride on Caspar. Why?"

"That's why!" I retorted, pointing to the steaming pile. "Presumably Caspar's?"

"What's the problem? Be good for the garden," said Jake.

"Humph!"

"You don't sound very happy. Bad day at school, was it?"

"Oh no," I said with heavy sarcasm, "absolutely great. I was accused of being a paedophile, bawled out the headmaster, pissed off a police sergeant and assaulted a colleague. Otherwise, just fine."

"Sounds like you need a pint to wind down. On me." A rare offer from Jake.

"No doubt you're thinking of town. With me driving." Though I was sorely tempted.

"We could wait for Benji," Jake suggested.

"And Uncle Tom Cobley and all, I suppose?"

"Eh?" The ditty from my native Devon obviously wasn't part of Jake's folk song repertoire.

Chapter 6

Something must have woken me.

I sat up quickly - too quickly to cope with the effects of the booze I'd consumed the night before. Little demons with sledgehammers were trying to smash their way out of my skull, and my tongue felt like used sandpaper. If I'd kept to the two pints at the Castle I would have been okay, even if slightly over the legal limit to drive. Jake however had appropriated a bottle of Highland malt whisky he'd discovered in his office. Probably squirrelled away by the previous Union President, a surly Scot.

"Twelve years' old, must be well past its sell-by date." he'd said, "Pity to waste it."

It had seemed at the time an excellent way to continue our reminiscences.

It was daylight. I rose, very gingerly, from my bed. I resisted the reflex action of drawing back the curtains. My eyes wouldn't cope with the sunlight streaming in.

There was a strange sound. Again. A sort of 'Wheeeiiiaaa.' Noise of any sort was unusual out here in the sticks, apart from the occasional passing vehicle. 'Wheeeiiiaaa' was not natural. But my few functioning brain cells couldn't think of any reason why aliens would descend upon Penybont.

I staggered downstairs in my dressing gown. Jake and Benji were already having breakfast.

"Hi. Feeling better?" said Jake cheerfully. No sign of a hangover with him. He waved a half-eaten slice of toast at me. "Want some?"

"Either of you got any aspirins?"

Benji reached for a small pill box on the table. "Here, try these. Nux Vomica."

"What the hell is that?"

"Homeopathic headache remedy. Or you could try

Belladonna." Benji said helpfully.

"I want to be cured not ruddy poisoned," I said.

"No danger. There's only a minute amount in it."

"How minute?" I asked suspiciously.

"Oh, something like one part in a few million, I think."

"I.e. bugger all! I'll stick to aspirin, thank you!" I remembered I'd left some in my guitar case.

"Please yourself. It worked like magic for Jake," said Benji. "Anyhow, excuse me while I go and feed Caspar."

I slumped into the chair he'd just vacated. I couldn't really believe the change that we were seeing in Benji. Two years ago you wouldn't have seen him before midday at the weekend. With his esoteric paintings and impressionistic creations he'd lived on a different ethereal plane to us mere mortals. Mind you, I suspected with his newly-found religion he'd still have his head in the clouds half of the time.

Which reminded me. "Jake, did you hear some strange noises this morning?"

"Like what?"

"Well, like..." I didn't need to finish. On cue, the eerie sound came again, closer this time, it seemed.

"That's Caspar. You haven't met him yet?"

"Only his gift of nature," I said, recalling the deposit of horse shit. "I thought he was joking - about the whole idea of riding, in fact. Has Benji really got him stabled in the garden shed?"

"Well, yes. Actually that's something we wanted to talk to you about."

"I'm not mucking out stables!"

"No, no. The shed's only a temporary measure. He needs pasture."

I wasn't sure where this was going but I had strong suspicions that I wasn't going to like it.

"I had this idea."

Oh God!

"There's the field on the other side of the stream. Goes up to the wood, you remember?"

"Uhuh."

"It doesn't usually have any livestock in it. Anyway, I mentioned it to Evan Jones, down at the cottage by the bridge. He knows the farmer who owns the field and has had a word with him. Seems he's quite happy for Caspar to graze there."

"Okay, that's good. So what's this got to do with me?"

"The farmer has asked us to arrange some simple fencing to stop Caspar straying up into the wood."

"And you want me to help put up the fence?"

"Well, that would be great, but also we need to bridge the stream at the bottom of our garden."

"Why?"

"Access. The gate to the field is up above the wood."

"Sounds like you need an engineer not a chemistry teacher."

"Sleepers, Rob!"

"Come again?"

"Old railway sleepers! I've seen them in the old goods yard next to the station. They'd be ideal."

"If you are expecting me to hump them back in Jessica, forget it! No way could I get them in the car."

"No, we'll use Caspar himself to tow them. All we need you to do is to drive slowly behind with your lights flashing to warn other traffic."

As I suspected, that wasn't 'all' I was asked to do. I was waiting patiently at the station yard, with Jessica stuffed full of wooden stakes and wire. I'd already done one round trip to Green Willy's Garden Centre a couple of miles the other side of Tencastle. Jake had gone off on his own to 'get some bits of gear', whatever that meant.

Jake returned just as Caspar clopped into view, Benji looking quite the professional jockey on the chestnut gelding. Borrowed from his uncle, so I was told. Trusting bloke, I thought.

I suppose I had assumed that Caspar would be harnessed to some kind of cart, though no such conveyance was in evidence.

I watched as Jake extracted four pairs of roller skates from a rucksack. With baler twine he secured a pair at each end of two creosoted old railway sleepers, which were more than eight feet long. Across the sleepers, fore and aft, he tied two short lengths of planking he'd persuaded the yard manager to throw in for free. Finally he unwound a new clothes line and looped the middle over the rear of Benji's saddle.

Jake stepped up onto the rear planking and took the end of the clothes line in his hand. "Right, let's get moving," Jake yelled.

"Haven't you forgotten your toga?" I called.

Fortunately there was plenty of room in the yard to turn. Caspar set off slowly and Jake wobbled precariously on his crude chariot behind him. In order not to be pulled forward off balance, Jake soon realised he had to place his feet behind the cross-brace and lean backwards. Jessica and I brought up the rear, her headlights full on. People stopped and stared at the strange sight as we turned out from Station Road and headed out of town across the river.

Although progress was slow, all went surprisingly well, even when we turned off the relatively flat highway and began the long climb up the minor road towards Penybont. Only on one occasion did we have to pull over to let a delivery van pass.

Suddenly I caught a glimpse of an animal - it could have been a fox - dart across the road in from of the horse. Caspar reared up, almost unseating Benji and allowing the clothes line loop to slip off the saddle. Jake reacted quickly with great presence of mind, flinging himself onto the grassy verge as the twin baulks of timber began to rumble backwards. Gathering speed they hurtled towards me. In a split second I had to decide whether to use Jessica to stop them or take avoiding action. I swung the steering wildly to the right and aimed for a muddy gateway to a field.

A sleeper caught Jessica a glancing blow on the nearside rear wheel guard as the pair careered off downhill. Ahead Caspar was fast disappearing out of sight. In my mirror I glimpsed the timbers catapulting skywards where they had failed to negotiate the bend.

I climbed out of the car, my shoes almost disappearing in the oozy mud.

Jake came down, limping slightly. "You okay, Rob?"

"Yeah! You?"

"Knocked the breath out of me. I'll probably have some ripe bruises in the morning."

"We're lucky there was no traffic on the road. Your contraption could have killed somebody."

"I didn't know Benji was going do stunt riding, did I?" Jake looked up and down the road. "Anyway, where is he?"

"He went thataway fast, " I said jerking my thumb uphill, "and your trolley likewise the other way."

I was concerned about the damage to Jessica. Fortunately, only a small area of paintwork was scratched. And only one front wheel was sunk in the mud, so with Jake's help I was confident I could extricate the car.

I hurried to join Jake who was striding off down the hill. A badly bent roller skate lay in the gutter by the bend. Just around the corner an old bloke sat gripping the steering wheel of his Morris Minor, rigidly staring through the windscreen.

"Are you all right, sir?" I said.

He turned to me, his right hand now shaking and pointing at the low bank opposite. "Di... did... did you see that?" he quaked, "Two torpedoes, coming for me... and...

and then they FLEW." He raised his finger, following it with his eyes. "Over... over there!" He looked at me, terrified. "They must have sunk the boat... oh dear me... I saw the explosion... and the wreckage!"

Torpedoes? Well, at a stretch of the imagination. But otherwise he wasn't making a great deal of sense.

He grabbed my wrist. "You must have seen it!"

"I'm sorry, sir, we didn't see a thing, did we, Jake?" I said, giving him a cue.

"No, nothing. We were walking down the road. No torpedoes and no explosions," said Jake.

"Oh dear!" said the old man, somewhat more calmly. "I was torpedoed during the war, you know. I sometimes have nightmares but never before in the daytime." He shook his head. "I could have sworn I saw them."

"Are you all right to drive?" Jake asked.

"I'm going to turn round and go back home."

We found the sleepers floating separately at the edge of a small pond with flotsam and jetsam of broken branches and twigs from a recently felled tree. The planking had shattered. With a considerable amount of effort and cursing, not to mention four wet and muddy feet, we eventually retrieved the timbers. We also recovered six undamaged roller skates.

"Any bright ideas how we get this lot home?" I said.

Jake looked at the timbers and then at my car still stuck a couple of hundred yards up the hill. "Well, if we can liberate Jessica, we could adapt the original plan."

"I'm not sure that would be legal."

"Why not?"

"Well, a towed vehicle is supposed to show number plates and also lights." I reckoned we had about an hour of daylight left.

We eventually made it home, at a snail's pace. I made Jake sit on the logs, which we securely strapped together. He held a torch in one hand and in the other a piece of cardboard with Jessica's number crudely scribbled in biro.

There was no sign of Benji or of Caspar at the cottage. Though peeved, we had other things to worry about, like having a shower and something to eat.

We heard the now familiar sound of iron-clad hooves on the road outside. Several minutes later Benji ambled in, looking somewhat dishevelled.

"Ah, the Lone Ranger returns," said Jake sarcastically. "Where the hell have you been?"

"Prospecting,"

"Come again?"

"No gold in these hills, Benji," I said.

"No, when you two didn't turn up I thought I'd have a look at the access to the field from the other side of the wood."

"Took you a darn long time," said Jake.

"Yeah, I sort of got lost on the way back. It was dark and it took me ages to find the gate," Benji looked at our egg-smeared plates. "Any of that left? I'm starving."

"In the fridge," Jake said unsympathetically. "We would have appreciated your help instead of gallivanting off into the sunset."

"Sorry, Caspar bolted. I was almost back here before I got her under control." He paused as a thought entered his head. "What happened to the sleepers?"

We told him.

"And tomorrow, it's bridge building time for you," said Jake.

Benji wrinkled his brow. "But tomorrow's Sunday!"

"So?"

"It's the Lord's day. It's a day of rest!"

"If you think we've slaved all day getting this gear together just for you to kneel on your prayer mat then you'd better offer your apologies to his Lordship right now." Jake's tone left no room for argument.

"But..."

"Be there, if you want any help from us."

Chapter 7

"Would you mind doing me a favour?" Jake asked.

"Depends," I replied warily. Knowing Jake, any request was unlikely to be straightforward. "What do you want?"

"Just a lift."

"Really? On a Sunday evening? You've only just got back from god knows where anyway."

"Oh, it's not for me."

"So it's not you that wants the favour?"

"Well, no… er, but yes… but not the lift."

"You're not making any sense, Jake."

Jake cleared a pile of newspapers from the sofa and flopped down. "You know Mary Williams?"

I did indeed, though not as well as I would have liked. After a brief snogging at a party in my first year at Tencastle any continuing relationship had been foiled by her sudden departure to nurse her sick father and Benji's subsequent unwitting concealment of her letter to me.

"Well, she's starting her final teaching practice tomorrow," Jake continued. "At your school."

Moby Dick's mention of student teachers at Carrick now clicked in my memory. But I thought I could see where Jake's favour was heading. "If you're asking me to make a detour each day through Tencastle, the answer's no. Sorry." Even though the company would be pleasant, it would add a considerable time to my journey.

"No, she's arranged digs in Carrick. It's getting there tomorrow morning."

"Hmm. And back on Fridays?"

"Not necessarily, she's there mostly for the duration. End of term would be good though."

"That I could do," I said. Then a thought occurred to me. "Where's the favour to you in this?"

Jake was not normally reticent about his activities.

"Er... well, we've been seeing quite a lot of each other recently. Hope you don't mind."

I wasn't sure whether my minding referred to the lift or to his relationship with Mary. He was aware of our history.

"No problem. Where and what time do you want me to pick her up?"

"Seven thirty by Goliath?"

The naked statue of an athlete so nicknamed by students was a convenient meeting point in the centre of Tencastle "Okay."

"Thanks, Rob. Oh, just one other thing."

I rolled my eyes.

"I suggested that you could also pick up Holly Dickens, our Carpiog dancer, from the bottom of her road. They're sharing a bedsit in Carrick."

Next morning I set out half an hour earlier than usual. I always made a point anyway of moving Jessica before Benji started clodhopping around on Caspar, who was still not properly toilet trained.

It usually took less than ten minutes to drive from Penybont to Tencastle. Not today. I'd gone less than a mile when, rounding a bend, I found the road blocked by sheep. Half the mutton population of Tencastle was heading towards me on the hoof. At least until Jessica's squeal of brakes panicked the leaders and sent then scurrying back downhill, where they were confronted by a portly gent in wellies - presumably the farmer - frantically waving his arms to halt the stampede. With his dog also worrying at their feet, the nervous beasts took the line of least resistance - up the road and verges past my now stationary car.

I thought I'd be able to make a quick escape as I saw in my mirror the last sheep snatching a mouthful of grass from the bank. But the dog had other ideas; streaking past my car it corralled the flock only a few yards behind me, as the farmer puffed his way up to my open window.

"Sorry about that, boyo," he wheezed, "Bit jumpy they are, not used to traffic."

"I understand," I said, more calmly than I felt, and added, unwisely, "I was brought up on a farm."

"Really? Well, in that case, if you wouldn't mind helping. I need to get the sheep into the field just up the road. If you could stand in the road to discourage any strays, Megan and I will have them out of your way in a jiffy."

I didn't mention that my father ran a dairy farm. Cows are a damn sight more intelligent and creatures of habit than sheep. I don't know quite what he expected me to do if any contrary animal made a break for freedom. Rugby tackle it, perhaps?

By the time I pulled up by Goliath I was running seriously late. Mary was looking anxiously at the watch.

"Sorry I'm late, Mary. Farmer decided to take his sheep for a walk all over the road."

"I was getting worried. Thought you'd forgotten us."

"Yeah, I'm sorry. I'd allowed plenty of time."

As Mary climbed into the back seat with her case, I had a thought. "Look, I think I'd better let the school know that we might be a bit late. I'll give them a call. Another couple of minutes isn't going to make much difference,"

As I opened the door of the call box across the road, I realised I didn't have the school's number.

"Come on, come on, answer, you pillock!" I muttered as the phone rang at Ty Melin. Neither Jake nor Benji were likely to have left the cottage - probably not even out of bed.

"Who's calling?" came Benji's sleepy voice.

"It's Rob. I'd..."

"Thought you'd gone to work," he slurred.

"Yes, now listen. Can you please ring Sir Wilfred Roberts in Carrick and say that the two students and I may be a little late?"

"Why?"

"Flock of sheep." I had no time to explain.

"I don't know his number."

I cursed silently. Benji could be pretty thick at times. "Not him, my school in Carrick. Use the telephone directory, for Chr... um, please." He might cause more delay if I blasphemed against his new-found faith.

"Right."

"And if Jake's there, please ask him to ring Holly's home number - that's Eric Dickens. She may have got tired of waiting."

"But..."

"Bye!" I hung up.

We shot off down the road through Pant Gorau, the run-down outskirts of Tencastle.

"Remember the party here?" said Mary.

"Very fond memories," I said wistfully. That's where I had first met her. Things could have worked out so different.

There was no sign of Holly where the bottom of a narrow lane joined the main road.

"Bugger!" I breathed out heavily. "She's probably walked back up to the house." We were nearly twenty minutes late.

"Can't you drive up and see if she's there?"

"Jessica doesn't like very steep hills." The lane up to the Dickens' house was at least a one-in-four gradient.

I got out of the car and looked up the lane. Holly was hurrying down.

"Got your message," she gasped, out of breath. "I was just about to ask my mother to run me to Carrick."

Fortunately we met no cavalcade of tractors or other hold-ups on the road, and by pushing Jessica to the limits of her power, we made it to school just as the registration bell rang.

"Catch up with you later," I called after Mary and Holly, having pointed them in the direction of Reception. I dashed off to my class.

I worked through morning break getting stuff ready for the next lesson, so it wasn't until lunchtime that I headed to the staffroom.

"Oversleep, did you?" John Rhys-Price was unavoidable as I entered the door.

"Pardon?"

"I was in the office when your message came through..."

"And you took the call?"

"No, the Secretary. I've never seen Miss Iceberg Ellis look so shocked. 'Lack of Sleep!' she repeated." John touched the side of his nose with his finger, "Mind you, if I'd been with those two gorgeous young girls all night I wouldn't have got any sleep either!"

"In your dreams! Either your hearing or hers is dodgy." Or, more likely, Benji's, I thought. "Flock of sheep is what I said. Blocking the road and made us late."

"Yeah, whatever!" John obviously didn't believe me.

I grabbed a coffee and wandered over to join Mary and Holly.

"How did it go this morning?" I asked.

"Well, after a distinctly frosty reception in the school office, everything's been fine," said Mary.

"Yeah, the secretary looked at us as if we were something the dog had brought in, but the Head of English is very nice," said Holly.

I could guess whom Iceberg had cast as the dog. "Don't know much about the English department," I said, "but I've worked with Mark Matthews, who is in charge of Humanities. You'll have no problems there, Mary."

"He's already asked me if I'd like to accompany a group on a field trip."

"To Dan Yr Ogof?" I said.

"Yes, that's right!" Mary looked surprised that I already knew about the caves on the edge of the Brecon Beacons.

"I went with him last year. Might come again," I said, half-jokingly.

"About our stuff in your car..." Holly began.

"No problem. I'm sorry that we didn't have time this morning but I'll run you round to your digs after school, okay?"

"Thanks, Rob."

***

"What exactly happened this morning?" Jake asked over supper. "I got this garbled message from Benji to ring the Dickens to say you'd be late."

"What exactly did he tell you?"

"Something about blocking the road and lack of sleep. Did you drop off while driving and have an accident?" Jake said with concern.

"The pillock!" I told him of my encounter with the flock of sheep.

"Just a case of baa humbug?"

Jake deftly dodged the remains of my bread roll.

Chapter 8

I was looking forward to half term. One reason was because I'd been working pretty well flat out on lesson preparation and marking - something for which teaching practice never really prepares you. The main attraction, however, was that I'd at last get the opportunity to meet up with Dilly again. The plan was that she'd come down to Tencastle on Saturday and I'd meet her off the train. I'd then take her back to Aberystwyth mid-week and stay a couple of nights with her parents.

Jake's room had en-suite facilities, and we'd quite happily shared the room previously when there had been four of us students in the house. He kindly offered to let me use an air bed and sleeping bag on his floor, to give Dilly a room to herself, if she wanted it, that is. I was rather hoping she would be amenable to sharing my room, if not my bed - which was a single, anyway.

The Monday before half term brought potentially a fly in the ointment. Actually, as it turned out, something considerably more substantial than a mere fly.

"Rob, I was wondering," Mary said at morning break, "since we're both going on the field trip this Friday..."

"We are?" That was news to me.

"You sound surprised. I thought you were keen to come. I mentioned it to Mark Matthews, and he's sorted out cover for your classes. Didn't he say anything to you?"

"Not at all. Anyhow, I'm happy to have a day out."

"Well, then, could I hitch a lift back with you? Jake's invited me over for the weekend."

"He has?" I didn't know about that either.

"Problem?"

"Um, no... not really." Jake's bedroom floor was definitely not going to be available. Perhaps we could persuade Benji to retreat to a monastery for the weekend.

"Are you sure?"

"Yes, of course it's okay. Just thinking of logistics. Dilly's also coming down from Aber for a few days."

I had a flash of inspiration. "Look, I'm going to suggest to Mark that I drive directly to Dan Yr Ogof and meet you there. It's a lot nearer for me than going via Carrick, and we could come straight back. We'd save an hour or so travelling."

"Brilliant."

Mark had been willing to agree to my request, which meant I had the luxury of an extra hour in bed, and I still got to the Dan Yr Ogof show caves in time for a coffee before the coach load of kids turned up. The party then intended to explore some waterfalls in the area. I parked Jessica near where I was assured the walk would end, and hopped on the coach for the short journey to the village of Ystradfellte. It was during this expedition the previous year that I'd inadvertently caused our coach to get stuck in a narrow lane at nearby Penderyn.

I was grateful for no mishaps this year, although we were a good half an hour later than expected getting back to where the coach was now parked behind Jessica. Mark and his colleague, Patricia Prior, shuffled the children aboard, and, as we stood watching the coach depart, Mary slipped her arm around my waist.

"That was a fantastic walk, Rob. Wouldn't have missed it for the world."

"Yeah, pretty spectacular," I agreed.

"How long do you think it will take us to get back to Tencastle?"

"Oh, we should be home by five o'clock. Darn sight quicker than going all the way round by Carrick, that's for sure."

Jessica, perversely, was unwilling to get going. She didn't respond to the starter and it took several swings of the handle to get her to splutter into life. Probably the light drizzle that had set in hadn't helped.

We chugged along the minor road from Ystradfellte into the heart of the Brecon Beacons, but through the steady flow of light-hearted conversation between Mary and myself I was aware that the old girl wasn't quite right. The odd missed beat of the engine and intermittent rumble below that I couldn't really attribute to the rutted road surface left me mentally crossing my fingers.

She just about made it to the top of a long incline, coughed and died.

"Why have we stopped?" Mary asked, curious but unconcerned.

"Don't know," I replied, truthfully. "Perhaps Jessica's tired."

I got out and was immediately struck by a strong whiff of petrol. I couldn't recall offhand the ignition point of octane but I thought it would be prudent for Mary to get out of the car as well until the engine had cooled down a bit. I lifted up the bonnet, though quite what I expected to see or do I wasn't sure. Still, it might have impressed Mary that I was doing by best to fix the problem.

After a few minutes contemplating Jessica's innards, tentatively testing the various leads for any loose connections, I tried the starter again. Nothing. I tried swinging the handle. A gentle cough but no encouraging sign of life.

"I think we're stuck!" I called despondently to Mary, who'd returned to the passenger seat to shelter from the drizzle falling from the thickening mist and low cloud.

"Haven't you got AA breakdown?"

"Yes, basic roadside assistance or tow to nearest garage."

"Well, that's okay then!" she said, optimistically.

"Ye...es, but I have to get in touch with them first." I pointed out. "Do you remember when we last passed a telephone box?"

Her brow furrowed, as she recognised our predicament. "Er, no. There was one in Ystradfellte I expect."

Which must have been several miles behind us - and bugger all habitation in between. Not even an isolated farmhouse that I could recall.

"How far's the next village?"

I shrugged my shoulders. "Two or three miles, maybe more." A dot on my old road atlas suggested that there might be a hamlet before we reached the town of Sennybridge - but it could have just been a speck of dirt.

"What are we going to do, Rob? We can't stay here!"

I wasn't sure that we had a choice, with respect to Jessica. I considered the options, which were limited and unappealing.

"Rob, the road looks as if it's downhill from here. Couldn't we just... er... free wheel? We might come to a house or something."

"Mmm." Mary had given me an idea. "We could try to bump start, I suppose."

Gingerly, I selected second gear, floored the clutch pedal, and released the hand brake. As the car started to roll I engaged the clutch. Jessica jerked, backfired and, to my relief, the engine began to turn over. For a hundred yards or so, until she once more juddered to a halt. I tried again. No joy. In desperation I was prepared to give Mary's suggestion a go.

"We're going to have to do this very slowly," I said. "A couple of hundred yards at a time. I can't let Jessica build up too much speed, or I might not be able to stop her. I just hope the brakes hold out."

Slowly is what we did. After every two or three short freewheels, I waited for a few minutes to let the brakes cool before proceeding. In the space of half an hour we probably covered two miles through country devoid of human habitation or any other mechanised transport. When we ran out of downhill slope we also ran out of options. We came to rest at a bend in the narrow road with barely room for a car to pass, and the road uphill in both directions. And the light was beginning to fade.

"Bugger, bugger, bugger!" I muttered. Not only were we immobile, we were almost invisible to oncoming traffic. We would probably have been safer on top of the hill.

"There's something coming!" Mary yelled.

I quickly turned on the ignition and hoped that my lights and horn still worked.

The flashing and hooting worked. The bonnet of a lorry poked slowly around the corner. Army colours.

Leaving the engine running and the lights on, the driver got out and strode over to us.

"What's going on?" he asked rather brusquely.

"We've broken down, I'm afraid." I said. "Is there a village or house back up the road? Somewhere we could make a phone call?"

"Aye, a few houses and a pub, about a mile back. Look, you'll have to move out of the way, we need to get through."

"That's not possible. There's no room for you to pass, even if we could move."

The driver wasn't happy. Audibly cursing under his breath, he glanced round at his passenger who had also got out of the vehicle.

"Problem, corporal?"

"This couple's old banger's gone kaput and blocking the road, sir."

The officer thought for a moment. "Think you could turn round? We passed a gate a couple of hundred yards back."

"We're not going the long way round, surely!" The corporal looked shocked, "Beggin' your pardon, sir!"

"No, we're going to tow their car to that village we passed. It's not far." He turned to us, "You should be able to get help there."

"Tha... thanks," That was far more than I'd ever hoped for.

"Perhaps your young lady would like to ride up front with us?"

Mary looked at me and nodded. A small price to pay to get us out of our immediate predicament.

They left us on the forecourt of a garage with a single petrol pump and a workshop, sadly closed. It gave me some hope for tomorrow morning.

"Really good of them to help," said Mary, as the army lorry pulled away.

"Yeah, that was unexpected."

"I gather they'd got a convoy of vehicles due to head up into the Brecons, so it may have been pragmatic to get us out of the way."

"Well, whatever. Here we are."

" What do you suggest we do now?" Mary asked.

"See if we can find some food." I nodded towards the hostelry a couple of hundred yards beyond the garage. "And make some phone calls."

I don't think I've ever been quite so pleased to see a pub - aptly named the Traveller's Rest. While waiting for our food - steak pie and mash - I mulled over our options with Mary. "It looks as if we're stuck here until the morning," I said.

"No bus or taxi?"

I shook my head. The barman's amused expression had confirmed what I already suspected; there were no buses from this outpost this evening, or indeed at any time. As to my enquiry about a taxi his answer was also unpromising. "Not much chance. Friday night the old boy in Sennybridge will be too busying ferrying young fillies to Brecon."

"Do they do bed and breakfast here?"

"Yes, but they've only got one room. A double." It was difficult to read Mary's expression. "You can have the bed. I'll sleep on the floor."

Mary shook her head almost imperceptibly, deep in thought.

"Or I could sleep in the car." Not that I fancied that option for one moment.

"That won't be necessary," said Mary, with a wry grin. "No choice really, is there?"

"We'd better let Jake know what's happening," I said.

"What? Tell him that you and I are spending the night together in a strange hotel?"

"Well, no, not quite in those words. I'll just tell him the car's broken down, and we've had to put up somewhere for the night."

I realised that I'd also have to ring Dilly. I was supposed to be meeting her off the train in Tencastle on Saturday afternoon. God knows whether I'd even be in Tencastle by then or have any means of transport.

"Jake's not worried," said Mary, as we took our limited luggage up the narrow staircase to the room we'd been allocated. Actually, probably the only room - the pub was quite small. "Did you get through to Dilly?"

"Left a message with her Mum. She'll ring me back."

The room, though surprisingly spacious, had seen better days. Faded carpets, off-white lace curtains hiding a stray cobweb on the panelled windows, drab brown drapes, chintzy armchair, an enormous heavy wardrobe, and, unbelievably, a huge four-poster bed.

"Romantic, or what?" said Mary, mischievously.

"Um," I wasn't quite sure what to say. I began removing the cushions from the armchair.

"What are you doing?"

"Preparing somewhere to lay my head."

"Don't be silly, Rob, the bed's big enough for both of

us."

"What!" Talk about confused emotions! Under other circumstances I'd have no qualms - well, not many - about sleeping with Mary, but Jake's girlfriend? And mine expected under the same roof in the next day or so.

Mary giggled. "You're such a prude, Rob! Look, if you're worried about virtues, we'll put the spare pillows down the bed between us, like courting couples did with a bolster in days of old."

I wasn't averse to her suggestion. "Suppose I clambered over?" I said light-heartedly.

"Just you dare!"

Invitation or warning, I wondered.

Back in the bar we'd been chatting for some time when I realised Dilly hadn't returned my call. I thought I'd better try again.

"Hi, it's Rob here again. Is Dilys back home yet?"

"She doesn't want to speak to you," came the frosty reply from her mother. I thought I could hear sobbing in the background. "I must say you've got a cheek!"

"What?" I was flummoxed. "Why? What's happened?"

"You! When she phoned the number you left, the receptionist said you'd just gone up to your room - with a young lady!"

My jaw dropped. Shit! "That's not..."

Mrs Morgan seized on the slight hesitation, "You're saying it's not true?"

"No... yes, er... no, I mean... I'm with Jake's girlfriend."

"Well, really! I think Dilys is better off..."

"No, no, please! Let me explain..."

"I don't want to hear..."

"Wait, please!" I pleaded. I thought she was going to slam the phone down. "My car has broken down. I was giving her a lift home from school... she's there on teaching practice." I burbled frantically.

"And?" Mrs Morgan said suspiciously. At least she

hadn't hung up.

"We got towed to this village. There's no way we can get anywhere until the morning. We're staying overnight at the local pub. I was helping Mary take her things to her room." I omitted to mention it was my room as well.

"Hmm." She obviously felt, correctly, that I wasn't giving her the whole story.

"Look, can you tell Dilys, please, that it wasn't what she thought. And I'd really like to talk to her if I can."

A short silence, then "Wait a minute."

I could just detect two female voices but not what was being said. I saw the barman looking at me. The phone wasn't coin operated but I expected a hefty phone bill in the morning. After what seemed ages, I heard footsteps.

"Rob?"

"Dilly? Oh thank God. I'm so sorry to have upset you. A terrible misunderstanding, I realise how it must have sounded."

"Was it? Was it a misunderstanding?" Fairly cool, flat response.

"Absolutely," I hoped I sounded convincing. "Look, did your mother explain what has happened?"

"Sort of."

"Well, we've been on a school field trip, and to save time I took my car so, rather than having to go all the way back to Carrick, we could drive straight to Ty Melin. Jake's invited Mary over for the weekend. You know Mary Williams?"

"Didn't you go out with her at one time?"

"Wanted to, didn't happen. Anyway that's three years ago. She's with Jake now."

"I see." Still distant.

"The reason I rang was that I'm not sure what time, or even how I'm going to get back to Tencastle. I don't know whether my car will be okay or not. I didn't want you hanging around at the station wondering where I was."

"Well, thank you for that, Rob." Did I detect a slight thaw in her voice? "I think in the circumstances it's probably better if I don't come this weekend, particularly if you've already got a house guest."

"I'd sleep on the floor." The second time that night I'd made that offer.

"No, best if you get the car sorted first."

"Can I still come up to see you later in the week? Even if I have to come by train?"

"If you want to," Dilly said, not exactly full of enthusiasm.

"I really would," I pressed. "I really would like to see you again."

"Give me a ring when you're back home then. Take care."

"Thanks, Dilly, See you soon." I breathed a sigh of relief. Our conversation finished on a much more encouraging note. Though I had been looking forward to a whole week together, postponing (hopefully the correct word) her visit would avoid some possible awkward situations.

I slept well. I hadn't tried to take advantage of the gentle kiss Mary gave me as we'd climbed into bed but contented myself with the thought that sleeping so close to a very attractive young woman was far more than I could ever have anticipated even six hours earlier. However, I'd set my mental alarm clock to be up and about reasonably early. I wanted to be at the garage when it opened.

I left Mary still sleeping, her shapely bosom clearly rising and falling beneath her nightdress. Unlike me, she had been prepared for a night or two away from home.

A wizened old chap in brown, oil-smeared dungarees was pushing open the door to the workshop.

"Good morning," I said, "I left my car on your forecourt last night."

"Ah, young man, I wondered where that had come from." He offered me his hand, freshly wiped on a greasy rag. "Ifor Ap Siencyn at your service. Problem, is it?"

"'Fraid so. Conked out completely on the top of the Brecons. I got a tow here."

"Right. You want me to have a look at it?"

"If you could, please."

"Well, I can't promise I'll be able to fix it, but if you come back in an hour, I should be able to tell you what's wrong."

"Thanks very much." Another thought struck me as I handed over the keys. "If you can't repair it today, is there any way I can hire or borrow another car?" Not that I entertained much hope.

"Um, well, that's asking!" He stroked his stubbly chin. "Possibly... I suppose... but let's see what I find out first, shall we?"

Back in our room, Mary was out of bed but still in her nightdress.

"God, you look beautiful!" I blurted out, my honest thoughts overcoming prudence.

Mary smiled and rewarded me with a peck on the cheek. "Thank you, Rob, for being a gentleman last night. I doubt I could have trusted other men in such a situation."

Despite myself, I blushed. "Let's hope you don't have to," I said.

"Rob, one thing," Her brow furrowed causing her nose to twitch upwards, "I didn't bring much money with me. I wasn't expecting to... er... spend a night in a hotel."

I had given the matter of our accommodation bill some thought. "It's not a problem. I've got my chequebook with me. And it's not your fault my car's kaput, so I wouldn't expect you to fork out."

"That's not what I meant!" Mary said, "I'm happy to reimburse you. It's just that I don't have the cash on me."

"No, really, Mary, that's not necessary, but thanks for

the offer."

"Talk about it later perhaps. Anyhow, any news about the car?"

"Being looked at. I'll know after breakfast."

After a hearty full English - or, rather, Welsh - breakfast, I headed back to the garage, leaving Mary to gather her things together upstairs.

"Well, young man," Ifor greeted me, "do you chew gum?"

"Pardon?"

"Chewing gum. I suggest you buy a packet or two."

I couldn't imagine what on earth this had to do with Jessica's problem. I wasn't gnashing my teeth in frustration - yet!

"The main problem is you ran out of fuel..."

"But that's impossible," I interrupted, "I only filled up yesterday morning!" Jessica's petrol gauge was permanently stuck on half full, so I kept a pretty close check on my mileage.

"That may be, but you've got a small leak in your petrol tank. Could have been caused by a sharp stone thrown up from the road. The tank's pretty well worn. You will need a new one."

He saw my face fall at this news. "But I've done a temporary job. Sealed the leak with chewing gum."

That didn't sound to me a standard procedure in car maintenance. "Gum?" I said.

"How far have you got to go?"

"To Tencastle. Fifteen, twenty miles or so."

"Well, you should be okay, but some chewing gum in reserve would be a good idea - I'll show you where the hole is - and I'll let you have a can of petrol just in case."

"That's... that's very good of you." I couldn't believe that we'd probably get home in Jessica.

"There is one other thing, though," Ifor looked serious. "I think your big end is on the way out. It needs looking at very soon but you should be good for a few more miles yet."

At least twenty, I prayed. I hadn't a clue what or where Jessica's big end was. "Thanks very much," I said. "How much do I owe you?"

"Petrol, mainly. I haven't done much else, and I won't charge for the chewing gum!"

"Thanks very much again," I said. All in all I felt I'd got away pretty lightly.

I took the journey very steadily, avoiding any unnecessary stops to minimise the chance of Jessica's lifeblood draining away again. But her future was causing me some concern since Ifor's diagnoses implied expensive remedies. When we got to Tencastle without incident, I felt a visit to Owain's Auto Emporium might be useful, while Mary collected a few things.

Initial impressions weren't good. Most of the cars were well beyond the limit of my modest savings. That had also been the case a couple of years ago when Jessica had been the only option.

Owain waddled out of his office. "The old girl still going strong, is she?" He nodded towards Jessica.

"Pretty well," I replied with some economy of truth. "I'm thinking of swapping her for something... er... more recent."

"Hmm," he wiggled a finger in his ear. "I'm afraid I wouldn't be able to offer you much for her, but have a look round, see if anything takes your fancy, and I'll see what I can do."

"Thanks," I said. Several cars had certainly taken my fancy but apart from an ageing Beetle with a ridiculously high mileage and a rusting Mini there was nothing close to my budget.

Mary arrived, closely followed by Jake laden with several heaving shopping bags. "You don't look happy," she said.

"Nothing I can afford," I shrugged my shoulders.

"Why?" said Jake, "Surely you're not thinking of getting rid of Jessica? She's almost part of the family!"

I explained the problem to him. He didn't say anything but I could see he'd got some scheme in mind. As long as it didn't involve hitching it up to Benji's horse.

"Holly mentioned that her mum is thinking of changing her car," said Mary.

"Really?" I was trying to remember what vehicles they'd had when they had invited Carpiog Morris back to their house for a barbecue - a couple of years ago, it must have been, soon after the group had formed.

"That baby Fiat?" said Jake. "Almost had to sit with my legs out of the window."

I wasn't fussy. "Might give her a call," I said. "Though I'm not sure what I'd do with Jessica. It wouldn't seem right just to dump her."

"I'll have her!" Jake declared.

"You're not serious?" I couldn't believe my ears. "She needs a lot of work on her, Jake!"

"I've got a friend who's into restoring old bangers."

"But you can't even drive!"

"I'll learn. You could teach me. It would get Jessica off your hands."

"Couldn't your friend just restore Jessica for me?" I said.

"Perhaps, but it would cost you."

Somehow I felt Jake was getting all the favours and I'd end up with zilch, but at least I could see a possible resolution. "You make arrangements with your friend, then. If I don't get another car, I'll pay for Jessica's repairs, otherwise you pay - plus, of course, new road tax and insurance."

"Fair enough."

"And I won't charge you for driving lessons."

Chapter 9

I'd set off for Aberystwyth on Wednesday morning. As the crow flies, it was not a great distance from Tencastle. Even by car the journey would not have taken more than two hours, either the shorter distance by minor roads or the longer, but less demanding, main road route. But I'd delivered Jessica for major surgery to Jake's mechanic friend that morning. The train therefore was the only way I was ever going to meet Dilly over the half-term holiday - and the most convenient connection via Carmarthen had been severed a few years earlier, no doubt by Beeching's heavy axe. As a consequence, the scheduled journey time was now in excess of four hours. All the way to Shrewsbury only to virtually double back through Newtown! That, of course, did not allow for operational contingencies, as the guard on the train had described the hour's delay. Cattle had somehow strayed onto the line in the open countryside beyond the small town of Caersws. Pity the diesel hadn't been fitted with the giant cow pushers you see on locomotives in those western movies.

Although I'd arrived, late, tired, and a little irritable, the few days with Dilly had gone much better than I had expected. I'd been apprehensive about the reception I'd get, not only from her parents whom I'd only met very briefly at the graduation ceremony back in the summer, but also from Dilly herself, given the circumstances of our aborted plans for her Tencastle visit. I needn't have worried. The Morgans had made me most welcome, and Dilly had shown me the delights of Aberystwyth, such as they were at the tail end of autumn. There had been little opportunity to explore any delights of a more intimate nature, however, but her agreement to a rescheduled return visit had given me great hopes.

The return journey couldn't have been smoother.

Feeling in a very pleasant frame of mind, I treated myself to the luxury of a taxi from the station back to Ty Melin. No doubt Jake would tell me of Jessica's fate.

"Hi," he said casually when I walked in. "Do you want the good news or the bad?"

I opted to retain my sense of well-being for a couple of minutes longer.

"We won't have to pay any rent until Christmas."

Not the news I was expecting. "Why not?" I asked, intrigued.

"I've done a deal. Decoration in lieu."

"Decorating the loo? What do you mean?"

"Not only there. The whole house."

I opened my mouth - and closed it again while I took in the implications of what Jake seemed to be proposing. And this was the good news?

"Am I understanding you correctly?" I said eventually, "We pay no rent but in return we decorate the house?"

"Absolutely!" Jake's enthusiasm was considerably greater than mine.

"And Benji's agreed to this... this deal?" "

"Yes. Well, sort of."

I raised an eyebrow.

"I mentioned it to him in passing, and he said, 'Whatever'."

I groaned inwardly. "And the bad news is?"

"We have to be out of the house by the New Year. Cousin's coming back from Oz."

We'd been led to believe that our tenure of Ty Melin was unlikely to continue into the New Year, so this confirmation wasn't in itself a surprise. However, it boded for a period of uncertainty while we all sorted out alternative accommodation.

"Any thoughts what you'll do?" Jake asked.

"I suppose it would make sense to look for digs in Carrick," I said reluctantly. "If I'm still there." Although I was hopeful my temporary position covering a maternity leave would be made permanent I hadn't yet had confirmation. "And you?"

"Dunno. May move in with Mary."

I was surprised that their relationship had developed that quickly. "And what about Benji?"

"He's making mutterings about the empty house down by the bridge. You know, next door to Evan Jones, where that posh family lived?"

I remembered. Two years ago, after rapidly melting snow had turned our normally placid stream into a raging torrent, we had helped to rescue them from the flood. "But he'll never be able to afford that!"

"He's got ideas about turning it into a retreat for meditation. Apparently one of the Jesus freaks he hangs out with has got pots of money."

"You could always ask if he'll have a spare cell for you." I suggested.

"Bugger off!"

Jake hadn't yet given me the news I really wanted, good or bad. "What's the situation with Jessica and your mechanic friend?"

"Waiting for parts, I think. Why?"

"Well, it would be nice to know. I've got to make a decision about the Dickens' Fiat this week. Holly's picking me up on Monday morning, so I can try it out coming back to Tencastle."

***

Whilst my old Ford Popular wasn't exactly spacious, the little Fiat 500 felt as roomy as a sardine can with myself, Holly and Mary crammed inside. Like Jessica, it laboured up steep hills, but on the positive side it had windows that you could actually wind down properly and had synchromesh on all its gears. And it had done barely

50,000 miles. Jessica's clock had shown 99,999 miles since the previous April.

"I'm surprised you're not taking this car on yourself," I said to Holly.

"Can't really afford to. Anyway, my twin brother would then want his own wheels as well."

"And where is he doing his final teaching practice?"

"Oh, Harry's up in Knighton. First time we've really been separated for any long period."

We made good time to Carrick. On the level the Fiat had reached over 50 mph, something Jessica could only achieve downhill with a following gale.

"I need to pick up a few things from our digs," said Holly. "You don't mind, do you?"

"No problem."

A few minutes later we pulled up outside a rather nondescript terraced dwelling in one of the residential streets that led up from the river.

"How did you come by this place?" I asked.

"Someone my father knew," said Holly. "I won't be long," she called as she opened the front door and slipped inside.

"I expect Jake's already told you that we've been given notice at Ty Melin," I said to Mary, while we waited. She'd been very quiet on the journey, making no reference, thankfully, to our predicament ten days earlier.

"He mentioned a leaving party."

That was news to me, but I wasn't unduly surprised. "I'm thinking of looking for somewhere in Carrick."

"You could always try here. We'll be gone by Christmas."

"That's certainly a possibility, Mary." It wasn't something I'd even considered until that moment. "What's it like?"

"Okay, I suppose. Landlady's a bit straight laced. And you won't have the freedom like you have at the cottage."

"Hmm. Still, it might do until I found something better."

"Why don't you pop round after school one day? We can have a word with the landlady in the meantime."

I made up my mind on the journey back after school. The little car jogged along quite contentedly and handled well. It would suit me fine, particularly as my daily mileage would be considerably less when I'd sorted out accommodation in Carrick. Nick Ramsbottom had just confirmed that my post would be made permanent, if I wanted it, since Jenny Pagitter, for whom I was covering, had decided not to return after maternity leave.

"Congratulations, Jake!" I called as I entered the cottage.

"Hang on a sec," came his voice from upstairs. The toilet flushed and Jake appeared, still hitching up his trousers.

"Did you say congratulations? What am I supposed to have done?"

"No, I meant it," I said. "Congratulations. You are now the proud owner of a car."

"What do you mean?"

"Jessica. She's yours."

"Why?"

"I'm buying the Fiat from Eric Dickens. You said you'd have Jessica."

"But... I can't drive!"

"So you said. You asked me to teach you."

"I... I... er, " Jake was rarely lost for words, but clearly his mind was racing through the various implications. "I didn't think you were serious," he concluded lamely.

"You seemed quite certain when you made the offer," I said.

"But - she's still at the garage!"

"Yes, well, you pay the bill and you get the car and driving lessons for free.

Jake remained speechless.

Chapter 10

"I'm ready," said Jake.

"For what?" I asked, as I helped myself to cereal in the kitchen.

"Driving lessons. You're not doing anything this weekend, are you?"

"Not specifically," I replied cautiously. Apart from the mountain of marking and lesson preparation I omitted to mention, knowing it would fall on deaf ears. "But aren't you forgetting something?"

"Such as?"

"Firstly, Jessica's not here, and secondly you haven't even got a provisional licence yet."

"Ah, well, Jessica's all sorted. And I've got the form here for the licence."

"But you haven't actually got the licence itself, have you? You're not legal to drive otherwise."

"Oh!" I'd burst Jake's bubble of enthusiasm. He thought for a moment. "Couldn't we go off road somewhere?" he said.

"You're joking!" But then I had an idea. "Possibly, though" I added.

Even though I'd only been driving the new car for less than a week, it seemed strange to get behind the wheel of Jessica again. We'd left Fi (Benji's idea - I never seemed to have a say in naming my own vehicles) in Tencastle, and collected Jessica from the workshop of Jake's friend. He seemed to have done a good job. Although the suspension was as rough as ever, she purred along without any extraneous rattles from under the bonnet.

I pulled into a makeshift car park where the road passed through high moorland. Stony tracks led off in several directions. We had the place to ourselves.

"Never been out here before," said Jake. "Where are

we?"

"On the route to where I did my first teaching practice."

"Pretty desolate, if you ask me."

"All the better for our purpose."

I spent the best part of half an hour trying to get him familiar with the position of the various hand and foot controls, together with their function and operation. Jake was impatient to take charge of the car for real.

Eventually I uttered a silent prayer and allowed Jake to start the engine. Many times he'd seen me give the handle a swing but I was confident that operation could wait until a later occasion.

"Okay, left foot down, select first gear," I said in my best schoolmasterly voice. "Now, gently down with your right foot and ease the pressure with your left foot until you feel the car begin to move."

The engine raced. "Gently!" I yelled, "Ease back on the accelerator!"

"Is that right or left foot?" asked Jake, lifting both feet almost simultaneously. Jessica lurched forward and stalled.

I took a deep breath. "Shall we try again?"

Again meant four more attempts before Jake got the correct degree of co-ordination to move Jessica forward more like a tortoise than a kangaroo. At least it wasn't my vehicle whose internal workings were being tortured.

"Right, let's try reversing. Same principle with the feet. Let out the clutch slowly and accelerate gently."

"What's that mean in plain language?"

"Left foot up, right foot down. You do know your left from right, I suppose?"

"I'm not an idiot!"

Matter of opinion I suppose. Jessica rolled forward slightly then shot back like a rocket into a tangle of blackberry bushes. I insisted that Jake extricated the vehicle himself without my assistance.

"Right, listen," I said a few minutes later. "You should always have the handbrake on before you get ready to move. It didn't matter this time because we are on almost level ground. Imagine you had to reverse up the road from Ty Melin. You'd also have to release the handbrake at the same time as you engage the clutch. And keep one hand on the steering wheel."

"Darn complicated this," Jake complained, "How on earth is my brain supposed to cope with each limb doing something different?"

"You managed okay with morris dancing," I said.

"Yeah, well, if I got something wrong I didn't end up with my arse in the brambles."

After the initial hiccups, Jake picked up the technique quite quickly, and was eager to move on. Beyond the confines of the car park.

Cautiously at first Jake guided Jessica along the track which appeared to have the smoothest, least rutted surface. Then as his confidence grew, I suggested he could change up into second gear. The track wound gently downwards between gorse and bramble bushes, with no end in sight. I was confident we'd find somewhere for Jake to attempt a three-point turn.

Jessica was gathering speed, still only in second gear, but the incline had become steeper. "Slow down," I advised Jake, then, as I saw the gate ahead, I yelled, "Brakes, NOW!"

Jessica slithered to a halt with a yard or two to spare. There was nowhere to turn. I got out and went round to take Jake's place at the wheel. While I didn't relish the prospect of reversing all the way up the track, I was at least confident I could do so.

"Why don't we just go into the field and turn round?" said Jake.

He had a point. The gate led into a large grassy

meadow, its far boundary obscured by the gently convex terrain. The ground looked firm enough. I thought perhaps I could also get Jake to practice a hill start.

I opened the gate and beckoned Jake to drive in, solo. More out of habit from being brought up on a farm, I also closed it again. As I strode over to join him for his next driving lesson I saw we were no longer alone in the field.

"Jake, for Christ's sake, get going!" I shouted, hoping he'd see the urgency in my hand signals. I sprinted for the gate, and prayed that Jake would notice the bull that was just about to charge.

Not a moment too soon Jessica let forth a blast of dark exhaust smoke and surged forward. Bucking wildly the car raced across the meadow with the beast in hot pursuit. And disappeared. I was considering options as to whether to stay put or investigate when, after what seemed ages but in probability less than thirty seconds, Jessica careered over the brow of the hill towards me. Jake appeared to have gained some ground over the bull, but not enough to escape through the gate.

Amazingly, Jake braked suddenly, swung the car round and charged back up hill with lights blazing and horn sounding. I waited for the inevitable crunch of metal and bovine muscle.

The bull veered away at the last minute and galloped away out of sight. Jake deftly swung the car round again and sped towards the gate, which I quickly opened to let him through. Jessica screeched to a halt.

"Bloody hell," Jake exhaled heavily, wiping his brow as he walked towards me. "I never realised a bull could move so fast!"

"You did well," I said. "Turning the tables like that was darn risky but impressive."

"Yeah, well, I'm done with being a motorised matador!"

"Probably Jessica's fault."

"What do you mean?"

"Red rag to a bull?" I said. "He probably took exception to Jessica's livery." Which was bright pink.

I heard the sound of another vehicle. I glanced back over the gate, towards which an old tractor was heading. The driver was yelling and shaking his fist in the air.

"We're going to have more than a bull to contend with if we don't shift," I ran to the car. "I'll drive!"

Barely waiting for Jake to slam the door, I gunned the engine and shot off up the track, indifferent to the discomfort from Jessica's ageing suspension. Nor did I stop until I'd put a dozen miles or so between us and the car park.

We sought refuge at a safe distance in the Black Cock at Llanbedrod. As a precaution I left Jessica at the rear of the pub out of view from the road.

"Christ, I've never been so desperate for a pint!" said Jake, quaffing the foaming bitter.

Chapter 11

I was already feeling quite chuffed that evening when I got back to Ty Melin. I'd sorted out accommodation in Carrick for next term, in the digs Mary and Holly were currently sharing. I'd run them home after school and had a word with their landlady. She was a bit of a sourpuss, but the flat, though compact, was functional. It comprised a small kitchenette-cum-lounge, one bedroom with a single bed and a convertible sofa, and a pocket-sized bathroom with loo and shower.

The icing on the cake was the letter I found waiting for me from Dilly. She'd agreed to come down the following weekend. I just needed to make some back-up dormitory arrangements with Jake.

He wandered in with Benji as I was finishing the reheated remnants of Sunday's stew.

"Benji give you a lift?" I said, jestingly.

"He did, actually."

"What, not on Caspar?"

"Yeah, why not?"

"Well, I... oh, forget it." I could think of a number of reasons why not, but it would have been flogging a dead horse, so to speak.

"All ready for the weekend then, Rob?"

"Yes, at last!" I replied, then paused, wondering how he already knew of my plans. No way would he have opened my letters. Unless, of course, Dilly had rung when I was out. "Er..." I began.

"That's really great! Now, we'll need to get some stuff in."

"Ye...es." I wondered where this was leading.

"Now, if you could stop by Green Willy's and pick up a step-ladder?"

"What?"

"To reach the ceiling."

I tried in vain to think what that had got to do with anything. "Why would..."

"And could you get the paint and some brushes?" Jake was ticking off various points on his fingers.

"Jake, I..."

"Cream emulsion and..."

"Jake, just shut up for a moment!"

"What? What's up?" He looked bemused.

"We're talking at cross purposes here. Dilly is coming to stay this weekend."

"Oh, is she?" Jake said, "No problem, she can lend a hand."

"Jake, my plan for a romantic weekend with Dilly doesn't include plastering the walls with paint!"

He frowned. "But you said..."

"I didn't know you were planning to decorate the house this weekend."

"I didn't know you were planning to invite Dilly this weekend," he retorted.

"Whatever. I'm sorry, I'm not available. Next weekend if you like."

"But that's when we're having our party!"

"We are?" That was news to me.

"Can't you postpone..."

"No way!"

"Oh, well, I suppose it will just have to be Benji and me - and Mary, she's offered to help."

Bully for her. Though I thought she was still in Carrick.

"What's just you and me?" asked Benji, returning from the kitchen with a jam sandwich.

"Decorating the house. This weekend, remember?"

"Not me. I'm meeting with the Seven Brethren."

"What's that," I said, "Seventh Day Adventists meet Plymouth Brethren?"

"Eh?" These God squad groups obviously weren't part

of Benji's religious conversion. "They're the ones putting up the funds for the house - you know, by the bridge."

"You're serious about that?" Jake said.

"Absolutely." Benji thought for a moment. "Hey, if I help with the painting here, perhaps you'd like to do the same at the house."

Jake and I looked at each other. We both shook our heads.

"Moses and Kiddecott - doesn't quite sound right for an outfit of interior decorators!" I chuckled. "But, seriously, Jake, let's get back to the issue of this house, this weekend," I continued. "If you want to make a start on your bedroom, fine, but I don't want to be paddling around paint pots in the living room or kitchen." A possible conflict of interests suddenly came to mind. "I was thinking of asking you if I could share your room, if necessary."

"You could borrow my hammock," Benji offered. "It's big enough for two."

"I'll pass on that," I said. I couldn't see myself swinging from the walls, let alone two of us possibly in an intimate relationship.

"Or you could use my room, I can stay down at the house."

"Thanks, Benji, that is helpful."

"How about we have a concerted effort on the decorating the following weekend?" I suggested.

"I suppose we could have a house-painting working party," said Jake.

"I think the guests might have other ideas about getting plastered."

"Perhaps you're right," Jake conceded. "I'll need to do some rescheduling." He thought for a moment, then added, "I'd still be grateful if you could get the step ladder."

***

In my eagerness to fine-tune my own plans for Dilly's visit I'd put Jake's plans to the back of my mind. Until he reminded me on Friday morning just as I was about to set off for Carrick.

"You won't forget to call at Green Willy's on the way home, will you?"

I had, of course. "No problem," I called over my shoulder. I was intending to come back via Tencastle anyway, to meet Dilly off the train. Unexpectedly her school had been closed for the day, so she was able to travel on Friday afternoon instead of Saturday morning.

I hadn't really given any thought to the practicalities of transporting a step ladder in a Fiat 500. It wasn't until I carried it out to the car that I realised it was as long as my vehicle. And I didn't have a roof rack. I thought about returning to the store and asking them to deliver it - but then Jake wouldn't have it for his weekend activities. One thing the Fiat did have, surprisingly, was a sun-roof.

Dilly looked gorgeous. Her petite figure was perfectly dressed in a smart powder blue skirt with matching jacket, and her dark eyes sparkled beneath shiny black shoulder-length hair. I restrained myself with a quick hug and a kiss and led her out to meet Fi, my new car.

"Are you joining the fire brigade, Rob," she asked, seeing the ladder protruding several feet out through the roof of the car.

"Sorry about that, it's just something Jake asked me to get."

She raised an eyebrow. "Okay..."

"There's plenty of room for you and your bag," I said, exaggerating Fi's capacity. "Though I'm glad you didn't bring a large suitcase."

Dilly was able to sit reasonably normally in the front seat once I'd moved the ladder more to my side, leaving me hunched over the wheel in order to drive.

It was unfortunate that the belt of heavy rain arrived several hours ahead of its forecast. A few drops at first, but as we reached the edge of Tencastle it was obvious that we'd be soaked well before we reached the cottage.

"Might just be a shower," I said hopefully as I pulled into a dark lay-by sheltered by overhanging conifers. "Didn't think I'd need a brolly!"

"I've got one," said Dilly, "in my bag." She scrambled out to rummage in her holdall.

Someone tapped on the window. "Good of you to stop, Rob!" came a familiar voice.

"Jake! What the hell are you doing here?"

"Walking home. At least I was, till it started raining."

"We're a bit overloaded already, as you can see."

"Ye...es, I see. Hi Dilly!" said Jake, as she held her brolly over them both. "Er, supposing I hang on to the ladder? It's only for a short distance."

"But you'll get soaked anyway stuck out through the roof!"

"Hmm." Jake thought for a moment. "I know, if I strip the plastic wrapping off the ladder, I could drape it around me." Immediately he set to the task, while Dilly and I looked on gobsmacked.

"There!" he said. He'd squeezed himself against the rungs, his head and torso protruding through the roof. The breeze caught the loose plastic, which flapped out behind him like a transparent cape.

"I think you should take your jeans off," I said.

"I don't understand."

"Superman wears trunks not trousers!" Dilly and I both laughed.

"Pillock! Sorry, Dilly," Jake added.

I drove very carefully back to Ty Melin, attracting a hoot on the horn from a motorist and a long hard scrutiny from the officers in a passing police car.

"I'd forgotten what a delightful cottage this was," said Dilly. We'd flopped out onto the sofa with a coffee to warm us up, while Jake took a shower. The cape hadn't been entirely successful; most of it had blown away and ended up draped across a hedgerow.

"Yeah, two years ago since you came to our bonfire night party." I put my arm round her shoulders. "But we've got to be out by the New Year."

"That's a great shame. What will you do?"

"I've got a small one-bedroom pad in Carrick, temporarily."

"I see."

In two words Dilly seemed to convey thoughts that had already been going through my mind. Would the landlady be amenable to female visitors and would Dilly be agreeable to sharing a room with me on a future visit? When I'd shown her to my bedroom and mentioned that Benji had offered to let me use his, Dilly hadn't suggested avoiding any inconvenience to him.

We were saved any possible awkward discussion by Jake breezing in.

"Good to see you again, Dilly. Sorry about the uncomfortable journey." He almost sounded as if he meant it. "All my fault, really."

"I thought you'd got your own car now - Rob's old boneshaker?"

I winced at her description of Jessica - even if it was true.

"I have, but I haven't passed my test yet, so I keep it down by the college. I get to practice whenever I can persuade Rob or another driver friend to risk their life."

A thought struck me. "Didn't you say Mary was staying this weekend?"

"Couldn't make it until tomorrow afternoon. Probably."

I suspect she'd got wind of Jake's intentions with paint

and paper.

"But don't worry, we're all sorted for this evening."

I wasn't worried until that point. "What do you mean?"

"Food! Dinner party for four. I found a great recipe for chicken curry." He noticed me glance at Dilly. "You weren't thinking of going back into town to eat, were you?"

Actually I was, though I hadn't broached the matter with Dilly yet, largely due to the intervention of Jacob and his ladder.

Dilly pre-empted my reply. "That sounds really good, Jake. Thanks!"

"But there's only three of us now," I put in my token objection. I assumed Benji would be keeping the company of his godly brethren.

"All the more for us," said Jake, "and I picked up a couple of bottles of plonk yesterday. On offer they were."

I hadn't intended to spend my first evening with Dilly in the company of anyone else but there really was no other option. In consolation Jake's culinary skills had greatly improved, though it was probably prudent not to enquire too closely what had actually gone into the dish. Dilly and I at least managed to claim the sofa to ourselves after dinner. The copious quantity of wine and port we consumed left us contentedly merry, relaxed and, as the evening wore on, increasingly soporific.

I wasn't surprised then when Dilly announced she was ready to turn in. I took that as a cue to follow her upstairs, 'to make sure she had everything she needed', I said to Jake. His leery grin clearly expressed doubt that those were my real intentions. But we enjoyed just a few minutes of passionate embrace and fumbling before Dilly extricated herself with a gentle, "See you in the morning, Rob," and a goodnight kiss.

I was certain of one thing. I wanted to be out of the cottage soon after breakfast and not return before the evening. Once I'd showered and dressed I waited until I heard stirrings from my room, then tapped gently on the door. I took her 'Hi, Rob,' to be an invitation to enter. She was sitting up in bed and patted the duvet for me to join her - though, unfortunately not under the covers. Perversely I had a flitting image of the recent occasion when I'd seen another girl in bed, every bit as attractive. But this time I had no reason to keep my distance.

"So what's the plan for today?" Dilly said, a little while later, as I lay beside her stroking her silky black hair.

"What would you like to do?" I asked, "Weather looks settled. Take a drive out somewhere?"

"I'd quite like to see Carrick, where you work."

"Ok...ay," I said tentatively. With my luck I'd be sure to bump into John Rhys-Price, and lurid speculation would be all around the staff room by Monday morning break.

"Or, why don't you show me those caves and waterfalls where you took the kids? I've never been that way before." There was a mischievous sparkle in her dark brown eyes. "You could even show me where Jessica broke down."

I suspected there might have been a hidden agenda behind her teasing, but I couldn't think of any better suggestions. However, I had no intention of stopping off at the Traveller's Rest in case I was recognised as having spent the night there in the company of a different woman. Mind you, were Fi to break down in similar circumstances...

Fi behaved herself impeccably. In the clear late November sunshine I was even able to enjoy the spectacular scenery of the Brecons, previously shrouded in low mist and fading daylight. Dilly hadn't come prepared for serious walking so we took in just the nearest waterfall and pottered around by the river near Ystradfellte where it flows into a cave. We then let ourselves get seriously distracted by the local pub.

"Dan yr Ogof or Carrick?" I said as I washed down the last of the sticky toffee pudding with my second pint of Felinfoel beer - a brew I'd not come across hitherto. I hoped the dessert and the steak and ale pie would soak up enough of the alcohol to keep me legal to drive.

"Can't we do both?"

"Depends if you want to do any shopping in Carrick. It's dead by six o'clock."

"Carrick then," said Dilly. "You know its Welsh name is Carreg Mawr?"

"Yes, indeed. It sounds beautiful the way you say it." I loved her soft, lilting accent.

"Flatterer!" She laughed.

One would never regard Carrick Major as a shopping metropolis but it did have character in an old- worldly sort of way. None of the major retail chains had yet displaced the independent stores which provided most of the requirements for the townspeople, and indeed for those in the outlying villages. I showed Dilly where I would be lodging after Christmas. I walked her past the imposing entrance to Sir Wilfred Roberts Grammar School where I worked. We strolled past the livestock market down to the bridge where the main road to Carmarthen crosses the river.

"Fancy tea and cakes?" I said. "There's a lovely little bakery and café in the main square."

Dilly nodded eagerly. She was quite petite and slender but she had a healthy appetite!

The chance of meeting John Rhys-Price in tea shop was zero. I reckoned he'd still be playing rugby somewhere, or else propping up the bar in the Bull and Dragon. We gave our full attention to the calorie-laden cakes on offer, so it wasn't until I turned to look for a table that I saw two familiar faces.

"Hi Rob!" Sandra waved. "Come and join us!" She was sitting with Janet Milward, the new music teacher.

I couldn't really ignore them. "Hi there!"

Dilly followed me over to their table. "Sandra and Janet are two of my colleagues at work," I explained, and introduced her. "Dilly and I were at Tencastle together."

"Do you still live there?" Janet asked.

"No, in Aberystwyth," replied Dilly. I sensed she was feeling a little uncomfortable. "Just visiting. I was interested to see where Rob worked."

"Pretty grey and daunting from the outside, isn't it?" said Sandra. "It's okay when you get to know it."

"Have you been teaching there long?"

"I don't actually teach. I'm a science lab technician, but Janet and I both started this term. Same as Rob, really, though as you probably know, he did his TP there."

"Uhuh," Dilly acknowledged. Though I may not have told her in so many words, I'm pretty sure she knew of my previous experience at Sir Wilfred Roberts - or at least some of it. She turned to Janet. "Are you a technician as well?"

Janet chuckled. A light, infectious laugh. "Not like that. No, I teach music."

"Rob plays the guitar, don't you?" said Sandra, looking at me with a mischievous grin.

"Really?" said Janet, with what sounded like genuine interest.

I nodded. Three years ago, Sandra had tried to use the excuse of guitar lessons to lure me into her house.

Dilly saved further probing on that topic. "He's a folk singer too. Won first prize at the inter-college eisteddfod."

An exaggeration - Jake had done the vocals and I'd played the spoons. So I felt it only fair to sing her praise as well. "And Dilly won first prize for Welsh folk dancing."

"That's very interesting," said Janet. "I'm toying with the idea of starting a folk club in Carrick."

Dilly was rather pensive for a while on the drive back

to the cottage while I burbled away about all manner of trivia with barely any response from her.

"Surprised Sandra knew about your guitar playing," she said eventually.

Flannel or truth. I opted for a bit of each. "She used to live in the village where I did my first teaching practice. Her daughter was at the school. She probably saw me taking my guitar in one day."

"I see."

"Quite surprised when I found she'd moved to Carrick and we'd be working together." Not the best way I could have put it.

"Right."

"You're not thinking I've got something going with her, are you?" I knew that was exactly what was in her mind.

"She's quite attractive."

"Yes, I don't deny that, but she's also a good bit older than me. And she's married. She's got a daughter who's nearly twelve!" I didn't elaborate that the daughter came from a previous relationship.

"And what about Janet?"

"Today's the first time I've really spoken to her." That was the truth.

We were almost back at the cottage. I wanted to direct her thoughts away from whatever she thought I might be getting up to in Carrick. "How about we go into Tencastle this evening?" Though after our generous lunch I doubted if we'd be spending the time in a restaurant.

Dilly thought for a moment, then flashed me a smile. More like her usual self. "Okay. But I'd like to change first."

That Jake had been busy was evident from the aroma of fresh paint that hit us as soon as we stepped inside the cottage. Dilly wrinkled her nose.

"Sorry," I said to her, "You probably already gathered. Jake's in D.I.Y. mode this weekend."

The handyman himself appeared on the landing, dressed in tatty denim shorts and T-shirt, both liberally spattered with white paint. Similar blotches on the ebony skin of his bare arms and legs suggested he had been stricken with a bizarre plague.

He waved a paintbrush in greeting. "Hi there, you two! Had a good day? Come and see what I've been up to!"

I rolled my eyes at Dilly. She grinned and nodded. We climbed the stairs and followed Jake into his bedroom. All the furniture was pushed together in the middle, covered, mostly, with an assortment of newspaper, a plastic sheet and a threadbare blanket. The steps were set up in the corner where a short length of curtain rail still awaited attention. Straddling his desk chair, a plank supported a tray of used brushes and a tin of paint.

"Well, what do you think?"

"Um..." He'd certainly effected a transformation, and, for a novice, I suppose it wasn't too bad. The tired wallpaper with its floral designs had been coated with a pale cream emulsion, reasonably evenly applied.

"Been at it ever since you left," Jake burbled. "I'm just about knackered."

"Jake! Don't..." I cried, as I realised his intention. Too late.

He plonked himself down on the end of the plank. Which promptly tilted, dropping him on the floor while the brushes cascaded onto his chest and the paint pot described an aerial somersault before bouncing off the window sill.

"Oh SHIT!"

White paint spattered the windows and trickled down the freshly-emulsioned wall onto the carpet.

"Flaming hell, just look at that mess!"

"Mmm, bit like one of Benji's early impressionist murals," I said, unhelpfully.

Dilly giggled.

"That's not funny!" Jake retorted.

I couldn't contain my laughter any longer.

Jake grimaced, and, realising he wasn't going to get any sympathy for his plight, turned to practicalities. "You're the chemist, Rob, how do I get rid of this ruddy paint?"

"You've got turps or white spirit, I suppose, for cleaning the brushes?"

"Yeah."

"Right, scrape off as much as you can, then paper towels or old cloths soaked in white spirit. Probably a good idea to wash the whole lot with hot detergent afterwards as well. You'll have to emulsion that patch of wall again, though."

"Yeah, whatever," Jake said, resignedly.

"I'll give you a hand while Dilly gets changed," I offered.

"What, are you going out again?" Jake sounded genuinely surprised.

"Thought we'd get a bite to eat in town."

He thought for a moment. "Can I join you? I haven't eaten yet. Didn't even stop for lunch."

I wished I hadn't mentioned food. I would have liked to have said no. We'd already done the ménâge à trois last night. But I felt some smidgeon of pity for him. "Well, okay. But only if you change into something that doesn't get us high on solvent fumes."

"Would it be okay if we pick up Mary as well?"

Tencastle wasn't well endowed with good eating establishments – or many eateries at all, for that matter – and I'd been thinking of something more inspiring that Ffion's Fish Fantasia, the local chippie. I'd heard that the Fox and Shepherd, down by the river, offered a reasonable menu under its new management. They would surely have room for the four of us without pre-booking. And I thought Jake would definitely appreciate a pint. We also discovered that they offered reduced portions for people with a small appetite – which suited Dilly and me.

Had the convivial atmosphere and the beer - I shouldn't really have had another pint - not dulled my senses I would have been more aware of the implications when Mary accepted Jake's invitation to come back to the cottage for the night. "So that we get to work early," he'd said.

The whiff of white spirit caught us even as we entered the front door. In Jake's room it would have been overpowering. Besides which, his room was still in a state of chaos.

Mary and Dilly headed for the kitchen to brew some coffee.

"Rob," said Jake to me in the lounge "we have a problem. We can't use my room."

"We weren't going to," I said, muttering "Pillock" under my breath.

"Rob, would you mind…"

"If you were going to suggest that I give up Benji's room for you and Mary, the answer's no!"

"But couldn't you and Dilly…?" He nodded towards the kitchen.

"No."

"Hey!" came Benji's voice from the landing, "You got coffee going?"

Jake and I looked at each other open-mouthed.

"What are you doing here?" said Jake, as Benji sauntered downstairs in his pyjamas.

"I live here, remember?"

"But… you said you were sleeping in the Brethren house?"

"That was last night."

"Why not tonight as well?"

"Hard floor and too cold. Didn't have any coins for the meter."

I was sure the Benji of old wouldn't have noticed such trivialities of discomfort.

"I've put your things back in your room, Rob," he added.

When it came to the crunch, there wasn't much argument about which option was least unattractive. None of us fancied decamping to a cold, barely furnished house, least of all Benji. I was not keen on making another round trip to Tencastle to take Mary back home, with or without Jake. So we dragged Jake's mattress into my room to give both girls a decent bed. Jake and I stretched out our sleeping bags on the floor of the living room.

Breakfast seemed strangely subdued. The makeshift sleeping arrangements had totally scuppered any hope of romantic dalliance that Jake and I might have harboured. And I hadn't slept well. Jake and I used to share a room when there were four of us in the cottage, and I'd forgotten just how loud he snored.

Dilly's train back to Aberystwyth left just after midday so if I whisked her away from the cottage we'd at least have a couple of hours to ourselves.

"Rob, I was wondering..."

"Tell me later!" Whatever Jake had in mind I didn't want to know.

I breathed a sigh of relief as we set out for Tencastle.

"I'm sorry, Dilly, about last night. This weekend hasn't really worked out well for you."

"I don't know," she said. "You could say it's been... er... interesting." She thought for a moment. "You know, you're really going to miss having Jake around when you move to Carrick."

"I'd not really thought about it, but, yes, you're right."

Even in my first year at Tencastle, as a fresher student over three years ago, Jake and I had been good mates, and over the two years in the cottage at Penybont there was rarely a dull moment when Jake was around. And it had been Jake's initiative that had got Dilly and me together.

We reminisced over our carefree student days for pretty much most of the morning, strolling leisurely arm-in-arm through the park and along by the river Tene, past the mound that was all that reputedly remained of the castle in the town. With half an hour to spare we made our way to the station café.

"Dilly, I was wondering... I've been up to your parents. Would you like to come and spend a few days in Devon over the Christmas holidays? I'll be back there with my parents."

Dilly took my hand. "I don't know, Rob. It's very sweet of you to ask, but it would be difficult. It's always like one big family party. Aunts and uncles and cousins, my brother and his wife at Christmas, then we always go up to Caernarvon to my mother's side of the family for New Year."

"I understand. It used to be a bit like that back home. Not so many relatives around now for one reason or another."

"I'm sorry, Rob." She saw my look of disappointment. She took a deep breath. "Look, Rob, I need to say this. I really do enjoy your company but I don't think it's really going to work for us, is it?"

"What do you mean?"

"Well, we're not able to meet up very often, and when you move to your bedsit in Carrick..."

"That will only be temporary!"

"Perhaps. You don't know."

"What I'm saying is, let's remain friends... meet up when we can... but, please, I don't think we can expect a more committed relationship. Not unless circumstances change."

This was not the farewell I wanted. "I don't know what to say." I bit my lip. "I love you, Dilly."

Dilly smiled. "I'm very fond of you, too, Rob, but let's just step back a while and see how things work out. I'm not saying never - and in case you're wondering, I'm not seeing anyone else."

"Okay." I tried to put on a brave face. "Thank you for being honest. But I do hope we will get together again."

Our last embrace on the platform was as passionate as one could be in a public place.

That Sunday afternoon Tencastle held little interest for me. It struck me, for the first time, how dead it was. There was no point in seeking refuge in the Students' Union since my erstwhile college friends were either still away on teaching practice or had left college. I sought some solace in a pint in the Castle Inn, musing over some of the hilarious times we'd had there with Carpiog Morris. Which, if anything, made me even sadder with the observation Dilly had made, that my way of life was going to change drastically in just a few weeks' time.

I could have got pissed. Instead I wandered, aimlessly, for a couple of hours. I even found myself up by Thomas Hall, the male student residence, at one point - a good twenty minutes' walk out of town.

Eventually, as the light began to fade, I drove back to the cottage.

"Hi Rob! Go well, did it?" Jake's glance at my face gave the answer. "Oh."

I was glad he didn't press me for details. He changed tack, hoping to uplift my spirits.

"Going to join us for supper? Mary's cooked a lasagne."

I realised I hadn't eaten since breakfast. "Yes, thanks, that would be good."

Jake prattled on during the meal about what they'd been doing during the day. "Got the bedroom all sorted now. Back to our own beds tonight!"

I was wondering whether that included Mary when

Jake's next comment made it obvious. "By the way, if Mary stays on tonight, could you run her to Carrick tomorrow morning?"

"No problem." I'd be glad of the company to take my mind off other things.

"I've also been thinking..."

Oh Christ! Another Jake scheme!

"... I think we've been a bit ambitious in trying to decorate the whole house. I'm going to tell my relative that it's not going to be possible. Technical difficulties, you know."

The best news today. I forgave Jake the use of 'we' in the ambitions.

Chapter 12

I'm very rarely down in the dumps for long. After the previous night's supper with Jake and Mary, I'd already begun to consider the positive aspects of life beyond Ty Melin. One worry less was that I now had a secure job, and the money, not to mention time, saved on the daily commute would certainly be valuable. And there was certainly no reason why I shouldn't continue to enjoy some social life in Tencastle, particularly if Carpiog Morris started up again after Christmas. I also resolved to write regularly to Dilly.

During the journey to school, Mary and I enjoyed an easy exchange of thoughts on our respective prospects for the New Year. I was very curious to know what part Jake might play in her plans but I exercised discretion by not asking her directly. I got the impression, however, that Jake hadn't raised the subject of moving in with her. Which made me wonder whether he'd really done anything at all about arranging alternative accommodation for himself. No doubt he'd fall on his feet, whatever.

Janet Milward was pinning up a notice just as Mary and I walked into the staffroom. "Oh, hi there, Rob! Can I interest you two in the PTA barn dance? Friday week?"

"Possibly. I went to it last year." I didn't elaborate that it had quite life-changing consequences for my partner, the former lab technician. "Are you organising it, then?"

"Oh no, just the posters. You could bring Dilly. You said she's into Welsh folk dancing."

"I don't think she'd be able to get away from Aberystwyth." I had an idea, though. "Mary, how about the four of us go? You and Jake, and Holly and me?"

"Sounds fun. I'll mention it to her, and you twist Jake's arm."

"Okay, Janet, put us down for four tickets,

provisionally."

***

"Got a date for you, Jake," I said, as soon as he walked in the cottage. Rarely did I have a chance to spring a surprise on him.

"What do you mean?"

"Foursome. Twmpath."

"You're not making sense!"

"It's a Welsh barn dance at the school in Carrick. I've got tickets for you and Mary."

"And the other two?"

"Myself and Holly, if she agrees."

"Um, just one question. How do I get there? And when is it?"

"That's two questions."

"Pillock!"

"Friday week. If you can spare the time, you could come over with me in the morning. Or get a bus later. I'll bring us all back."

Jake thought for a moment. "Actually, I might be able to drive myself by then. I'm taking the test next Thursday."

That was a surprise. "Really? I didn't think you'd had any time to practise!"

"I've been having some lessons. Instructor says I'm a natural."

"Naturally."

***

The day before the barn dance my plans suffered a setback.

"Sorry, Rob, I'm not going to be able to get to the dance after all."

"That's a shame, Holly. Something crop up?"

"Yeah, I'd forgotten that we were supposed to be going away that weekend. Big six-o birthday party for my aunt."

"Never mind. I haven't bought the tickets yet."

Which reminded me that with the event fast approaching I needed to get them from Janet anyway. No time like the present. I had a few minutes before afternoon registration and diverted to the purpose-built music suite.

"Hi stranger! What brings you to foreign parts?"

"Hi Janet. Just remembered I haven't paid for any tickets yet. It will only be three now, I'm afraid. Holly can't come."

As she rummaged in a drawer, I had a thought. "You'll be there, won't you?"

"I don't know. I don't really fancy going on my own."

"Why not come with me then?" I said instantly, then added, "If you'd like to, that is, and make up the foursome."

I thought I saw her eyes sparkle. "Okay, yes, I will."

At the end of the afternoon, Janet returned a visit to my room. I wondered if she'd had second thoughts. After taking in the strange surroundings and wrinkling her nose at the lingering traces of sulphur dioxide, she sat down on a bench stool.

"Rob," she began, "I was wondering. You'll have three or four hours between the end of school and the start of the dance. Would you and your friends like to come back to my place for a bit of supper?"

Wow! "That's very kind of you. I'd love to, and I'm sure Jake and Mary will agree."

"I have an ulterior motive," she confessed, "I'd like to sound out your ideas for a folk club in Carrick. I did mention it briefly in the café the other week."

"Yes, I remember. Well, it's Jake who's got more

experience in that area. He's quite a star performer at the college club. Plays the banjo."

"Great! Well, ask him to bring his banjo and you can bring your guitar."

"Really? Do you play?" I realised immediately my gaff. "Sorry, that was a stupid question. I mean, what do you play?"

"Piano, of course. Also violin, and I've recently taken up the piano accordion."

***

As Jessica wasn't parked outside the cottage when I got home, I assumed Jake had failed the driving test. His glum looks offered confirmation.

"What happened?" I felt bound to ask.

"Imbecile for an examiner! Blamed me for his own stupid mistake."

"How come?"

"Well, everything was going well. I'd done all the compulsory manoeuvres without a problem, then the pillock told me to take the next left."

"So what was wrong with that? Mix up your left and right?"

Jake glared at me. "No way! Didn't give me much notice, but I signalled and braked and turned in time."

"So?"

"It was a one-way street! And not the way I was going."

"Didn't you see the sign?"

"There was a delivery van in the way. Anyway, I assumed that the examiner knew where he was going."

"What did he say?"

"Went ballistic! Accused me of not taking due care and attention. He didn't like it when I told him I was only following his instructions. Declared he meant the next turning after the one-way. I said that in which case he should have said so! I didn't know the road systems in the town."

Jake slumped in the armchair. "Didn't even take my perfect reversing into a driveway into account to get back on course. I've a darn good mind to appeal."

"I don't think you can do that."

"Whatever. Anyhow, I've put in for a re-test. Pity I can't take it in Tencastle!"

I turned to more immediate practicalities. "So are you going to come with me tomorrow morning to Carrick?"

"Dunno. I don't fancy moping round the town all day. Probably come on later."

I had an idea. "It's possible you might be able to get a lift with Eric and Kathryn Dickens. They are going to pick Holly up after school for some family gathering. Why not give them a ring?"

"Will do. Thanks. I've got a fair bit of Union business tomorrow." He thought for a moment then added, "Who are you going with if Holly's away?"

"Janet Milward, the music teacher. I did tell you last night."

"Sorry, I had other things on my mind."

"She's invited us round for supper. Oh, and bring your banjo."

***

Janet had suggested that when Jake arrived with Holly's parents, at the end of afternoon school, we could all walk to her flat, just a few minutes away. We waited for half an hour in vain.

"Can't think what's held them up, said Holly. "Dad's usually so punctual."

"Perhaps aliens have landed in Tencastle and he's holding the front page," I joked. Eric Dickens was editor of the local rag.

"Look, you three go on, and if you give me your address, Janet, we'll run Jake round when he arrives."

From the outside it looked dreary and run down – a nondescript terraced house tucked away down a back street a short distance from the town centre. Inside, however, Janet's first floor flat was bright and tastefully furnished. To what extent that was due to her work I had yet to discover.

"How did you come by this?" I asked, impressed by the view over the river from the compact kitchen, which was separated from the living room just by a doorway hung with strings of beads.

"Bit of luck, really," said Janet. "Parents of a college friend lived here. That's how I first got to hear of Carrick. He put it on the market after they had both passed on."

"So you're renting the flat?" Mary asked, as Janet finished showing us round the rest of the accommodation - the pocket size bathroom, main bedroom and a long, narrow room with integral upright piano.

"Well, sort of, I suppose." She saw our puzzled looks. "My Mum and Dad bought it. They didn't want me living in a poky bedsit. They'll probably make a profit on it such times as I move on. And renting out the downstairs flat pays the mortgage."

She transferred a large casserole dish from the fridge to the oven, and filled a saucepan with water. "Chilli con carne okay for you?"

We nodded.

"Please make yourselves at home."

While the pots bubbled away, Janet was keen to pick my brains about the college folk club in Tencastle. Not that I'd been there much in my last year; Jake would know more about the current activity.

I glanced at my watch – five o'clock and he still hadn't turned up.

"Have you had any experience in running a club?" I asked.

"Not at all, but I used to go to a couple of clubs when I was at uni. Really enjoyed it."

"Where was that?"

"Exeter."

"Really?" Knock me down with a feather. "I'm from Devon, but much further north."

"You're not familiar with the Exeter folk scene then?"

I shook my head. "I wasn't into folk music until I met Jake."

"Main one was the Jolly Porter, near the station. Didn't see many instruments there - they were more into unaccompanied traditional song, so sometimes I used to take the train or bus out to Crediton where they had a club in the back room of the Railway Hotel."

"Have you sussed out a suitable venue in Carrick?"

"Well, I did wonder about the school but I guess it would lack the atmosphere."

"And the booze," I added, helpfully.

"Yes, so possibly the Bull & Dragon, or there's the Quarryman's Arms just at the bottom of this road, by the river."

I could see a good excuse for a pub crawl. Something Jake would appreciate. Still no sign of him. At this rate I hoped the barn dance caller had a good repertoire of dances for threesomes.

When supper was ready we decided to go ahead without him. But with the first mouthful came muffled thumping from below. Janet rose to investigate, and I followed closely, in case of intruders.

Jake stood at the door, looking damp and dishevelled. He caught sight of me. "Rob! Thank God!" Then remembered his host. "Sorry, pleased to meet you. I'm Jake." He held out his hand to Janet. "Christ, I'm just so glad to have found your place."

"Wasn't Eric going to drop you off?" I asked when we'd got him inside and he'd given Mary a hug.

"Well, he was running a bit late so I said I'd walk. Holly gave me the address."

"So what kept you?"

"I've spent over an hour searching all over this town for Arthur Street."

Janet wrinkled her brow. "But this is Cyfartha Street"

"Yeah, I know now. It was only when I went in the pub to get out of the rain and ask for directions I found the road didn't even exist!"

I grinned.

Jake glared at me. "If someone hadn't suggested this place I'd have had to stay in the pub for a couple more hours."

"Such hardship!" The girls joined in my laughter - and so did Jake.

With a hearty meal inside him, and the opportunity to play some music, Jake soon put his streetwalking behind him. Janet had a pretty good repertoire of folk tunes, most of which Jake didn't know but it didn't stop him busking away on his banjo. By recognising the chord shapes he was using, I followed about half a bar behind on the guitar. So that Mary wasn't left out, Janet found her a tambourine to keep the beat - more or less.

We could probably have kept going all evening had not Janet glanced at the clock. "Hell, we'd better shift. The dance will be starting soon."

Though it was nigh on eight o'clock when we got back to the school, I was surprised that there was no music coming from the hall, as I had expected. Instead, the stage was all set up with a P.A. system but otherwise deserted, and a chap with a thick dark beard was pacing around by the entrance looking anxiously at his watch.

I presented our tickets to the woman on the door.

"May have to give you all a refund. Band hasn't turned

up yet."

"But it's all set up," I said, nodding towards the stage. The hall was already comfortably nearly full of people just chatting.

"Yes, the caller's been here since half six with all the gear. No musicians yet."

Blackbeard sidled over. "Sorry about this, they should have been here an hour ago. Can we give it another ten minutes?"

"Perhaps we can help," said Jake, "we're musicians..."

"Jake, we can't just..." I began, then noticed Janet was showing nothing like my level of consternation. She was deep in thought - and totally unaware, of course, of Jake's impetuous schemes.

The caller looked uncertain. "What do you play?"

Janet promptly stepped in before Jake, "Fiddle, mainly. And my friends do the rhythm on guitar, banjo and percussion. They're very good."

Christ, and I thought Jake did bullshit!

"But you won't know my dances, will you? And where are your instruments?"

'Our stuff's in the car," said Jake.

"I can be back in ten minutes with mine," said Janet, "And just tell me what kind of tune you want and we'll manage."

"Okay... we'll give it a try. And thanks!" Blackbeard ran his hand through his tousled hair. "I'm Tom, by the way." He offered his hand. "Suppose I'd better let the punters know what's going on."

Gobsmacked, I just stood there... until Mary jogged my arm. "Come on, Rob," she said with a wry grin, "let's help our two virtuosos get the show on the road!"

The punters didn't seem unduly concerned that the dancing started nearly half-an-hour after the scheduled time, though Tom had got them up on the floor to walk through the figures while we made some final adjustments to the microphones. I strummed quietly while Janet and Jake took the lead, and Mary beat out the rhythm on the tambourine. Janet conjured up a tune that seemed to fit the dance - not that I was taking a great deal of notice of what was happening on the floor. I was trying my best to look as if I actually knew what I was playing, and surreptitiously turned my microphone down. By the time we came to the end of the second dance I was feeling quite relaxed.

We were well into a frenetic jig for Strip The Willow, as Tom called it, when I saw him wave his hand in greeting. By the entrance stood three fellows laden with instrument cases and looking rather bemused.

As the dance ended, Tom grabbed the microphone and addressed the audience. "Ladies and gentlemen, I'd like you to show your appreciation for these fine musicians who offered to step in at a moment's notice to enable the evening to go ahead. Please give a big hand to..." he whispered to Jake, "What's your band called?"

Jake muttered something.

"... a big hand to the Accidentals!"

I guess it was the first time many of the audience had really noticed who was up on stage, and there were a few looks of surprise as some parents and students recognised us members of staff. The applause was tremendous.

"And now, we'll be taking a short break, during which my regular band will be setting up for the second half."

Tom's colleague dumped a bass drum by the stage and spoke to him briefly.

"Big accident apparently. Traffic at a standstill. I really am grateful to you guys." Tom stroked his beard, before continuing, "Can I give you something for your efforts?"

"That's not necessary," said Janet. "We were pleased to help."

"I'll be in touch with you again then, if you're up for doing a full gig for money."

"We'd be up for it!" Jake replied immediately, just assuming that we'd all concur.

"The Accidentals?" I said, over a pint, courtesy of Tom. "Where did that come from?"

"Spur of the moment," said Jake. "Seemed appropriate. It wasn't exactly planned!"

"I like it!" said Janet.

Just dancing for the rest of the evening could have seemed like a bit of an anticlimax but the adrenalin buzz kept us on a high.

"Wow!" I gasped as I flopped, drenched in perspiration, onto a chair, "I'm knackered!"

"Me too," said Jake. "We must do that again, though."

"Rob, if you don't want to drive back to Tencastle tonight, you're welcome to stay over. There's room for all of you, if you don't mind a floor."

"Might just do that, Janet. Thanks," I said. "Jake? Mary?"

"Well, I've still got my room here in Carrick," said Mary. Then, seeing Jake's uncertainty, added, "I'm afraid I can't offer you floor space though, Jake. The old bat's a bit fussy about late night visitors."

"Why don't you all come back for coffee anyway, and you guys can decide later?"

Later - much later - when we'd pretty well wrapped up the plans for the future of folk music in Carrick, not to mention the rest of Wales, Jake prepared to walk Mary back to her digs.

"Give my regards to Arthur Street!" was my parting shot as I headed gratefully for the spare room bed. Jake could have the sofa.

Chapter 13

I did not want the term to end. I was enjoying my job, enjoying an easy working relationship with Sandra, and sharing common interests with Janet. Despite the heavy work schedule and long daily journey in poor weather and little daylight, I did not want the term to end.

Most of all I did not want the term to end because it also meant the end of our life at Ty Melin. After nearly two and a half years in the vibrant madhouse of shared accommodation with Jake and Benji -not forgetting former housemates, Dan and Sunny - I was about to sever a major link with my student days. The farewell party that Jake had planned hadn't happened - our friends were still largely dispersed on teaching practice, or gainfully employed anywhere from John O'Groats to Land's End.

The more immediate problem, however, was what to do with my belongings - the clothes, the books and paraphernalia that had inevitably accumulated. There was no way Fi could cope with transporting it all the way to my parents' home in Devon, and, of course, back again to my new digs in Carrick in the New Year.

That penultimate Saturday before the end of term I sat nursing my second cup of coffee and looking dejectedly at a few cardboard boxes I'd already packed with my stuff. A pair of Christmas cards - one from Dan, one from Dilly - were the sole decorations on the mantelpiece.

"Hi Rob! Any coffee left?" Jake trotted down the stairs in his pyjamas. He'd good reason to be cheerful. He'd just passed his driving test at the second attempt and Jessica was now keeping Fi company outside.

I waved my hand towards the kitchen.

"Down in the dumps?" he said when he returned with a steaming mug.

"Yeah. Sorry to be leaving this place."

"Mmm, me too." He paused for a moment. "I, er… it's not really my business but I've been wondering… what are you going to do with the greenhouse?"

"You what?"

"The greenhouse. Your dad bought it. It didn't come with the house."

"Well, I can't exactly fold it up and put it on Fi's back seat, can I? I don't even know what I'm going to do with all this in here." I said, quite curtly.

"Okay, no need to get shirty. Just asking."

"Any bright ideas?" Which I realised was the wrong thing to say to Jake the moment the words left my mouth.

"Actually, yes."

I groaned inwardly. "Go on!"

"We could move it down the road to Benji's new hermitage."

"And why would we want to do that?"

Jake counted off points with his fingers. "One, you don't want it. Two, you could store all the stuff you don't want to take to Devon until such time as you shift it to Carrick. Three, Benji's into being self-sufficient and would make good use of it. Four, I…"

"Okay, okay. You've spoken to Benji then?"

"It was his suggestion. But he didn't think you'd take him seriously."

"Unlike you, I suppose." Jake had the knack of making any hare-brained scheme seem plausible. "And how are we supposed to move it?"

"Newton," said Jake.

"Pardon?"

"You know, Isaac Newton – what's goes up must come down."

"I'm sure he didn't have greenhouses in mind."

"No, but it came in kit form. You and your father put it up. Should be easy enough to take it down again." Jake pointed at the boxes, "You've probably still got the instructions there somewhere."

"For Christ's sake, Jake, there's no way I'm searching through those boxes for a piece of paper that may or may not exist." I took a deep breath. "Look, if Benji wants the greenhouse, he's welcome." I could see it might solve my storage problems, so I added magnanimously, "I'll even help you take it down if you two do the reconstruction."

"Thanks, Rob. We'll get to work on it."

I had a sneaking suspicion I wasn't hearing the whole story. "Jake, what's your particular interest in this?"

"Didn't I tell you? Benji's offered me a room down there until the summer."

"What about the rest of his god squad?"

"Oh, there's still a lot of work to do before it opens as a retreat for meditation next autumn. He doesn't want any rent, so I'm going to help him decorate."

I questioned Benji's judgement, in view of Jake's previous experience with a paintbrush. "Thought you were going to move in with Mary?"

Jake look surprised. "Why would I want to do that?"

Sometimes Jake could be so naïve.

***

I was beginning to regret my offer. The three of us had already spent an hour sheltering from the intermittent heavy showers in the greenhouse, while working out the best way to dismantle it. We could see it had nuts and bolts, but we didn't have a spanner. There were aluminium clips but we weren't sure how to remove them, fearful of breaking the glass. Without a plan we weren't sure we'd remember which part went where even if we did get it apart. Benji's offer to make detailed sketches at each stage didn't seem terribly practical either.

"It's a pity we can't just lift it up and move it, lock,

stock and barrel," I said in frustration.

"That's a brilliant idea, Rob." said Jake, "Why not?"

"Think of the weight, for a start, Hercules!" I objected, "And think of the glass and the aluminium frame moving and..."

"Okay, I'm thinking!"

Jake continued pondering the problem while we got ourselves warmed up in the kitchen. I half listened to Benji chatting away to me about saving mankind while I thought of saving a hell of a lot of time and effort by just buying another greenhouse.

Jake started pacing up and down, a sure sign that another scheme was hatching.

"Right," he began, "We'll obviously need more people to help lift it, and we'll need to secure it to a firm wooden base..."

"Why? You're not intending to float it downstream, are you?"

"Hey, that's good. I'd not thought of that!"

"Forget it, Jake. You'd never get it under the bridge, and no way am I paddling about in a freezing cold river."

"Yeah, you're probably right. But... hang on, Benji, you won't need those old railway sleepers over the stream any more. We could use those."

"Jake, they weigh a ton on their own!"

"There are some wooden pallets down by the cottage," said Benji. "Builders' merchants left them. Would they do?"

"Let's have a look." Jake grabbed his coat and strode for the door.

Benji and I looked at each other, shrugged, and followed in his wake.

***

Jake, of course, directed the operation. He'd cobbled

together the four small pallets we'd hauled back into a base large enough to take the greenhouse and then attached the roller skates we'd used previously to transport Caspar's bridge. He'd acquired several lengths of stout rope and press-ganged most of the Union Executive to help. Benji's contribution of praying to the Almighty for fine calm weather also paid off.

Removing the metal bolts that secured the aluminium frame to the ground was no problem. The tricky bit, however, was to raise the greenhouse sufficiently in situ to slide the wooden base underneath. First we had to slide three ropes underneath, then, while three people on either side used them to lift the structure, two more of us attempted to slide the pallets into place.

"All ready?" said Jake, "All lift when I give the word."

"How about a hauling shanty?" I asked, and offered, with a finger in my ear.

"Poor ol' Jacob Moses - haul him away
Wants a place to grow his roses - haul him away
So we're sending him a glasshouse - haul him away
He's got us working off our arses - haul him away."

"Pillock!"

On the fourth attempt, after much sweating and cursing, to which Benji turned a deaf ear, we achieved our first goal. Then, gingerly - very gingerly - with all hands at the ropes, now threaded through the pallets, we inched the greenhouse out of the garden and into the freestanding area beside the house. Jessica and Fi were already parked in the road, crucial to the next stage.

The plan was for Fi to be linked up behind the greenhouse, acting as a brake, and a team of six to take ropes either side of it, slowly moving downhill to the bridge, a process which called for very precise co-ordination on my part in the car. At the bridge, Jessica would be hitched up at the front to ease the load over the hump. Benji had suggested using Caspar for this purpose but the consequences of a horse galloping away with a glasshouse in tow didn't bear thinking about.

Eventually, we were all in position and ready to roll. Now, normally the road to Penybont is quiet, with little traffic even on weekdays and virtually nothing on Sundays. Not today. Sod's law with a vengeance. We'd barely moved a few yards before I noticed a car behind me, and very soon at least three more.

Jake realised we could have a more serious problem. "Benji, can you stop the traffic beyond the cottage on the other side of the bridge. We don't want some idiot haring round the bend."

"What shall I tell them?"

"Wide load."

As we advanced at a snail's pace the queue behind me grew longer, and less patient - I heard one horn hooting loudly.

Jake signalled me to stop. In my side mirror I could see a well-dressed bald-headed man striding towards me. He didn't look happy.

"What the blazes do you think you're playing at?" he yelled, rapping on my window.

I wound down my window, just a little. "I'm sorry, sir," I said politely, "We are only moving this load to the other side of the bridge."

"You're blocking the road. Now move out of the bloody way!" His face was getting redder by the second, not helped by the fact that I found the situation rather amusing.

"And where do you suggest we move to? We can't exactly pull over."

"You've no business blocking the road like this. I'll have you know I'm on the Highways Committee for this county and you need permission to block the road."

I was getting tired of his rantings. "Then you should know that we have as much right to be on the road as you have. Permission is not needed if we are moving."

"You're holding me up on an important journey!" he shouted.

"It's actually yourself who's prolonging the delay," I pointed out. "Nobody's going anywhere till you get back in your car and show a bit of patience, like the rest of the drivers."

The message obviously got through. He stamped away, loudly muttering, "Morons." I was really chuffed to see he got a slow handclap from the other drivers on the way back to his car.

We proceeded slowly. There was enough space, just before the bridge, to pull over enough to let the other vehicles through. I saw one of our helpers give a V for victory sign as the self-styled VIP drove by. At least that's what it looked like from a rear view.

Crossing the bridge was touch and go. More touch than go. The combined width of greenhouse and pallets left literally just a couple of inches leeway between the stone walls of the bridge, and no room for the manual rope handlers except at front and rear. Fi and Jessica worked together fantastically as a team - under the guidance of Jake and myself. I thought we deserved a medal for our driving skills and co-ordination.

"Where do you want us to put the greenhouse, Benji?" Jake asked when we'd finally done the last bit of manoeuvring from the road to the track at the back of the cottages. And cleared the road for traffic – not that any more vehicles had come our way.

"Um, I don't know. I hadn't really thought about that."

"So now you tell us, you pillock!" I said.

There weren't many options. The only suitable level space was the car parking space by the front door. Jake would have to make some other arrangements for Jessica.

"I was thinking," said Benji. "Rob, you could put all your spare stuff in the cottage here until after Christmas."

Benji had good ideas. Pity they didn't come in the right order.

Chapter 14

I almost collided with Jake who was intent on urgent business with a mop.

"What are you intending to do with that?" I asked him. I couldn't really believe he was going to be any more meticulous in keeping Benji's retreat clean than he had been at Ty Melin.

"Oh, hi, Rob." He waved the mop in greeting, and headed towards the garden path. "It's backed up," he called over his shoulder.

"What...," I started to say, but thought I'd get more of a clue by following him.

He knelt beside a hole in the path I'd not noticed before. An unpleasant odour assailed my nostrils.

"Drain's blocked," he explained, "Took me ages to find this manhole cover. All covered over with mud and weeds."

Where waste water went after flushing the toilet or pulling the bathplug I'd never really had cause to think about. I suppose there was a septic tank somewhere, like on our family farm, but perhaps a mains sewer did indeed extend beyond the fringes of Tencastle.

Jake poked and prodded the evil smelling grey sludge with the mop. I hoped he wasn't going to use in the house again.

"Something's stuck down there," he declared.

Obviously.

Whatever was causing the obstruction was eventually freed, and the sludge gurgled away, leaving a sizeable amorphous lump.

"Flush the loo, will you, Rob," Jake called. "Give this thing a rinse. I've trapped it with the mop."

I came back out a couple of minutes later to find Jake holding what looked like a small soggy brown bag at arm's length.

"Ruddy stuffed toy, would you believe?" Jake wrinkled his nose. "Who on earth would chuck a teddy bear down the bog?"

"Christopher Robin?" I suggested. Though it was probably the young daughter of the family that had lived in the house previously.

"Come again?" said Jake, puzzled.

"Poo Bear!"

I narrowly avoided the dripping animal as it flew towards me.

After we'd given Winnie the Pooh a decent burial and Jake had showered, we flopped out on the sofa with a beer apiece.

"Happy New Year, Rob!" He raised his glass. "Have a good Christmas?"

"Pretty fair, Jake, thanks." Actually it had been a very low-key festive season on my father's farm. My brother came over for lunch on Christmas Day, and a few relatives and family friends popped in at various times. Apart from a long chat with Dilly on the phone it was pretty boring. "How about you, other than auditioning for Dyno-rod?"

"Yeah, good." Jake didn't elaborate but prattled on enthusiastically. "Now, you'll be pleased to know Min and Huw are back and they'll be having a belated engagement party and Carpiog Morris will be starting up again next week and I thought about having a ceilidh with our new band and, yeah, talking of which, we'll organise an exchange with Tencastle students' folk club and your lovely lass from Carrick and I'd like..."

"Hang on, Jake!" I held up my hand. "One thing at a time! Have Min and Huw fixed a date and venue?"

"Er, yes, fortnight today, I think. May be at the Union, maybe at that new nightclub place round the corner from the Castle Inn? Know it?"

"Pub yes, club no. Anyhow let me know. I'll not be able

to get along to Carpiog on the first night -another staff meeting and the Head waffles on for hours. But I'll definitely be there the following week!"

"Do you think Janet would be interested? She'd be a great asset."

"Possibly. I'll also have a chat with her about getting together for more music sessions, and the folk club as well. And by the way, she's not my girlfriend."

"Shame," said Jake sincerely.

"Right, now I'd better get Fi loaded up with my boxes and head over to Carrick. I've got the rest of the weekend to get settled in before term starts on Monday."

"Give you a hand," said Jake.

"By the way, what was the other thing you were going to tell me about?"

"Dunno."

I realised something was different about the cottage from when I'd last seen it. "What's happened to the greenhouse?"

"Oh, we've moved it up the garden."

"We?"

"Yeah, myself, Benji, and Evan, next door. He helped me clear a space. Took it apart and put it together again, too. Quite easy really."

I held back on a few choice comments.

***

Number 14, Heol Llanfair, Carrick Major, was my new abode. Mrs Edwards, the landlady, welcomed me, though 'welcome' implies some kind of warmth. Her face looked as if she'd breakfasted on raw lemons. Before she even let me cross the threshold she demanded the month's rent in advance, plus a breakages deposit. She handed me a stapled bundle of paper - 'conditions of tenancy' she called it, which I suppose I should have read before I signed up. Not that she actually asked me to sign anything. I had to remind her to give me a key for the front door as well as one for the first floor flat. Her rooms were on the ground floor.

The flat, too, lacked warmth. Like a refrigerator it was. No radiators for central heating, just a couple of small convector heaters in lounge and bedroom, all serviced by a coin-operated meter. I suspected I'd be paying premium rates for my electricity.

Moving in my belongings and unpacking took far less time than I had anticipated. By mid-afternoon, therefore, I sat slumped in the old armchair, wondering what to do with the rest of the day. Shop for provisions, obviously, since I'd not had the foresight to bring even some coffee and milk with me.

I felt in need of company. Even on the occasions when I was in the house alone at Ty Melin, I felt the presence of my house mates and knew that Jake could be guaranteed to breeze in at any time, eager to expound his latest scheme. I thought of calling Janet. But I didn't know her number, and, looking round the flat, I didn't have a telephone either. Bugger! I hadn't noticed a payphone in the hall and I guessed that asking the landlady if I could use hers would be a waste of time.

There was no need for me to relinquish the parking space virtually outside my digs, as it was just a few minutes' walk into town. Actually, it took longer, taking a fruitless detour via Janet's. There was no reply when I rang her door bell.

Having purchased sufficient food and drink to tide me over until Monday from the supermarket - a very modest establishment despite its superlative aspirations - I ambled along the pavement, undecided whether to head back to the flat and eat alone, or splash out and dine alone at the Bull and Dragon. I put my bags down to look at my watch. Nearly five o'clock. Would the pub even be open yet?

I became aware of someone waving their hands from the inside of the shop where I had halted. Beyond the display of properties for sale and rent, the blonde hair was unmistakeable even though I couldn't yet see her face clearly.

"Rob!" Sandra called from the doorway, "I thought it was you. Come on in for a minute!"

With nothing better to do, I entered the premises of Morgan and Maxwell, Estate Agents and Auctioneers.

"Bill's just shutting up shop," Sandra said, and then put her hand to her mouth, "Oh, I forgot, you haven't met my husband, have you?"

I didn't really have any preconceived ideas of what Sandra's hubby might look like. But if I had given it any thought, I would undoubtedly have been way off the mark. Bill Maxwell was short, plump, bespectacled and balding, not at all the sort of catch that Sandra could have commanded. I hoped her experience with Terry, her former partner and Fanny's father, and my rejection of her advances hadn't made her desperate.

No Adonis perhaps, but Bill exuded charm - a positive asset in his job, I suppose - and offered me his hand. "Pleased to meet you, Rob. I've heard quite a lot about you from Sandy."

"Not too much, I hope, and it's probably not true," I replied.

"I was surprised to see you out there," said Sandra, "I didn't think you'd be back until first day of term."

"I've just moved into digs here in Carrick."

"Oh, right!" She sounded surprised, then added, "So what are your plans for this evening?"

"Pie and pint and an early night." That precisely summed up my expectations.

"Come and have a bite with us!" said Bill, then looked at his wife for her agreement.

"I... I'm, um..."

"It's no problem, Rob, really," said Sandra. "And Fanny's away with her dad all weekend."

"Okay... thanks very much, I'd love to."

I felt rather tiddly after several glasses of wine before, during and after the excellent casserole that Bill and Sandra had laid before me. I thought that walking back might sober me up a bit, but Sandra insisted on running me back to my digs. Which was probably just as well since their modern four-bedroom house, with all mod cons and huge garden, was a fair way out of Carrick, on the other side of the river.

"Aren't you going to give me a goodnight kiss?" Sandra said as I heaved myself out of her car and offered profuse thanks for a most pleasant evening.

"Er... "

"Don't worry, I'm not going to seduce you," she said mischievously.

I leant through the open driver's window and gave her a peck on her cheek. As I withdrew my sleeve caught on her door handle. "Oh, bugger it!" I exclaimed.

"What's the matter?"

"I've just dropped my front door key! I think it's fallen down the drain."

"Hang on, I've got a torch somewhere. Let's have a look."

We crouched down beside the car. No sign of the blessed key. Sandra moved her car forward away from the drain, and we searched again. The drain had obviously not been cleaned out for some time, and there on a tuft of grass clinging to the side of the drain was the key. About six inches down.

We looked at each other. "Any suggestions?" I asked.

"Try to get the drain cover off?"

Tyre levers and screwdrivers would not budge the cover. I was also wary of dislodging the key.

"You could knock on the door and get the landlady to let you in."

"I don't think she'd appreciate being disturbed at gone midnight!" Another idea was forming. "Do you by any chance have a length of string or twine in your handbag?"

"Yes, I have as matter of fact. Why?"

"Well, I've got a little horseshoe magnet in my car – came out of a Christmas cracker, and I thought it might come in useful sometime. Put the magnet on the string, lower in into the drain and hey presto!"

A police constable came across us peering down the drain, Sandra shining the torch while I dangled the string. "Fish not biting?" he said sarcastically.

I lost concentration momentarily and the key which was almost within touching distance caught the underside of the drain cover and disappeared, with a plop. "Oh shit, shit, SHIT!"

"May I ask exactly what you are trying to do?" the bobby asked.

I explained my predicament.

"You live here?" he enquired, rather superfluously I thought.

"Just taken digs here. It's my first night."

"Well, there's no way you're going to get that key now, however good an angler you may be. Best just knock up your landlady. She does live on the premises, I assume?"

I nodded, and before I could repeat the reservations I'd made to Sandra, he thumped on the front door. No response. I winced as he thumped again, "Open up, police."

A light came on, and I saw a curtain pulled back. Shortly afterwards the front door opened and Mrs Edwards stood there in dressing gown and hair in curlers. Open-mouthed she took in the scene - myself standing beside the constable and Sandra leaning by her car door.

"Does this young man live here?" the policeman asked.

The look she gave me would have withered a florist's entire stock of blooms. "What's he done?" She demanded curtly. Her nose twitched. "You're drunk!" she snapped in my face.

"Nothing. He's being trying to retrieve his front door key. It dropped down the drain."

"Well, I'm not having a drunken lecher in my house! He can go back with his floozy!"

I was about to respond forcibly to defend my honour and that of Sandra, but the constable spoke first. "That is most unhelpful, madam. I ask you again, have you rented out accommodation to this man?"

Mrs Edwards pursed her lips, and gave the briefest of nods.

"Then I insist that you let him take up his accommodation this evening. You can settle any differences you may have in the morning."

I thought for a moment she wasn't going to budge, but she moved aside with bad grace to let me in.

"Thank you," I said to the constable. I waved goodbye to Sandra.

There would be consequences, of that I was certain. Mrs Edwards struck me as the kind of person who would not let matters rest. Munching my toast and marmalade next morning, I'd barely started to consider possibly conciliatory approaches when the knock came on my door. It was just past nine o'clock.

"Mr Kiddecott, I want to speak with you!" came her curt voice.

"Just a moment." I stood and opened the door. "Please come in," I said politely.

"I don't need to be invited into my own property!" she snapped.

I held back from responding about a tenant's right to privacy. "I apologise for the inconvenience I caused you yesterday evening," I began, attempting to mollify her.

"I want you out of here. Now!" Uncompromising.

"And why is that?" I replied calmly.

"Rolling up here drunk, bringing this house into disrepute with the police calling in the middle of the night, and some ridiculous story about losing your key."

"I was not drunk. I'd had a few glasses of wine in the company of Mr and Mrs Maxwell - the estate agent, you know? Mrs Maxwell kindly gave me a lift back. The key slipped from my hand when I was getting out of the car. The policeman was most helpful."

"Hmph!" Her eyes darted around the room and fixed on a couple of cans of beer I'd bought in. "No matter! You are already violating the terms of the tenancy!"

"What?"

"No alcohol on the premises, and I expect my tenants to keep reasonable hours. And no members of the opposite sex in your room, if you were thinking of bringing that woman back here."

"You must be joking!" Not even Thomas Hall, the male student residence at Tencastle was that strict.

"You had the terms of tenancy when you signed up. I presume you have read them?"

"Haven't got round to it yet. If I had, it's very unlikely I would have accepted such conditions, for Christ's sake!" My patience was wearing thin.

"And I'll thank you not to blaspheme, particularly on the Lord's day! You will not stay a day longer under my roof."

"Frankly, I've no wish to stay here any longer. If you return my cheque I'll be gone." Though where to I had no idea.

"Out of the question, Mr Kiddecott. You've broken the terms of the tenancy. You forfeit your rent."

I took a deep breath, mentally counted to ten, and resisted the desire to tell the stupid old bat what she could do with her rooms. "The only thing I've signed is the cheque for a month's rent and breakage deposit and I shall put a stop on it first thing tomorrow morning. I will pay you for the one night's accommodation and for the loss of the key."

Her jaw dropped. "You can't do that! I won't have that!" she screamed. "I shall call the police!"

"Go ahead, if you really want to make a fool of yourself." I guessed it was an empty threat, not that she'd get much sympathy as I hadn't done anything wrong. "Now if you'll leave me a few minutes to pack up my stuff, you can have your room back as I found it."

She stormed out. Almost in tears I thought, though I felt very little sympathy for her.

It didn't take me long to throw my belongings together. I made sure that I gathered everything in the foyer, then propped the front door open and moved the boxes outside, just in case she got some idea of retaining any items in lieu of lost rent.

A bright crisp January morning and nowhere to go!

Actually that wasn't quite true. I would have to go back to Tencastle to drop in a letter to my bank cancelling the cheque, and I still had a few items to collect from the Benji house.

I hadn't expected to find the gates to the school car park padlocked. The small gate for pedestrians was, however, open, suggesting that there might be someone - the caretaker, perhaps - on site. I'd hoped to park just by the science block and dump my stuff in Nick's office for a day or two until I found somewhere to stay. Now it looked as if I would have to hump the boxes across the large expanse of tarmac. I took the least bulky box first and parked it on the ground while I fiddled with the key to open the science block.

It had not even occurred to me that the block might be alarmed. Normally by the time I arrived on a school day everything was open anyway. I looked frantically for a control box to turn off the constant wah-wah and flashing lights but realised that I had no idea what the code was. I quickly relocked the door - it didn't stop the alarm - picked up my box and sprinted back to the gate, hoping to make myself scarce before anyone came to investigate.

"Well, well, young man, we meet again," said the bobby from last night, as I got back to my car. "Care to tell me what you've got in the box?" He glanced inside the car. "And what else you've got there?"

"It's all my stuff from my digs - former digs, I mean."

"Oh yes?"

"I'm no longer there, in Heol Llanfair. Landlady was totally unreasonable. You saw what she was like."

"Uh huh," he said. "So what are you doing here?"

"I work here. I'm a science teacher. I was going to leave my stuff here overnight. I didn't know that the building had an alarm out of hours."

"Can anyone confirm you work here?"

The alarm fortunately died away.

"The lady I was with last night - Mrs Maxwell - she's the lab technician."

"Oh really? Anyone, shall we say, more independent?" The implication that Sandra and I had something other than a professional relationship was evident in his tone.

"Well, any of the staff could confirm my position here but the only other two whose addresses I know in Carrick are Janet Milward and Mark Matthews."

"Okay, I'm inclined to believe you. I'm actually off-duty. I was on my way home when I heard the alarm. The station will probably have received the alarm and contacted a senior member of staff."

I winced. The last thing I needed was Moby Dick turning up. Fortunately, it was the car of deputy head, Eric Rigby, that screeched to a halt behind Fi.

"Rob?" he said, looking at me. He introduced himself to the policeman, "What's going on?"

"I'll leave the young man to explain, sir."

***

Bleary-eyed, I arrived for work early on Monday morning. Bleary-eyed because I'd set out before daylight from Benji's house, where I'd spent an uncomfortable night curled up in my sleeping bag on a hard, cold floor. And that after several beers at the Castle relating my woes to Jake and Mary, who seemed to find it all one big joke. Early because I wanted to be there when Nick Ramsbottom turned up, to explain why his office was filled with my junk. Eric Rigby had kindly helped me with that task yesterday.

Sandra was keen to know what had transpired but I only had time to tell her the bare essentials before lessons began.

By lunchtime it seemed that the whole staff knew I was homeless and speculation had grown faster than bacteria on bullshit - I was camping out in the science lab, sleeping in my car in the school car park, even rumoured to have spent a night in the cells for vagrancy!

"So where are you going to sling your hammock tonight?" asked John Rhys-Price, always going for the direct approach. "Got a bed at my place if you're desperate."

"Being sorted, thanks." I wasn't that desperate. Yet.

"My wife's parents own a caravan on the site just out of town," said Mark Matthews. "It's not used this time of year. Want me to ask?"

"Possibly," I said, "but I'll hold fire for the moment, thanks." It would probably be even colder than Mrs Edward's flat or Benji's floor.

Sandra and Janet cornered me almost simultaneously. "You first," said Janet.

"Rob, I could ask Bill whether he's got anything

suitable on his books. In the meantime, we do have a spare room, if you don't mind sharing with us and Fanny."

"That's very kind of you, Sandra. Please do ask your husband, but I really don't want to impose on you if I can find something else."

"I may be able to help you then," said Janet. "You know the downstairs flat at my place?"

I nodded.

"Well, the old boy that lives there is going to move in with his son and family."

"When?" That really sounded interesting.

"Not certain, but he's given a month's notice. My guess is that he'd be willing to go sooner than later."

"That would be brilliant, Janet." I had a thought, "How much is the rent?"

"Er, I'm not certain, but I'm sure we could come to some arrangement with my parents." She brushed the hair from her eyes. "And I have got a spare room in the meantime."

Chapter 15

I suspected that a few items were being taken from my lab. Nothing particularly valuable, but the number of test tubes seemed to be decreasing far more quickly than could be accounted for by breakages. I also appeared to be a little light on spatulas and crucibles.

It was, of course, the Head's policy to use the laboratory as a form base, and as such he expected the room to be available for the students during break and lunchtime. I was reluctant to believe that my own form of eleven-year-olds could be responsible for possible pilfering but the fact that the room was unsupervised for significant periods during the day meant that anyone could have access. Although some equipment and most of the chemicals were in locked cupboards, many of the drawers and cupboards in which common, everyday equipment was kept were not fitted with locks. And it wasn't always convenient to have materials required for a demonstration or awaiting clearance from an earlier lesson to be kept out of sight, though Sandra did her best.

I expressed my concerns to Nick.

"Hmm, funny you should say that. I've noticed a couple of things missing from their usual place, but assumed I'd mislaid them."

"So what do you suggest we do?"

"Short of full-time supervision, I'm not sure."

By the following afternoon I was in no doubt. A beaker half-full of copper sulphate solution had disappeared from the fume cupboard over the lunch break. Sandra confirmed that she had not removed it.

Next morning, Sandra caught me almost as soon as I entered the science block. "Something, I thought you'd like to know, Rob," she began. "It may or may not be relevant to the missing items."

"Go on!"

"Well, I asked Fanny casually whether she has ever noticed any older students hanging around your lab. She sometimes pops over to see me during the breaks, particularly if she's forgotten her pocket money."

"And?"

"Well, you know her friend, Daisy Colville?"

I nodded.

"Apparently Daisy's elder brother and a couple of his mates are often in the loos upstairs. Smoking probably."

"Okay, thanks." Interesting, though far from proof.

"Don't mention that you got this information from Fanny, will you?"

"My lips are sealed." I grinned.

I told my form that for a while they might not have free access to the lab, as we needed to do some security tests. I assured them it was not because of anything they had done. I locked the lab door at morning break and at lunchtime. I was rather hoping Nick would follow suit, but though offering his support, he declined.

"Let's see how things pan out," he said.

Things panned out very quickly. Before the end of that same lunch break, I got a summons to Moby Dick's office.

"Mr Kiddecott, I found the door to your laboratory locked this lunch time."

"Yes, sir."

"Why?" he demanded. "I have given very explicit instructions that form bases must be available to pupils during their free time."

I explained my concern about incidents of pilfering.

"You are responsible for the security of your equipment. You must make sure everything is locked away properly."

I pointed out the inadequacies in suitable lockable storage space.

"Then the laboratory must be properly supervised at

all times when pupils are present."

"I agree. Are you suggesting that I must spend all my breaks in the laboratory?"

"No, no, of course not!" he flustered.

"Then how do you suggest I deal with the problem, Dr. Bedford-Dickson?"

Adept as a politician at avoiding a direct answer, he barely drew a breath before repeating, "The lab must remain open. That is paramount!"

"And I am responsible for the security of the contents of the laboratory?"

"Yes, yes! Of course!" He snapped.

"Very well. Then in my professional judgement, until such time as adequate secure storage is provided or alternative arrangements for supervision are made, the only way I can guarantee security is to lock the laboratory at times when neither I nor another member of staff is present."

"You dare to defy my orders?"

"With respect, sir, your orders, as they stand, are contradictory. I will follow security requirements but I will not accept responsibility for an open, unsupervised laboratory. If you wish to unlock the door, then the responsibility for anything that happens as a consequence is yours, not mine." I took a deep breath. Confronting authority was not something I enjoyed. "I am quite happy to put my views in writing to the School Governors. Mr Ramsbottom is prepared to support me on this." I'm not sure how far Nick would have gone in backing me up but I felt the limited degree of bluff was worth using.

"You are dismissed!" Moby Dick barked. I hoped he only meant dismissed from his presence.

I heard no more of the issue for several days, though it was something of a stand-off with regard to laboratory access. I routinely locked the lab when I left. Sometimes I found it unlocked when I returned after lunch.

***

"Moby's in a stink!" John Rhys-Price declared to no-one in particular as he entered the staffroom just before afternoon registration.

"So who's upset him this time?" I said, being nearest to John.

"No, no, he's really in a stink – his office, that is. Full of stinky fumes. Christ, you could smell rotten eggs all the way down his corridor!"

"Hmm," I pondered. My last lesson in the morning with an 'O' level group had included the reaction of metal sulphides with dilute acid, so my room also had a lingering bad eggy aroma, despite the use of the fume cupboard. I had a strong suspicion that Moby's problem was more than coincidence.

Sirens heralded the arrival of a fire engine. We could see the crew donning breathing gear as Moby Dick gesticulated towards his first floor office, apparently oblivious of his audience of staff and pupils gazing down from every convenient window. Further entertainment was curtailed by the registration bell.

I wasn't surprised when the Headmaster wanted a word with his Chemistry staff, though to meet us on our home ground was unusual. At the end of the afternoon, Nick called me into his office where Moby had already taken the one comfortable seat, or rather, the only one that wasn't piled high with books and leaflets.

"Gentlemen, do you recognise this?" he began. He held up a small porcelain crucible. "The firemen who attended my... my, ah... incident found it hidden behind my door. They are sure it was the source of the fumes."

I looked at Nick, who nodded almost imperceptibly. "I think it's one of the items that was taken from my lab last week." I'd found my lab had been unlocked again this very lunch hour.

"I see." He obviously expected me to say more.

"This morning we were using the chemicals which produce hydrogen sulphide - that's the foul smelling gas. It's possible that someone could have filched some of the reagents from the fume cupboard at lunchtime."

"And why weren't the chemicals locked away?"

"There's no lock on the fume cupboard, and it's not the sort of stuff you want to flush down the sink."

Moby glowered. He clearly thought I was responsible for polluting his airspace. Mind you, the lads (I guessed) who'd sneaked into his room certainly had balls to carry out such a prank.

"If I may," Nick interceded, "Mr Kiddecott has already spoken to me about security in the laboratory, and I share his concerns. There is the potential for even more serious mischief in which someone could come to harm."

Moby's brow puckered as some undesirable consequences were no doubt dawning on him. "What do you recommend?" he barked.

"Well, firstly, if it is your desire that the laboratories remain accessible as a form base..."

Moby nodded.

"... then we must have much more lockable storage facilities in the laboratory. It will mean some inconvenience for us personally at the start and end of lessons but we can cope with that. Secondly, I would suggest that we have a prefect on duty in the laboratory block during morning break and lunchtime."

"Yes, yes, I will see to that!" Moby readily agreed. "But I want the culprits for this... this outrage apprehended!"

Nick stroked his chin thoughtfully.

I had an idea. "Dr. Bedford-Dickson, I have some suspicions as to who might have been responsible but it would be impossible to prove. They will be in a group I teach after break on Wednesday morning. I'll do another practical exercise to tempt our miscreants. I'll stay in the prep room during the lunch hour and see if they take the bait. In the meantime, we'll keep the lab unlocked and any other sensitive material out of sight."

"Thank you, Mr Kiddecott, that is a very commendable suggestion."

Wow. Praise from Moby Dick was a very rare commodity.

***

"You look like the cat that's got the cream," said Janet when I walked back with her to her flat after school on Wednesday. I'd taken up the offer of her spare room until the tenant below moved out.

"I caught Dennis Colville and his mate red-handed trying to nick some chemicals from my lab. And I was really pleased to see his smug detective sergeant father called in to face Moby's wrath. I even got a few brownie points with Moby as well." I didn't mention that his carpet would probably have been crackling with minor detonations and puffs of iodine had the lad succeeded.

"By the way, Janet, are you willing to give Carpiog Morris a try tomorrow?"

"Yes, I'm up for it."

Chapter 16

"Rob!" Min enveloped me in one of her famous cuddles the moment I stepped inside the room, and planted a kiss firmly on my lips. "So lovely to see you again!"

Barely over five feet in height, and with a rather mousy appearance, whatever slight disadvantage she had in physical characteristics she more than made up for in her vivacious and friendly personality. But one difference was immediately obvious.

"What have you done with your glasses?" The Min I'd known for the last two years always wore huge spectacles.

"I've still got them, but I'm trying out contact lenses."

"You're looking as gorgeous and bubbly as ever though!" I'd never known her any other way, even when she'd been hospitalised after a freak accident some two years ago. "Your leg's fully recovered now?"

"Pretty much." The odd twinge but it won't stop me dancing!"

She noticed that I wasn't alone. "Hi, welcome to the ranks of Carpiog Morris. Like a drink?" She led Janet off to the bar, and called over her shoulder, "Usual for you, Rob?"

I nodded and surveyed the small group already gathered in the back room of the Castle Inn. Jake was chatting to Huw, Min's fiancé, who'd put on some weight and grown a beard since the previous summer. Holly, whom I'd got to know well during her teaching practice, and her twin brother, Harry, were the only other people I recognised. Evidently Min and Jake had been beating the drum for new recruits to replace those dancers who, like me, had left the university college of Tencastle, mostly for more distant employment.

I caught Jake's eye. "Hey, Rob, come and meet the

new gang." He looked over my shoulder. "Janet's not with you?" He sounded disappointed.

"Min's already taken her in hand."

"Splendid! That means we`ll be at least as strong as last year."

Assuming they persevered and weren't cursed with two left feet, I thought. They seemed quite a promising bunch. Johnny O'Toole - 'from Belfast' he declared - was about my height, wiry, with long brown hair, and a mischievous grin. Stocky, gaunt and altogether more serious, Baz Barrington told me he had been born into a morris family in Essex though had hitherto declined to don the baldricks and bells.

"I'm Priscilla Possett," said the tallest girl I'm sure I'd ever come across, "but my friends all call me Posy." Surprisingly deep voice too. Her companion, April, was the complete antithesis - a good head and shoulders shorter, dumpy and well-rounded in every dimension.

One person I'd expected to see was absent. "No Gron?" I asked Jake. Goronwy Griffiths, a lecturer at Tencastle and former morris dancer himself, had been instrumental in getting Carpiog Morris up and dancing.

"No, he thinks we're quite capable of shaping our own destiny now," said Jake, "I'll be running the practices." Seeing Min and Janet slip back into the room with brimming pint glasses he continued, "Right, let's get started. Most of you have already got to know each other but I'd like to welcome Janet, from Carrick."

Janet blushed at becoming the centre of attention and waved, "Hi!"

"Janet, have you brought your accordion or fiddle? Or would you prefer to dance?"

"I'll have a go at the dances first, Jake, if you don't mind," she replied. "I can pick up the tunes later."

"Okay, ask Huw to let you have the dots." Although Jake occasionally joined in on his banjo if he wasn't dancing, Huw had hitherto been our sole musician. Mind you, his Welsh bagpipes didn't really need any other support.

Jake soon got us started with probably the simplest dance in our repertoire, which involved little more than a weaving figure, or hey as we knew it, in between thrashing each other with sticks. Border Morris is basically pretty straightforward if you can manage the simple step-hop footwork and know your left from your right in order to avoid collisions in the figures. Unfortunately these two attributes don't come naturally to everyone.

"No, no, right! Right shoulders!" he reminded April for the umpteenth time. Whilst the other new recruits were shaping up really well, her attempts at keeping in time with the music failed consistently, and her stepping resembled that of a waddling lame duck. But she was keen, very keen.

"I really enjoyed that," she declared when we took a beer break after a vigorous hour.

Although it was early days, Jake, I suspected, was already feeling that April might be a lost cause in getting her movements in any kind of co-ordination with the rest of the set.

"I've been thinking about an animal," he said inconsequentially when we'd all refilled our glasses.

"And we have to guess what it is?" said Min, puzzled.

"A pet?" Harry suggested.

"He probably means a mascot," Baz contributed.

"What, like a live goat?" said Harry.

"Or silly ass," I volunteered, never sure quite where Jake's thoughts were leading.

Jake glared at me. "Not a live animal, pillock! A symbolic one!"

"You mean like a unicorn or dragon?" I said.

"Something like that - a ritual beast to entertain the crowds and extract money from them."

"But isn't that what we do already?" I said.

"It's all part of the tradition. I've seen a side in London with a unicorn." I was about to ask Jake how many pints he'd had prior to the apparition, but he continued, "Fellow dressed up with a painted papier maché unicorn head and long cloak over his shoulders."

"I've seen a similar thing back home with a dragon's head." said Janet. Which reminded me I didn't yet know where Janet's roots were.

"So would we go for a Welsh dragon then?" Min suggested.

"Or a Mari Llwyd?" said Huw, to blank looks. He didn't elaborate.

"Might be better to go for something more relevant to Tencastle, perhaps less controversial than the national symbol," said Jake.

"What about a sheep?" said Holly.

"Perfect!" said Jake, "You're a star!"

Holly blushed.

"We could call it Baasil!" said Harry.

"Baarney!" Johnny chipped in.

"Or Ewegene?" I added.

Posy put her hand up, "'Scuse me, but aren't we getting the genders mixed up? Is the sheep male or female ."

We looked at each other, briefly silenced.

"Well," I said. "A ram is a male sheep and a ewe is female."

"Baabara, then," said Johnny, shrugging his shoulders

"Ewegenie?" Baz suggested.

"I like it!" said Jake, "Hands up for Ewegenie?" No one dissented.

Ewegenie the Sheep was thus conceived. Who was to be responsible for bringing her into the world was not even discussed. Had Benji still been in artistic mode we might have asked him. He'd done an imaginative job on our very first publicity poster for Carpiog Morris in blending an image of a pig with a Morris Minor.

We capered around the back room of the Castle for another forty-five minutes. I declined the offer of another pint from Jake, conscious that I now had a much longer drive home.

"See you all next week," April called cheerfully. I wondered if she might be feeling sheepish before too long.

"That was great fun, Rob," said Janet as we drove back to Carrick, "Absolute crazy lot but great fun."

"Really glad you enjoyed it."

"By the way, Min's invited me along to her engagement party this Saturday. You know about it already, I guess."

"Yes, Jake mentioned it before Christmas, though he wasn't sure of the date."

"I think she assumed we are, er, together," Janet added tentatively.

"Well, in a way, I suppose we are," I said. "We work together, we are sharing the same house and we have common interests." I'd not really given more than a passing thought about any closer relationship up to that point, really being content to let things take their natural course. And I was sort of still in contact with Dilly. "You're good company," I added.

"Thanks, Rob. You too."

"Tell me, I was quite intrigued, where was it you saw the dragon you mentioned?"

"Oh, that would have been in Sompting, one Boxing Day. The local group always dance there and perform a mummer's play."

"And where exactly is Sompting?"

"It's near Worthing, in Sussex."

"And you live there? Your family home, I mean?"

"Yes, or rather a couple of miles away in Shoreham, on

the coast. I went to school in Worthing."

"That's amazing!"

"Why?"

"Dan, my former house mate, is now teaching in Worthing. And last year I practically got stranded in Shoreham trying to get to a job interview."

"Really? What happened?"

"Car broke down, Beeching cuts to railway, and bus route blocked. Otherwise I might have been working in Steyning rather than Carrick."

It took the rest of the journey to Janet's flat to tell the full story of my aborted interview and my experience in the town.

***

It would, in retrospect, have been prudent to have checked with Min at the morris practice where exactly she would be holding her party. I'd assumed that she had told Janet, and Janet assumed that I already knew.

For a Saturday evening the Students' Union was relatively quiet. The upstairs refectory which doubled as a function room for concerts and private parties was deserted.

"Not here then?" Janet said, superfluously.

"Hmm, no." I thought for a moment. "Jake did mention a new night club venue near the Castle Inn. You know, where we were the other night?"

Janet nodded. "You probably won't be able to take these bottles of wine in."

"Good thinking. I'll drop them back in the car." I paused. I'd parked Fi in the opposite direction from the Castle. "Do you want to go on and I'll meet you there? You know the way?"

"Okay."

"I won't be long."

I was pretty quick, but there was no sign of Janet when I got to the club, The Naked Dragon, as it was called. I could hear the throbbing sound of heavy rock from the top of the steps to the entrance.

I checked the Castle to see if she was waiting there instead. No joy. I couldn't really see how she could have got lost within four hundred yards from the Union in a town the size of Tencastle.

I began to climb the steps to the club entrance.

"Where do you think you're going, boyo?" A beefy giant emerged from the door, blocking the entrance.

"The party," I said, more calmly than I felt, "I've been invited."

"Show me!"

"What?"

"Your invite. Show me!" He thrust out huge gnarled hand.

Min hadn't given out any invite cards as far as I knew. Still, I made a show of rummaging in my pockets. "Sorry, I must have left it at home." A lame excuse.

Beefy thought so to. "Then you're not coming in. Now bugger off."

I just stood there, gobsmacked.

"You heard me, get lost."

"Yes," I stuttered. And grasped at one last straw. "Tell me, did you let a girl in just now? Slim, bit shorter than me, in a brown coat?"

"What if I did?"

"She's.. er... she's my girlfriend. I asked her to wait for me."

"Yeah?" he said dismissively. "Looks as if she's stood you up then."

"But..."

"You," he jabbed a fat finger at me, "Leave. Now!"

Arguing or pleading with him was obviously going to be pointless. Reluctantly I slowly began to descend, still clueless as to what to do next as I reached the pavement.

"Rob! Rob, wait!"

I quickly turned at the sound of her voice. Janet had pushed past Beefy, her coat dragging under her arms and flew down the steps.

"Oh Rob, thank God!" she cried as she collapsed into my arms.

"It's okay, it's okay."

Janet took a deep breath and exhaled. "That was so damn weird. There was no-one there I recognised at all. No Min, no Jake. No-one I knew. Must have been someone else's party. And then this bloke, pissed as a lord, tried to haul me on the dance floor. I grabbed my coat and ran."

"Why didn't you wait outside?"

"The doorman." she glanced back up the steps. "I told him I was waiting for someone but he told me I could wait inside in the warm. He was quite insistent." She sighed, "God, what a fool!"

"No matter, it's okay now." I held her tight. "I was dead worried where you'd gone. No way was that bouncer going to let me in." And I whispered in her ear, "I'm not as pretty as you."

She drew back and looked at me. And smiled. "You're very sweet, Rob! Thank you."

She knitted her brow, "But what do we do now? Go back to Carrick?"

"Honestly, I don't know. You're absolutely sure that Min told you the party was tonight?"

"Yes, definitely."

"Well there's nowhere else I can think of in Tencastle." We started to walk back to the car.

"Min and Huw's place?"

"Unlikely, it's the size of a shoebox." But Janet had given me a flash of inspiration. "One possibility. Do you fancy a short drive out of town?"

Janet shrugged. "I'm in your hands."

Signs were that I'd guessed right. There was just enough space to squeeze Fi between Jessica and another car below Ty Melin. Two more cars were parked on the other side of the bridge at Penybont as we walked down to Benji's retreat. Not that it was a place for meditation and temperance that evening. Laughter, music, and the sounds of people having a good time distilled out into the night through the open front door.

Jake stood just inside, dressed incongruously in a long golden kaftan and a bathroom towel turban. He was holding his banjo in one hand and a bottle in the other.

"Hi there, what kept you?"

"We've been in Tencastle," I said. "Er, what's with the outfit?"

"Fancy dress party. Didn't Min tell you?"

"No, and neither did she tell us that the party was out here in Penybont. We've been faffing around the Union and the night club for the past hour."

"Oh." Jake didn't seem at all concerned. "But you're here now!"

"What about Benji? This isn't really his scene now, is it?"

"He's away for the weekend to some hermitage. I'm looking after the house." He saw my sceptical look. "Seemed like a good opportunity since we never had a proper farewell party for Ty Melin either." He saw I wasn't fully convinced. "Evan and Bessie from next door are also away," he added.

I doubted if Benji would ever be aware of Jake's house-minding venture.

We eased past him into the lounge, which was heaving with most of Carpiog Morris and several people I didn't know. We both felt rather overdressed for the occasion. Particularly as Min was clad in nothing more than few strategically placed plastic fig leaves – evidently Eve to

Huw's caricature of Adam the Gardener from the Sunday Express, complete with flat cap and fluffy beard. Holly was, well, holly - a dark green bin liner cut to shape with dangles of red berries, while her twin brother, Harry, was almost swamped by a hessian sack entwined with garden string on which pieces of green plastic were threaded.

"Holly and Ivy?" I suggested.

Janet chuckled. "But what's he supposed to be?" she pointed to a chap clad from head to toe in white plastic.

Chap caught sight of us and waddled over, his leg movement being severely restricted. "Rob and Janet, isn't it? I'm Johnny." he said in a strong Irish accent. He looked at Janet's puzzled face and whispered to me in a loud aside, "I'm a condom. See?" He pointed to the attached label bearing the letter C with the little hook-like cedilla attached underneath. "It's French."

Janet collapsed with laughter. I'm glad she wasn't prudish.

"Quiet everyone!" Min called out. She'd climbed up onto a chair to make the announcement, and was waving her hands to gain attention. Whatever was keeping the fig leaves in place was being put to a severe test.

"Time for a dance, now we're all here." She winked at me. "Who's up for Upton?"

The most vigorous dance in our repertoire, the Upton-on-Severn stick dance, needed plenty of space both laterally and vertically. Dancing space could probably be condensed but I had serious concerns for the ceiling and light fittings with half-a-dozen two-foot-long hazel poles thrashing around. Others seemed to be equally hesitant.

"Celery sticks," yelled Min, "on the table!" As some Carpiog members moved towards the buffet, Min called to me, "Give me a hand down, Rob."

I toyed briefly with lifting her down with both my hands on her bare skin or fig leaves, but prudently just offered my hand in hers to steady her balance as she jumped down.

With no celery left I grabbed the longest cheese straw and joined the other five dancers in the set. Huw's bagpipes squealed into life and away we went, prancing round on a four-foot square of carpet. My cheese straw was no match for Jake's celery stick and disintegrated into crumbs at the first slash. The replacements offered by willing onlookers fared little better until I was finally handed a cucumber – a much superior weapon.

Following loud applause we declined demands for an encore, pleading a dearth of long thin stick substitutes. Instead, Huw kept on playing. Jake retrieved his banjo from the corner where he had parked it out of the way while he danced.

"Have you brought your instruments?" Jake asked.

I nodded. I'd told Janet that a jam session was highly likely. "Be back in a mo," I said to her.

In the couple of minutes or so it took to retrieve my guitar and Janet's fiddle from the car most of the guests had acquired something with which to contribute to the music - Johnny the Rubber on a tin whistle, and a harmonica among the recognisable instruments, while others improvised with comb and paper, spoons, and Baz was making farting noises with a now empty demijohn. I assumed Baz had himself downed the quart of cider that it had contained. One lass was doing absolutely amazing percussive things with four walnut shell halves.

But even the musicians were flagging after playing almost non-stop for an hour or so. No stopping Jake, though, who crooned a gentle song, 'I Never Will Marry' - perhaps appropriate as the relationship with Mary seemed to have ended. "Anyone else for a song?" he asked when he'd strummed the last chord, "Janet?"

"Okay, if you like." And then added, "I'm not very good."

I'd never heard Janet sing, so I had no idea whether

she was being modest or honest. With fiddle cradled in the crook of her arm she played an introduction and then continued with a simple but highly effective accompaniment to a beautiful rendering of a slow ballad, 'She Moved Through The Fair' in a voice crystal clear. As she finished with a long draw of the bow across two strings, you could have heard a pin drop in the few seconds of awed silence before everyone clapped enthusiastically in appreciation. Almost a standing ovation if we hadn't been sprawled over sofas and floor.

"That was absolutely amazing, Janet!" I said.

"Thanks, Rob."

But I got very little opportunity to have Janet's undivided attention for the rest of the evening. Jake was encouraging her to firm up arrangements for the launch of a folk club in Carrick – something that seemed to have been on the back burner since Christmas, and Huw was quizzing her about fiddle techniques and offering to extend her repertoire of Welsh tunes. All that in between more songs from her, Jake, and Baz, who seemed to have an almost limitless repertoire of drinking songs, delivered with great gusto.

Eventually, at some time after midnight, Janet whispered to me, "Do you think we should be heading back home?"

"Okay, if you're ready." I said. I'd purposely kept off the beer for the last couple of hours. Not so most of the other partygoers. It would only have been a matter of time before Min attempted her inebriated party piece of horizontal morris dancing.

"Leavin' a'ready?" she said, "Y' c'n shtay a'night."

"Thanks, Min, but we've got a full day tomorrow - today, I mean." Though I didn't know what would be filling it exactly.

"Givus a hug then."

Christ, it was difficult to suppress an erection with so

much silky smooth bare skin pressed close to me. I'd seen Min strip naked when completely blotto but I trusted that tonight it would be in her fiance's arms.

Min gave Janet a hug for good measure, too.

Chapter 17

The pub crawl was Janet's idea. Perhaps not to test the ales as such but to find a suitable venue for her folk club. She'd been pretty fired up about it after chatting to Jake the previous evening.

Although I'd more or less discounted the Bull and Dragon, the largest and most central of the Carrick watering holes, it did have a function room, according to Janet. Far too large, as it turned out, and way out of our non-existent budget! The landlord of the Eagle Tavern, just off the main square, was very keen and the beer was excellent. Unfortunately, with more than a quartet of singers and musicians, the snug would have been, well, very snug indeed, to the point of intimacy. The Sportsman was loud and brash - enough said. We also looked in a couple of others but settled on the Quarryman's Arms which was in effect our local. They were happy to offer us free use of the small dining room on a Monday evening when they didn't serve food, provided we bought a few drinks of course. No problem.

"How about having a bite to eat here?" said Janet, examining the menu card in the restaurant. "I haven't got much in the house."

"Yeah, why not?" I agreed. "Let's celebrate the birth of folk culture in Carrick." I added with alcohol-induced pomposity.

"It's also my birthday tomorrow."

"Even more reason to celebrate! Red or white?"

"Eh?"

"Wine. Can't celebrate your birthday without wine!"

"Red, then, please."

A couple of hours later when we staggered back up to the house, I was feeling a bit squiffy but very happy. Janet made no objection when I put my arm around her waist, though it was more in self-interest to keep me upright. I collapsed on her sofa, a great beam of a smile on my face.

"Black coffee?"

"Mmm, you haven't got any Alka-Seltzer by any chance? Must be something I ate."

Janet raised an eyebrow. I don't think she thought the food had anything to do with it. She popped into the kitchen and came back with a glass of water and a tube of tablets. Then returned to the kitchen.

I fiddled with the tube and eventually got a tablet into the glass. Where it floated.

I was staring at the glass in confusion when Janet reappeared with two mugs of coffee. "The darn tablet won't dissolve," I said.

Janet hooted with laughter, "Could be because you've put the plastic cap in the glass instead of the tablet, you daft pillock."

If my cheeks weren't already rosy I'm sure they were now glowing red in embarrassment. "Sorry, Janet," I mumbled, "I'm not usually like this."

"You're very sweet even when you're pissed," she said softly, and sat beside me. Her arm went round my shoulders.

I'd no idea how long I'd been asleep when I was awakened by the telephone ringing.

"For you," said Janet. "I think it's Jake."

I staggered to my feet and took the proffered handset. "Rob here."

"Go. a ..ig f... ..and." a voice crackled.

"Sorry, Jake, can't hear you properly."

"Acci...ls...ys..g...n ...day."

"Jake, you're breaking up, I can't get what you're saying,"

"Us. ..aying. ..e get ..aid"

"Don't forget to tell Jake about the folk club," said Janet.

"Okay. Only hope he can hear what I'm saying. The line's terrible."

"We . m...t... ra...tice."

I more or less got that. "Okay, Jake, we'll talk at practice. By the way, we've sorted out a venue for folk club. Quarryman's Arms, starting next Monday."

"What was all that about?" asked Janet.

"Don't really know. He sounded like a Dalek with laryngitis. We'll find out on Thursday."

We actually found out much sooner.

***

My brain wasn't really back into full gear on Monday morning, though I'd slept well. I suspect Janet had steered me in the direction of my bedroom but I obviously hadn't got undressed. Her cheery greeting at breakfast helped to convince me that I hadn't made a complete fool of myself.

"Happy birthday!" I replied and gave her a peck on her cheek.

Somehow I lumbered through the day without too much demand on my mental capabilities. Apart, that is, from covering for a colleague's lesson. Gerry Kipling had stumbled past me into the staffroom at morning break looking extremely flushed and muttering angrily to himself, "They'll regret this. I'll make them regret this!" I hadn't had a great deal of contact with him but it was obvious he smoked like a chimney. I'd heard also that he had some problems with discipline.

I found I'd lost my free period after lunch to cover for his G.C.E. French class. Even as I approached the language suite, I could hear the chant, "Kip, Kip, Kipper!"

"Kip, kip..." The voices faded as they realized the taunting was misdirected. Mr Kipling was not taking the lesson. I was.

Thirty teenagers looked at me warily. None of them

were in my chemistry groups. I glanced at them unsmiling and turned my attention to the blackboard. Every inch was covered with fish skeleton graffiti, some with a gross caricature of Gerry's bespectacled face. And the cloying gut-churning smell suggested something putrefying in the teacher's desk. I lifted the lid. The half-eaten kipper must have been at least a week old.

Someone sniggered. "You," I snapped at the culprit, a tubby lad with a shock of ginger hair, "Get rid of this!" I held the offending specimen between my fingertips.

"'S'not mine," he sneered.

"I don't care whose it is. Get rid of it!"

He curled his lip, ready for another defiant comment.

"Now!" I said, "Or I shall personally stuff this down your backside."

I heard a couple of stifled giggles. With bad grace Tubby grabbed the kipper from me. "In the bins at the back of the kitchen," I commanded. They were at the other end of the school site. "And you," I pointed at a tall youth with bad acne in the front row. "Get the blackboard cleaned off!"

Gerry hadn't left any work for the class. I thumbed through a textbook one girl had placed on her desk. "Right," I said, "Page 22, read the passage and answer the questions." The title of the exercise was 'M. Leclerc goes fishing'. "And I strongly suggest you leave out any reference to kippers."

***

Janet was back at the house before me.

"Hi Rob," she said. "Faculty meeting?"

"No, I had a small errand to do." I pulled a small parcel out of my briefcase. "Here, something for you, for your birthday."

"Rob, you shouldn't have! You paid for the meal

yesterday!"

"My treat."

Janet unwrapped the box of Milk Tray, and put my card along with the dozen or so others on the mantelpiece. "Rob, thank you so much. You really are such a kind person." She flung her arms around my neck and kissed me full on the lips."

"Hey, I could get to like this!"

She punched me playfully in the chest. "Oh, there's one letter here for you as well," she said.

I recognised the handwriting. Dilly. Not something I wanted to open at that moment. "Thanks. It's from my cousin I think. Not urgent." And to deflect any queries I offered to help get supper ready.

Some people think that teachers have it easy because we get long holidays, conveniently overlooking the fact that during term time our working day doesn't end at four o'clock when the kids go home. Marking and lesson preparation often takes up most of our evenings and much of our weekends.

Both Janet and I had our heads down in work after supper. Until the doorbell rang.

"Expecting visitors?" I asked.

Janet shook her head. Whoever was at the door now knocked loudly.

"I'll go," I offered.

More knocking and bell ringing. "Okay, okay," I shouted. "Hold your horses!"

Jake did not look happy.

"What on earth are you doing here?" I asked.

"I've been down the Quarryman's for the last half hour waiting for you two morons to turn up."

"Why?"

"What do you mean, 'Why'? You told me the folk club was on."

"That was next Monday."

"That's what you said yesterday. And the 'next Monday' was this evening."

I thought Jake was being pedantic but I could see how technically he had got the wrong date. "Look, you'd better come in."

He stepped in and led the way upstairs.

"Oh, hi, Jake. Pleasant surprise." said Janet, with a smile. Which dispelled some of Jake's grumpiness.

"Yeah, well," he said.

"Jake thought the folk club was this week," I explained.

"Oh." Janet was surprised. "Oh, I'm sorry. You poor chap, driving all the way over unnecessarily. Rob did say that the phone connection was bad."

I found a couple of cans of lager. "Least we can do is offer you a drink," I said. "And we do need to sort out what you were trying to tell me on the phone. You kept breaking up."

"Ah yes," said Jake. "I've got the band a gig at Ynysgwyn Manor. You remember it?"

Indeed I did. We were paid a very generous fee to perform our rag mummer's play there a couple of years ago. But a band gig?

"Come again?"

"Our barn dance band - The Accidentals. They want us to play for a wedding. Good fee."

Janet and I looked at each other open-mouthed. Standing in to salvage the PTA dance was one thing, doing a professional gig at a high-class country hotel was in a different league altogether.

"When..." "What about..." We both started raising some important issues at once. Janet laughed. "You first," she said.

"Okay, when is this wedding taking place?"

"Second Saturday in March, I think."

"Christ, Jake, that's barely six weeks away!"

"So? What's the problem?"

"The problem, Jake," I said, "is that we have virtually no experience of playing together and we have no amplification equipment." Another thought crossed my mind. "And who would be doing the calling for the dances? Have you thought of that?"

"Um, no, not exactly," Jake admitted. "Couldn't you do it?"

I rolled my eyes. "I hardly know a do-si-do from a strip the willow!"

During this exchange Janet had been deep in thought.

"Jake, let's take this one step at a time," she said. "Do you know how long they want us to play for?"

"Oh, they mentioned a couple of hours max. Probably less. They're having a disco afterwards."

"I trust you haven't signed us up for that as well!" I said.

Jake glared at me.

"Right, I could hold that together," said Janet, "And I'm sure we could borrow the P.A. system from school. It's pretty good." She paused. "Who else would be playing?"

"Well, us three, obviously. And Huw, probably. And I've heard Baz Barrington's a whiz on drums."

"Hmm, it's do-able, I guess," said Janet.

"What about the caller?" I asked. "I don't mind having a go but not at such short notice. I'd be way out of my depth."

"What about asking Tom, from the PTA band?" Janet suggested. "He gave us his phone number, I think."

"Janet, you're brilliant!" said Jake. "And he owes us a favour!"

Jake rummaged in his wallet and extricated a dog-eared business card. "Can I use your phone?"

The phone seemed to ring for ages before someone replied. Confirming that he'd reached the right person, Jake described the gig enthusiastically and laid on the bullshit that it would be an honour to have Tom call for us. Evidently he bought it.

"He'll do it!" said Jake, triumphantly, when he'd hung up.

"Did you ask him how much he'd charge?" I said.

Jake frowned. "No, I didn't."

"You'll need to sort that out," I said. "If you haven't already said otherwise to your client you can suggest that the caller would be an extra charge. They probably won't bat an eyelid if they can afford to hire Ynysgwyn Manor."

Over another beer and the remains of a bottle of wine, we toasted the future success of the Accidentals, and also Janet on her birthday. We also discussed plans for the folk club launch, with the question as to whether to run it weekly, fortnightly or monthly. Play it by ear seemed to be the consensus.

When Jake eventually left sometime after ten o'clock, continuing with our school work had very little appeal.

"Must have been quite an experience sharing a house with Jake," said Janet, "He's quite a whirlwind when he gets an idea in his head."

"Can't disagree with that," I said. I felt quite exhausted. "Going to turn in early, I think."

"Okay, see you in the morning."

I wanted the privacy of my room to see what Dilly's letter was about. I'd last written to her earlier in January to say that my intended digs had fallen through but I was pretty sure I hadn't given her my new address. All in all quite intriguing.

I wasn't really prepared for the bombshell.

Dear Rob,

This is a very difficult letter for me to write. I've agonised for some time over whether I should burden you with my problem but I know you have had strong feelings for me. I too have always enjoyed your company. Under different circumstances I like to think our relationship would have blossomed.

Since Christmas I have not been well. At first I thought I had just caught a seasonal bug but the tiredness, sickness and stomach pains would not go away. In short, the doctors don't know what is wrong but they suspect I may have cancer. I am due to have various tests.

My parents have not taken the news well, and try to avoid any discussion, more to avoid their discomfort than mine, I regret to say. I'm trying to continue working but it's not really fair on the school for them to never know when I'm going to be well enough to turn up. But being housebound most days just makes me feel even more depressed.

I would like to ask a big favour. Would it be possible to come and stay with you for a few days over the half term? I desperately need to get away from home for a while though I shall understand if you are not able to help. You told me what happened about your original digs in Carrick and I guess you have now settled in elsewhere. I asked Jake for your new address. I hope you don't mind.

Love,
Dilly

***

I had been red-eyed and uncharacteristically taciturn at breakfast.

Janet had known something was troubling me. "Your cousin?" she'd enquired.

"Eh?" I'd briefly forgotten what I had said when she'd handed me the letter. "Yes, that's right," I'd nodded.

She'd asked if she could help but I'd thanked her and declined until I'd had a chance to think things through.

I was thankful when final bell rang. I'd drifted through

the day, going through the motions of teaching like an automaton. I'd hardly slept a wink the previous night.

I needed to be alone. I sat in the driver's seat for a few minutes before starting the engine. I headed Fi out of town on the Carmarthen road, the opposite direction from Tencastle. I drove steadily, aware of the road conditions and light traffic but not my precise whereabouts. And all the while considering various options.

I'd probably been on the road for about half-an-hour when a café sign caught my attention. I pulled in to the near-deserted car park. Apart from a burly stubble-faced trucker who left shortly after I entered, I was the only customer. I ordered a mug of coffee and a toasted sandwich from the middle-aged woman serving behind the counter and took a seat at a table by the window.

I suppose I must have looked a rather sorry sight, sitting there, elbows on table, head resting in my hands and gazing vacantly into the darkness.

"Something troubling you, young man?" the woman asked gently when she brought my order over.

"A dilemma, I suppose," I replied, "Not sure what to do for the best."

"Girl problem?" Then added hastily, "I'm sorry, I shouldn't be intruding,"

"No, no, that's okay," I waved to the seat opposite, inviting her to tarry a while. "I've just had some sad news from a friend. She thinks she might have cancer."

"Oh dear, I am so sorry."

"We were close, and I'm still very fond of her, though we've rather gone our separate ways since leaving college."

"But you want to see her?"

"Well, yes, or rather she has asked if she can come and stay with me for a few days."

"Is that a problem? New girlfriend?"

"It's a bit complicated. A colleague at work offered me a room in her house when my lodgings fell through, and shortly I'll be renting her downstairs flat when the current tenant moves out." I took a deep breath and continued. "We've not been living together as a couple but we get on very well together with common interests, and, well, I'm hopeful that... that things might develop."

"I see."

"I don't want to jeopardise my prospects with Janet, my colleague, but I don't want to turn down my friend Dilly when she needs my help."

"Do Janet and Dilly know each other?"

"Yes, they have met. That was back in the autumn. I was living elsewhere at the time and Dilly was staying with me. We haven't seen each other since." I realised my coffee was getting cold. "Look, I'm sorry, I really shouldn't be burdening you with my problems."

"No problem. No-one else to talk to and no customers queuing up. It can help to get things off your chest to someone not involved."

"That's true," I said. Though pouring out my personal thoughts to a stranger is not something I would normally do. "So what do you think I should do?"

"You should talk to Janet. Show her the letter perhaps, unless there are intimate details you want to keep secret."

I shook my head.

"In the circumstances I'm sure she'd want you to help Dilly. Unless you think she's likely to be very jealous of your former girlfriend."

"No, I'm sure that's not the case."

"You might need to think about sleeping arrangements. If you have the use of the ground floor flat, then perhaps Janet and Dilly could share the upstairs. Then neither of them would have cause to suspect you of sleeping with the other!"

"That's brilliant!" That solution had never even entered my head. "I'm really so grateful to you. I really couldn't decide what to do." I stood, ready to leave. "Thanks... I'm sorry, I don't even know your name."

"Chrissie."

"Rob," I shook her hand. "Thanks so much, Chrissie."

As I set off back to Carrick I felt as if a whole weight had been lifted from my shoulders.

***

Janet was aware of my change of mood from the morning before I'd even taken my coat off.

"Problem solved?" she said.

"I think so," I replied. "Janet, I..."

"That's good," she called as she ducked into her bedroom, and quickly reappeared with a sheaf of papers. "Something I want to show you. I've done some posters for the folk club." She spread the papers on the table. "What do you think?"

I looked at them. "Very good, very good indeed." They were, too, bold and eye-catching, uncluttered but with all the necessary information. I tried to get back to the key matter. "Janet, about half-term..."

"Oh yes, meant to talk to you about that." Janet jumped in, "I'm going to my parents for a few days, so I won't be here. So there's no hurry for you to move into the flat." She paused and then added, "You don't really have to move at all, you know."

She caught my open-mouthed expression. "What?"

I was unprepared, certainly, for the implications of what she had said. "Sorry, Janet, can I backtrack a bit?" A flash of concern across her face. "No worries, though."

"You remember the letter you gave me? It wasn't actually from my cousin but I needed time to think. It's probably best if you read it for yourself."

Janet took the letter and studied it. Her hand went up to her mouth, "Oh, the poor girl!" she exclaimed, and looked at me in sympathy, "You'll ask her to come down, won't you?"

"I'd like to."

"But you were worried, yes?"

I nodded.

"About how I'd feel about a girlfriend staying with you? Or how she'd feel about you sharing a house with me?"

"Both," I acknowledged.

"But if I'm not here, then it won't really be a problem, surely?"

"You'll know. Even if I had realised earlier that you were going to be away, I would have wanted you to know."

"I really appreciate that. But I don't have any exclusive claim on your attentions." She paused. "You're a lovely person to be with, Rob, and I'm very happy with what we share in our lives. And I trust you to do what's right."

"Thank you for being so understanding,"

"You will write to Dilly?"

"Tonight."

We hugged each other without speaking. She didn't draw back when I put my lips to hers.

Chapter 18

I can't explain why, but the prospect of the weekly drive from Carrick to Tencastle for morris practice seemed far more demanding than the daily return trip I'd undertaken without a thought while on teaching practice and during my first term as a full-time teacher. I had no real reason to complain, however. Anything but, since I shared the journey with Janet as a passenger on most weeks, and I invariably felt uplifted after an evening in the company of the zany characters that made up Carpiog Morris. It was different, I suppose, in that instead of a couple of miles drive home it was thirty odd, and I felt I had to be more careful of my alcohol consumption.

We also took the opportunity to practice, informally, for our forthcoming band gig, with a music session in the Castle bar once we'd finished prancing about with sticks and bells.

I got Jake and Janet a second pint, with ginger beer for myself, before we launched into a fast and furious music session.

"Y'know," said Baz, extricating a pair of drumsticks from his rucksack, "why don't we put ourselves about a bit?"

"What do you mean?" I said.

"Carpiog Morris. My old man's always gallivanting off somewhere with his side – Holland, Germany, whatever."

"Interesting," said Jake, stroking his chin.

"Baz, it's dangerous to trigger Jake's thinking processes," I said. "He'll probably have us dancing in Timbuctoo by Easter."

Jake glared at me. "Actually, as it happens, I've been talking with our infamous Councillor Bowen-Martin about a cultural exchange to Brittany."

"Why?"

"Why not? They're Celts, like us in Wales."

I looked around our dancers. "Apart from Huw, most of us aren't Welsh," I pointed out.

"Doesn't matter, they wouldn't know the difference."

Huw raised his eyebrows but refrained from commenting.

"How would it work?" said Janet, ever practical.

"Well, we'd probably take a coach, us plus a few civic dignitaries. Your father, too, perhaps." he said to Harry and Holly, who rolled her eyes. "Long weekend, dancing, drinking, lots of ooh la la."

"I'm up for that!" said Min.

"Anybody else interested?" Jake asked.

Most hands went up. Mine slowly. "Have to be school holidays," I said.

"No problem. Easter?"

Janet also put her hand up.

"I'm also thinking about..."

"One thing at a time, Jake," I cautioned.

"... a folk festival," he concluded lamely.

***

"Nervous?" I said to Janet as we started walking down to the Quarryman's.

"Not really. I just hope some people turn up." she said. Jake had already brought apologies from Min and Huw.

To our pleasant surprise there were already half-a-dozen people gathered in the back room when we arrived a good twenty minutes before the advertised start time. Two of them had guitars. While we introduced ourselves and sorted out drinks from the bar, the room began to fill up comfortably. Apart from ourselves we attracted five other performers and about a dozen people who had just come along to listen. Not bad for a new venture, we thought.

Janet and I had discussed beforehand whether we'd run the evening as a formal folk club, with each performer given a short spot enough for two or three songs, or as a more casual singaround in which everyone was invited to do one number in turn, going round the room twice or more, as time permitted. We opted for the latter, thinking that we'd probably get a better balance with singers hitherto unknown to us.

Jake had just started his first song when I became aware of intrusive music from a speaker above the door. I hadn't noticed it when we'd been checking out possible venues. I excused myself to speak to the landlord.

"Can't turn it off when the juke box is being used," he said, "but I can turn it down as far as possible."

Which he did. The speaker still issued forth a background buzz, slightly irritating but ignorable during the first round of acts which included a chap with a deadpan delivery of a hilarious parody, a young girl singing in Welsh to a harp accompaniment, and a tall fellow with a soft voice and intricate guitar style. With unkempt shoulder-length hair and a long straggly beard it was impossible to guess his age.

The noise from the speaker seemed to be rising. The bearded bloke started his second song, 'Oh No John, No' - definitely not the bowdlerised version I'd heard in Primary School -

"Madam may I tie your garter just a little above your knee

And if my hand should slip a little further would you think it amiss of me?"

"*IT'S NOW OR NEVER...*" Elvis blared forth from the speaker with impeccable timing, as our singer paused for breath.

What happened to John and his woman we never found out. Janet announced a beer break once the laughter subsided.

"Sorry, folks, nothing I can do about it tonight," the landlord apologised. "Switch must be faulty but I'll get it sorted for next time."

I reported back. Janet grimaced, "That's it, then."

Jake looked at the speaker and then at Janet. "Can you take off your sweater?"

"What?"

"Your jumper... oh and your scarf. I'll tie it round the speaker. Should muffle the sound enough." He paused. "Are you decent underneath... I mean, you are wearing a blouse?"

Janet nodded and began to peel off her bright pink woollen sweater. She handed her long turquoise scarf to Jake as he clambered up onto a chair.

The thump of an electric bass could still be detected but the raucous twanging and vocals were effectively silenced. Enough for us to continue into a third offering from each performer.

I was surprised to see John Rhys-Price lounging in the doorway. He raised his half-empty pint glass in acknowledgment. He looked as if he'd already emptied a few more. As the Welsh girl finished a quiet unaccompanied song which she'd said was about a blackbird, John swayed into the middle of the room.

"G'you a song," he mumbled, and launched into a loud and definitely off-key chorus of a rugby song, which I knew had some pretty obscene verses.

I stood up to intervene. "Sorry, John," I said, "Not here."

"Whaddyermean?" he snapped and belched.

"Save it for the clubhouse bar."

He glared at me. "Right. Letshavva duet." He lurched towards Janet, "Miss Milward, you c'n play a prett' tune wimme." John lost his balance and would have fallen onto Janet had Jake not caught him by the shoulders and pulled him back.

"Get your f***ing hands off me, you f***ing coon!"

I thought for a moment Jake was going to land one on John. Out of the corner of my eye I saw the landlord glance in to see what the commotion was all about.

"Out, John, now!" I said, more politely than I felt. When he stood his ground, Jake and Longbeard helped me manhandle him, still cursing profusely, towards the door. One flailing fist caught Janet's dangling scarf and brought her pink jumper down on his head.

"What the f***!" he yelled and lashed out, his fist catching me a glancing blow on my nose. Which started to bleed.

Two policemen arrived just in time to witness the incident. One firmly escorted John out of the room while the other - the same one who'd helped with my misfortune on two previous occasions - came over to the chair where Janet had sat me down to staunch the blood with her handkerchief.

"Well, Mr Kiddecott, you do seem to be making a name for yourself as a victim of unfortunate circumstances."

"I'm shorry," I gurgled.

"Do you want to press charges?"

I shook my head.

"Well, I'll leave you in capable hands, sir." His expression clearly showed that he had noticed that I was in the capable hands of a different young woman.

No-one really had the inclination to sing any more, and it was getting near closing time anyway.

Janet stood to address the assembly before they all drifted away. "Thank you all for coming. I'm sorry that the evening has been, er, rather incident prone. If the landlord is agreeable the folk club will meet again next month - without canned music or drunkards."

Although we didn't feel that the incident with John Rhys-Price was in any way down to us, we thought it best to offer our apologies to the landlord, in the hope that we could use the venue again.

"Not your fault, gentlemen - and lady," he said. "He's been warned about his behaviour before. He's already been banned from the Bull and Dragon, and he won't be welcome here in future - nor, I suspect any of the other pubs in Carrick Major."

This was quite a revelation to me. I certainly hadn't been aware of my colleague's reputation.

"Are we okay then for next month?" Janet asked.

"No problem - and I'll get the loudspeaker sorted by then." He stroked his chin. "Really good to see some live music. Would you like me to lay on chips or something next time?"

"Brilliant - and thank you!" I said.

Unexpectedly Jake declined the offer of a nightcap back at the house. "Early start tomorrow," he declared. I didn't enquire about the reason. I was happy just to share the sofa with Janet and a cup of strong coffee.

"That was some evening," she sighed, and leaned her head on my shoulder.

"Memorable indeed," I said. "The prospects look good. Good call to leave it for a month." We hadn't decided beforehand on the frequency of the club.

"What do you think will happen to John?"

"Night in the cells to sober up I expect."

"No, I mean at school. I recognised a couple of parents in the pub."

"Dunno."

There was no sign of John in the staffroom next morning. I suspected that a heavy hangover would be the least of his problems.

When I was asked to the Head's office 'at my convenience' I had no doubt that Moby had heard of the shenanigans. As I thought it very likely that Janet would also have received a similar request, I thought it prudent to ensure over coffee at morning break that our accounts didn't throw up any inconsistencies. Surprisingly, Moby hadn't yet contacted her.

Moby got straight to the point. "I understand that Mr Rhys-Price assaulted you in a public house yesterday evening, is that correct?"

"No, Sir, that is not correct."

"He didn't punch you on the nose?" Moby was clearly taken aback by my denial.

"His fist did make contact with my nose, unfortunately, but it wasn't deliberate."

"Explain yourself!"

"I got too close when he was waving his arms about."

"Why would he do that?"

"I guess he was a bit upset when I asked him to stop singing a rugby song at the folk club. There were ladies present."

"You had an argument, then."

"No, not really. I suggested he should return to the main bar, and I was heading there too. That's when I was caught by his hand."

"So who called the police?"

"I don't know. Possibly the landlord or someone in the bar worried that things might get out of hand."

"Was Mr Rhys-Price drunk?"

"He wouldn't have been fit to drive, certainly, but incapacitated, blind drunk, not in my opinion."

"Are you aware that he was detained overnight in the police cells?"

"No." An honest answer, though I had guessed that that had been the outcome.

"And the police tell me you do not wish to press charges?"

"That is correct."

"Hmm." Moby stroked his chin in thought. "That would not have been good for the school. Thank you, Mr

Kiddecott." He paused. "You might wish to reconsider your presence at rowdy pub events."

I refrained from correcting his image of a folk club and from telling him that what I did in my leisure time was none of his business.

Chapter 19

Very few passengers disembarked at Tencastle. Dilly was not among them.

I'd received a letter from her several days earlier in which she had asked me to meet her off the ten o'clock train from Shrewsbury on Tuesday morning.

She could have missed the connection, I guessed. I knew from my own experience that the service from Aberystwyth was subject to unexpected delays. The next train wasn't due for nearly three hours. Enough time to go back to Carrick, although there seemed little point in making an unnecessary return trip. Over the weekend I'd already prepared the spare room in Janet's place for Dilly and moved my stuff to the sparsely furnished downstairs flat. It had seemed quite strange being alone in a house overnight for the first time in years – apart, of course, from my one-nighter at Mrs Edwards' flat. Janet had set off early on Saturday. I'd offered to run her to the Carmarthen station but she'd been quite happy to take the bus.

On the off-chance that Dilly might have let her mother know of a delay I rang her home number from the box outside the station. No reply.

With time to kill and no particular place to go I began to saunter up towards the Student's Union, where a coffee or pint with Jake might be on the cards. Halfway there I bumped into him. Under one arm was an aluminium ladder while the other was clasping a huge bundle of material.

"Oh, hi, Rob. What are you doing here?"

I might well have asked him the same. "Killing time between trains."

"That's good. I mean, if you've time, you can give me a hand."

"Doing what exactly?"

"Putting up banners."

"Right. Er, what for?"

"Our French visitors. You remember I mentioned a twinning exchange with Brittany? Well, they're coming over tomorrow for a few days, so we're putting up some welcome signs."

"'We' being 'you' I take it?"

"Council have paid for them, the Students' Union are putting them up. Only problem is most of the students are in lectures or on teaching practice!"

Not surprising. "So what do you want me to do?"

"Okay, I've got one banner to go up this side of town and one on the other road in. If you can hold the ladder steady against that tree," he said, pointing to an oak on the corner of the park by Goliath, "I'll shin up and tie it to a branch. Then the same with the lamp post opposite."

"What about the traffic?" Although Tencastle wasn't by any means busy late on a Tuesday morning, there were several vehicles using the road.

Jake thought for a moment. "No problem, I'll keep all the stuff this side until I've finished then you can hold up the cars until I've lifted the banner high enough on the other side."

I was dubious about my role but fortunately we struck a quiet spell at the crucial time and I only had to ask a cyclist to wait a minute. He dismounted and wheeled his bike on the pavement around our obstruction.

As Jake climbed down the ladder I noticed a problem. Or two, in fact.

"Who's Ben?" I asked.

"What do you mean?"

"Look." I pointed to the sign, which read '**WELCOME CROESO BEN VENUE**' in green letters on a yellow background.

Jake stared at the banner with a wrinkled brow for

several seconds until the penny dropped. "Oh shit!"

"I think you'll also find that 'bienvenue' is all one word." My schoolboy French was, though, a bit rusty.

"Oh shit," Jake said again. "I'll have to take the bugger down."

"That's another point, Jake. I'm not sure you've got enough clearance for a high vehicle."

My observation proved correct. Jake had untied the banner from the tree but had left it loosely supported over a branch while he disconnected the lamp-post end. At which point a tractor trundled down the street. Its attached mechanical shovel held aloft at the front snagged the banner, and Jake, clinging to the ropes, was whisked off the ladder. Like a puppet on a chain or like one of those small soft toys in a car rear window, Jake dangled in front of the tractor driver, swinging precariously from side to side.

The driver brought his vehicle to a halt and slowly lowered the shovel until Jake's feet touched the road.

"You okay, boyo?" the driver called as he climbed down from his cab, "Gave me a fright, Lord you did."

Jake brushed himself down, thankfully unharmed, "Not half as much as the fright you gave me!"

With the driver's help we untangled the banner from the machinery. It too had escaped undamaged.

"Here, hold this," said Jake thrusting the bundle into my arms, "Need to have another word with the tractor man."

"What was that all about?" I said a couple of minutes later.

"Had this idea. He's agreed to come back later this afternoon to help me put the banners up."

I raised an eyebrow.

"I climb into the bucket. He raises it up so I can fix the banner higher. Q.E.D."

Only Jake could think of that. I warbled a few words of

an appropriate song,

"He flies through the air with the greatest of ease, that daring young man on the flying trapeze."

"Pillock!"

"You're forgetting something, aren't you? The spelling mistake? You're not going to get a new banner done in a couple of hours."

"Daffodils," said Jake.

"Eh?"

"National flower of Wales."

"Yeah, I know that. So what?"

"We cover up the letters with daffodils. Should be easy to insert an extra stalk to make up for the missing 'I'"

I opened my mouth to speak but between incredulity and impracticality, nothing came out. "It's not the season." I said lamely at the second attempt.

"Not in bloom in the park yet. That's where I got the idea, swinging from the tractor. But I'm sure they'll be in the florists."

"Yellow flowers won't stand out against that background," I said. "And they'll wilt."

"Ah, yes, you've got a point," Jake mused. "A few tulips or something as well then. They've only got to survive for two or three days." He looked at the banner on the pavement. "How many do you think we'll need?"

I shook my head. "No idea."

On condition that I helped him with the banner Jake agreed to postpone his floral arrangements until after we'd had a pie and a pint in the Castle. "Half-an-hour or so," I offered.

We made a strange pair, Jake with his ladder and bundle, and me with an armful of blooms. A couple of students held the double doors of the Union building open for us.

"Someone die?" one of them asked.

"No," said his mate, "Belated Valentine gift for his

girlfriend, mark you!"

I sneezed. Probably had a nose full of pollen.

Fortunately we only had to deal with one banner, as the other, unexpectedly, had no cock-up in the French lettering. Jake started to clear up the sprinkling of green compost on his office floor.

"Hey, what's this?" he said, waving a piece of paper. "'If you meet her apologise'. What the hell does that mean? And why would I need to apologise to whoever this female is?"

I looked at the scribble. The writer was obviously intent on becoming a doctor. "Er, I think it could be 'meet R' and 'apologies'."

"So?"

"It might be a message from Dilly. I was supposed to meet her this morning at the station. She probably thought that there was a chance you might see me in Tencastle when I found she wasn't on the train."

Jake frowned, "But you're not seeing Dilly any more, are you?"

"Explain later," I said, "I've got to see if she's on the afternoon train."

A few people were waiting on the platform. And one, on seeing me, quickly enveloped me with a hug, and a kiss full on the lips. She then wrinkled her nose.

"What's that smell?"

"Sorry, Min. Jake's flowers. Long story."

"Oh, right." She didn't enquire further. She knew it would be a long story if it involved Jake. "Where are you going to, then?"

"Nowhere, I'm meeting Dilly off the train." Hopefully. "What about you?"

"Off to my parents for a few days," said Huw. "We need to sort out some details for the wedding."

"You will come, won't you?" said Min. "And Janet, too. We're inviting all Carpiog Morris past and present."

"Wouldn't miss it for the world."

"There'll be camping in the field. You remember?"

Indeed. I hoped Huw's father had updated the very primitive facilities since our previous visit a couple of years ago.

Min gave me a puzzled look. "Did you say you were meeting Dilly? Are you two, er, you know, together again?"

The arrival of the train from Shrewsbury again saved me from making a reply when I wasn't even sure of the answer myself.

Still no sign of Dilly.

I checked a couple of things with the Stationmaster. As far as he was aware there had been no problems or delays on the Aberystwyth line, and there was indeed one more train from Shrewsbury, at seven o'clock. Nearly four hours. Another phone call to the Morgan home still received no response. Decision time.

At the risk of getting roped into more floral decorations, I popped back to the Union. Jake owed me a favour, I felt. He agreed to meet the later train, and, in the unlikely event that she was on it, to drive Dilly over to Carrick.

Uncertainty is not good. Speculation is even worse, as any number of worrying scenarios for Dilly's non-show passed through my mind on my return journey to Carrick, particularly as I felt she had probably tried to get a message through.

I was tempted to phone again as soon as I got back but decided to wait until the evening when there was more likelihood of someone being at home. A long, fidgety, nail-biting wait.

"Morgan household." At last.

"Oh hi, Mrs Morgan, it's Rob Kiddecott here. I was supposed to be meeting Dilys today."

"Oh!" she sounded surprised. "Didn't she ring you last

night?"

Bugger! Downstairs I wouldn't have heard Janet's phone ringing.

"She may have tried, but I wasn't in," I said diplomatically. "Is she all right?"

"She had to go into hospital, I'm afraid."

"Oh my god, what's happened?" My heart was racing.

"Nothing serious. She's been waiting for some tests, and yesterday the hospital rang to offer her a cancellation."

"Is she all right?" Silly question, really.

"They are keeping her in overnight, but she should be back home tomorrow."

"Can I come and see her?" The question was out of my mouth without any thought.

Mrs Morgan paused, then replied, "I'm sure she'd like that. You're welcome to stay in the spare room again, of course."

"Thank you so much. Er, what would be the best time to come?"

"Give me a ring in the morning. We'll know then what's happening."

***

No way was I going to trust the train. Fi and I set off early. I threw a change of clothes into a duffle bag - just in case I stayed overnight. I allowed a couple of hours for the journey along unfamiliar roads, and planned to ring Mrs Morgan once I was well on my way. The first phone box I tried was out of order, but not before it had swallowed my coins. The next few miles were barren of any habitation and certainly of any modern means of communication. At last, almost on the outskirts of Aberystwyth I struck lucky, inasmuch as the phone worked. But no-one replied.

"Shit," I muttered. I guessed her mother had already left for the hospital. I had no option, I reasoned, but to go there myself. Aberystwyth is not a huge town so I assumed it would have only one hospital. But obviously its location was a well-kept secret, as the two people I asked for directions were very vague.

"North side of town," one said. "Just follow the signs." He didn't say which signs.

"Sorry, I don't live here," said the other, "but I think I saw it on the way in."

I drove slowly - not that fast was an option anyway - through the centre of town, past the station. At a major junction I caught a glimpse of a sign to a hospital. It would have been helpful if the next junction had also displayed a sign for I soon found myself approaching the station from the opposite direction. Amazing that they can send a rocket to the moon and back but finding one's way around an unfamiliar town is much more difficult. Some day, perhaps, a boffin might invent a gizmo that could help.

Frustration gave way to a sense of achievement when I finally pulled into the hospital car park.

"Hi," I said to the young woman on reception, "I'm here to visit Miss Dilys Morgan. Can you tell me which ward she's in, please?"

"Just a moment, sir." She consulted some ledger on her desk, flipped a few pages, and wrinkled her brow. "I'm sorry, we don't seem to have anyone by that name as a patient."

"Not signed out this morning, by any chance?"

She shook her head. "I'm sorry. Do you know when she was supposed to have been admitted."

"Yesterday, I guess. She was awaiting some tests and she was offered a slot at short notice because of a cancellation."

"Oh, I see. Do you know what kind of tests?"

"Not exactly, but there was concern that she might be suffering from stomach or bowel cancer."

"If it were for cancer tests then it is possible she would have been referred to a specialist oncology unit elsewhere."

Bugger! "Any idea where?" Not that it really mattered, I had no intention of searching hospitals the length and breadth of Wales on the off-chance of finding her.

"Sorry, sir."

"Okay, thanks."

Sipping a coffee from the hospital cafeteria I considered my options. A phone call had again gone unanswered. I could go to her parent's house but though I knew the address I had no idea where it was. On my previous visit I had come by train and had given no attention to the route her father had taken to their home. I could try contacting the University and ask to speak to Professor Morgan, always supposing he was there and available. I wasn't sure what his particular specialism was, however.

On the assumption that the Morgans would be returning home sometime that day, hopefully with their daughter, I thought the best thing to do would be to spend the afternoon pottering round Aberystwyth. Perhaps even try to find the pub where Jake and I had enjoyed a brilliant music session with other students up for the inter-varsity eisteddfod during my first year at Tencastle. It was also the occasion when I'd first got to know Dilly.

When I rang again just after six in the evening, it was Dilly herself who answered the phone. "Rob! I'm so glad you called. I'm so sorry to have let you down but I did try to get in touch."

"I admit I was really worried about you."

"That's very sweet of you." She became more serious, "Look, I don't think I'm going to be able to come down to see you this week..."

"No problem. You can see me in Aberystwyth. I'm in town."

"What! Really! You're in Aber?" Her mother of course had no reason to believe I'd already made the journey. "Oh, Rob, that's the second wonderful bit of news today."

Ten minutes later, having followed detailed directions, I was on their doorstep. When I recovered from the hug she gave me on opening the front door, I was surprised to see her looking so bright and cheerful. A little bit pale and gaunt in the face perhaps but otherwise not a haggard and sickly person I had been prepared to meet.

The nature of her ailment and the hospital tests were obviously off-limit to the conversations that continued throughout the supper and into the evening. Neither Dilly nor her parents made the slightest reference to the matter, and gave me no opportunity to satisfy my curiosity without appearing intrusive and insensitive. Indeed, Dilly was keen to hear what I'd been up to since moving out of Ty Melin. I thought it best to give the impression that I'd been living in my own independent flat in a colleague's house for some time rather than a couple of nights. I still wasn't quite sure of how Dilly regarded our relationship. I wasn't even sure whether I'd be heading straight back to Carrick in the morning. When we eventually had a short time to ourselves - her father had some work to do and her mother busied herself in the kitchen - Dilly resolved that uncertainty for me.

She snuggled up to me on the sofa. "Rob, do you have to go back to Carrick tomorrow?"

"No, not really. Nothing planned for the rest of the week. I'd kept it free for your visit."

"Yes, I'm sorry I've messed you around. Look, I've said I'm not able to come to Carrick now, but..." she paused, "... can you stay here for a couple of days?" She looked into my eyes, worried, I think, that I might refuse.

"Very happy to." I could feel the tension in her body relax.

"I was thinking... could we go out somewhere for the day? You know, take the car somewhere?"

"Yeah, certainly. Anywhere in mind?"

"Perhaps Nant-y-Moch and Plynlimon. If it's a fine day."

I hadn't a clue where either were.

If you wanted to get away from it all, Nant-y-Moch reservoir was definitely the place. Miles of open moorland, wooded valleys and spectacular vistas over a large inland lake. Not a soul in sight on this still, bright February morning. I sensed that Dilly had wanted to be alone with me, away from her parents, and out of the town where she was known. Ever since we had headed out on the main road eastwards from Aberystwyth soon after breakfast, however, she had been fairly reticent, responding cheerfully enough to casual conversation but obviously with something on her mind that she didn't want to share with me - yet.

At her suggestion we pulled into a rough lay-by where the road ran quite close to the reservoir.

"Shall we take a stroll down by the water's edge?"

"Fine by me," I said.

With a padded anorak and scarcely any breeze, the temperature wasn't uncomfortable. We wandered along the shoreline for a short distance until we found a suitable large boulder to sit on and admire the scenery. Arm in arm, contemplatively, until I broached the subject.

"You know, yesterday, on the phone, you said something like I was the second piece of good news that day?"

Dilly nodded.

"What was the first?"

"I haven't got cancer."

"Dilly, that's wonderful!" I gave her a big hug and

looked into her deep brown eyes. Still something worrying her, I thought. "So... er... did they find out what was actually wrong?"

"They think so. It's definitely not any form of cancer, it's not a serious bowel disorder, and if I'm careful, it's not life threatening." She threw a pebble into the water and watched the ripples spread.

"It seems I've probably got some chronic food allergy which has been causing me a lot of discomfort and a considerable amount of pain."

"Nuts?" I suggested. It was the only food allergy I'd heard of.

"Probably gluten - as in wheat products, and possibly something else as well. I've got to have more tests, but I'll be on a controlled diet, I guess, whatever."

"Well that's manageable. You've got your life - and your charm and beauty." I thought that might lift her spirits but she looked at me with a surprisingly serious expression.

"Yes, well..." she hesitated. "Look, Rob, I don't know quite how to say this, or whether I should say anything at all."

I was puzzled. "Is there a problem?"

"I've been wrestling with my conscience. I feel I want to tell you but I'm worried what you'll think of me if I do."

I had no idea what was in her mind. I know I hadn't got her pregnant - we hadn't gone that far in her room after the graduation ball last summer. Besides which she would certainly have been showing the signs by now. "It's okay," I said, "I won't storm off and leave your here in the wilderness. I'll try to be calm and understanding."

"Thank you, Rob. I know you're a good person." She took a deep breath. "When the doctors thought I might have cancer, I was very frightened. I knew someone only a little older than me who died barely three months after being diagnosed. It seemed so unfair. I thought of you and of the last thing you said to me when I visited you last Autumn."

"I love you?"

"Yes, that's right. I wished we lived nearer each other. I've never really had a steady boyfriend ..." she faltered.

"Go on!" I said gently.

"When I asked if I could come and stay with you, it wasn't just to get away from my parents. They actually have been very supportive. I thought I was going to die. I didn't want to die without... without... I didn't want to die a virgin. I wanted you to make love to me."

Jeez!

Dilly clung to me, her head in my arms, her body trembling with sobs. "I'm sorry, Rob, I'm so sorry."

"It's okay," I murmured. I really didn't know what to say.

"God, what must you think of me?"

"I think you're a brave lass who has been through a very traumatic time."

She looked up at me with wet eyes. "Tell me, would you... no, I've no right to..."

I knew what she was asking. "I honestly don't know, Dilly, really I don't." Though I can't say the thought of sleeping with her in a soft warm bed had never entered my mind. "But the situation didn't actually arise, did it?"

"I'm not even sure myself, especially when I found out my illness wasn't so serious." I felt her relax a little. "I've treated you so badly," she said softly, "I feel I ought to... if you wanted..."

"Dilly, you've got nothing to apologise for. No way was I expecting what you told me, and I'm, well, sort of honoured that you thought of me in such circumstances. But I don't think it would be right for me now to take advantage of your distress."

"Thank you, Rob. Thank you so much!" Her lips pressed close to mine for so long that I thought my resolve might waver.

"Shall we take a walk by the lakeside?" I suggested after we had sat for some time, arm in arm, enjoying the view and fresh air.

"I'm actually feeling quite peckish. How about we drive on and find a pub or cafe?"

"And hope to find something on the menu you can eat?"

"I'll be careful," she said with a smile. Good to see her spirit rising.

We certainly hadn't passed any pubs, or for that matter hardly any signs of habitation on the several miles of narrow winding roads that had brought us to the reservoir. So driving onward might prove more promising.

Onward, however, soon brought us to a point where the road degenerated into a rough track so we retraced our route back to an unsignposted junction. Dilly thought that we would eventually come out on the main road between Aberystwyth and Machynllech. She was a lot more chatty now, asking about the school where I worked and where I was living.

"My original bedsit lasted one night," I explained. "I've now got the downstairs flat in a colleague's house."

"That was good of him," said Dilly.

"Her, actually. Janet - you met her and Sandra, our lab technician, in a café in Carrick."

Dilly thought for a moment before replying. "Yes, I remember. Young and pretty. The music teacher?"

"That's right. Her parents own the house, and she has the upper part."

Another pause. "Forgive me asking, Rob, but are you and Janet... you know, are you together?"

Crunch time. Dilly had been very frank with me, so I felt I had to be completely open with her.

"Not exactly. We obviously see a lot of each other, we get on well together and we share some common interests. She's joined Carpiog Morris and we've started a folk club in Carrick. But we're not sharing a bed."

"Seems as though it might have been awkward if I had stayed with you, given my original intentions."

"Janet is away all week in Sussex visiting her parents."

"So she didn't know about us?"

"She knew. I showed her your letter, and she insisted that I should ask you to come."

Dilly digested the information. "I think I could get to like Janet."

After half an hour or so of open moorland, we reached habitation, a main road and the White Lion hostelry. Apart from an old gaffer in a shabby coat perched on a stool at the far end of the bar we were the only customers.

"Do you do food?" I asked. There were no obvious signs of a printed menu and the thin-as-a-rake young woman behind the bar wasn't a good advertisement for wholesome nourishment.

She pointed to a blackboard next to the spirits optics. The chalked handwriting which covered it was so small that I could only guess at most of the offerings.

"Can you recommend anything gluten free?" Dilly asked hopefully.

The barmaid looked puzzled. "Is that like veggie? We've got cheese and pickle sandwiches."

"Um, no, it's, well, something without bread, no flour in it."

"Oh!" Wheels turning in her mind, and she brightened up. "Well, we could do you a sandwich without the bread, I suppose." She seemed to be a sandwich or two short of a picnic.

Dilly and looked at each other, trying not to laugh.

"Could you, say, do cold beef with some salad?"

"Yes, I think so," she nodded enthusiastically, "I'll just check with the chef."

As we turned away to hide our giggles, we heard her call, "Ma, beef sandwich and salad? No bread though."

"Make that another," I said, "with bread."

Though I wasn't certain, I suspected that beer might have gluten in it, so Dilly settled for a red wine while I quaffed a pint of best bitter.

When it came the food was tasty and the portions generous. "Help yourself," said Dilly pointing to the bread which had been carefully laid to one side on her plate. Some of the butter had transferred to the beef.

Over a cup of coffee, Dilly once again seemed pensive.

"Something on your mind?" I asked.

"I was wondering… would you like to stay on another day? Unless you've got to be back in Carrick?"

"Not really. As I said, I'd kept the week free for you."

She smiled. "How do you feel about railways?"

"Um." I'd never had any feelings about them. "What do you mean?"

"There's a fascinating narrow gauge railway goes up into the mountains near Cader Idris. And the main line to get to it goes all along the Dovey estuary and the coast. You won't have to drive."

"I thought there was a narrow gauge railway from Aberystwyth."

"There is, up to Devil's Bridge. Do that instead if you like."

"No, I'm happy to go along with your suggestion."

It was a good choice. I suppose I'd never really considered travelling by rail as anything other than the means of getting from A to B, often inconveniently via C. The coastal route lived up to its expectations, all the way down one side of the River Dovey estuary to Machynllech, then, on a different train, along the other side and round the coast to Barmouth, on the far side of another estuary. It was a little further than originally intended but thence we retraced our tracks back to Tywyn for the rattling journey across open fields, through woodland, deep into the wild Welsh hills to the middle of nowhere. Or rather a small terminus station called Abergynolwyn. Why anyone should have wanted to take a railway there in the first place I didn't know. They probably had more sheep as passengers than humans, or perhaps it was to serve a quarry or mine. I had heard there was gold in those hills - somewhere. The best part of all was seeing Dilly enjoying life again - a smile, a twinkle in her eye and very relaxed. My part in her therapy was enjoyable too - and without any complications that her original intentions might have generated.

To be honest, I was somewhat reluctant to leave, but it was in effect by mutual, unspoken understanding that I should head back home - to Carrick - on Saturday morning.

"Will we see each other again, Dilly?" I wasn't really sure what I was implying by raising that question.

"I was going to ask you the same thing." She said softly, "I'd like to. I'd like to meet Janet."

She saw a look of surprise flash over my face. "I'm not jealous, you know. I'd just like us to remain good friends, whatever."

"We'll do that, Dilly. I promise."

If I'd been a poet I would have undoubtedly written a sonnet or two about unrequited love, lovers parting, and so on, all very much a fanciful interpretation of recent days. As it was I drove home on cloud number nine.

Janet heard me arrive back. "Hi, Rob, fancy coming up for a coffee?"

"Great, thanks," I said.

"Wondered where you'd got to," she said, as she set the percolator going. "Dilly didn't come after all?"

I was happy to tell her the good news about Dilly and an abridged account of my trip to Aberystwyth to see her. Some details were not for sharing. In return I enquired about her few days in Sussex.

"Yes, pretty good," she said, and talked about places with which I had only a very sketchy familiarity. "Perhaps you'd like to come down with me next time?" she said at the end.

Feeling happy, relaxed, and slightly soporific I nodded in agreement, and added, "And you could come to Devon.

Chapter 20

A larger than life sheep's head isn't what you expect to bump into in the gents. Even more so when it greets you by name.

"Hi, Rob, can you help me get this thing off?" Jake's voice, sounding sheepish.

With a few tugs from me and curses from Jake he eventually managed to extricate himself, sweating profusely. "Needs a few adjustments," he said.

"Ewegenie, I presume?" In truth, whoever had put the beast together had done a good job, utilising an old sheepskin rug on a wire frame, sackcloth, and natural wool around a dried animal skull. The whole lot was fixed to a long broom handle. It weighed a ton.

"Yes, Posy's work. She's an arts and crafts specialist."

"And who's going to be lambkins?"

"Well, probably whoever's not so good at dancing. April?" he suggested. "Or we could take it in turns."

My look conveyed what I personally thought of that idea.

"Have a word with you after morris," he said as we rejoined the rest of Carpiog in the back room of the Castle.

The new recruits had come on well in just a few weeks. Baz was a natural, but then he had morris dancing in his genes. Even April had managed to master the step-hop, most of the time, but it was anybody's guess as to which direction she would go, whatever figure was called. Janet, too, was becoming familiar with the tunes, playing alongside Huw when surplus to the number of dancers required in the set.

"Right, the news you've all been waiting for," Jake declared dramatically when we'd all filled our glasses at the half-time respite from practising.

I rolled my eyes. The others listened attentively.

"We had the party from Brittany here in Tencastle last week. They've invited us - and that includes Carpiog Morris - back. It will be during the Easter holidays." He gave the dates. "Now, can I have a show of hands from all those who can make it?"

Min's hand shot up immediately. Most of us followed.

"Sean? April?" Jake asked.

"Not sure yet," said Sean, "I may be in Ireland."

"I'm sorry, Jake, my brother's getting married then, and I'm one of the bridesmaids," said April.

"What about travel and accommodation?" Harry asked.

"Still need to check some things out. I'll have more info next week."

After the dance practice had ended, those of us with instruments - except Baz, who'd left his drums at his digs - stayed in the back room for another run through some tunes in preparation for fast-approaching band booking.

"We have a slight problem," Jake began.

"Snap," I said. "I've been meaning to tell you."

"Oh, really?" Jake grimaced. "You first then."

"The P.A.," I said. "We can borrow the stuff from school, but there's no way I can get it all into my little car. We'd barely have room for my guitar and Janet's accordion and fiddle."

"How about if I came over in Jessica?"

"The speakers are pretty large, Jake. I doubt if you'd even get them through the doors."

"Hmm."

"Also, if I remember rightly, there's no vehicular access to the island. We'd have to lug everything across the footbridge."

"No problem," said Jake brightly, "We can use those..."

"No roller skates!" I interrupted.

Jake glared at me. "Or I can borrow a porter's trolley. I

know a chap who works at the station."

"I was wondering, since they often have various functions and concerts there, whether they've got their own sound system we could plug into." Janet suggested.

Jake stroked his chin. "Yes, that would make sense. I'll check."

"And what was your slight problem?" I reminded him.

"Tom, the caller. He can't come."

"You call that a slight problem!" I exclaimed. "Why not?"

"He's broken his leg. He'll be in plaster for weeks."

"Can't he suggest a replacement?"

"Apparently not. They're a rare breed. You'll have to do it, Rob."

"What!"

"Well, you did say you'd be prepared to have a go."

"But... that was ages ago!" I wished I'd kept my mouth shut. "The gig's Saturday week, for Christ's sake!"

"Yes, I realise that, but what else can we do? It's only for a couple of hours."

Couple of hours! I had absolutely no idea how many dances one would expect to get through in that time.

"We'll manage somehow, Rob." Janet put her hand on mine and smiled in encouragement. "We can play a few instrumentals."

I wished I could have shared her confidence in my capability. I exhaled deeply. "Okay, I suppose."

"These might help," said Jake, who handed me couple of dog-eared booklets entitled 'Community Dance Manual' and a handwritten notebook. "Gron's Welsh folk dances," Jake explained. "Don't lose it - he'll want it returned."

I glanced inside. All the notes were in small, cursive script, and in Welsh. I handed the notebook back.

What with trying to recall folk dances from my very limited experience of such events, and with worries about making a complete mess of a couple's wedding day celebrations, I didn't sleep very well that night. And when I did drop off I dreamt that Carpiog Morris had all morphed into sheep in the middle of a square dance.

The following evening I studied the booklets Jake had given me. They certainly contained descriptions of more than enough dances to get me through the gig, though what some of the terms actually meant I wasn't sure. Hands across? Across what, I wondered. And 'right and left through' conjured up all sorts of possibilities. I picked out a few that seemed unambiguous and, crucially, simple.

"Yes, those look okay," said Janet. I'd taken up her offer to return to the spare room. Seems her parents were quite happy for the downstairs flat to be let again, while I would save some money by sharing with Janet.

"I still don't know whether I'm going to get my head round these in time," I said.

Janet thought for a moment. "Some suggestions, Rob. You could write down the details on small cards. You know, as an aide memoire, to hold in your hand?"

I nodded. Made sense.

"I'm happy to run through the tunes while you try calling the instructions."

"That would be helpful."

"And how about asking the kids to help out one lunchtime? We could sell it to them as a project we're working on and we need some willing guinea pigs. I expect your class would go for it. You'd then have some experience of live calling."

"Janet, you're brilliant!

***

Curiosity rather than enthusiasm for whatever bullshit yarn we had sold them produced a dozen or so youngsters, mostly female, to our chosen grassed area beyond the Science Block. It was out of sight of the main buildings and playground. Tentatively they found a partner, the two lads deciding to stick together, and formed a large circle. No problems with the first dance, nor with the second, also a circle, once I'd explained the difference between left and right, clockwise and anticlockwise.

Attracted by the sound of the accordion, a small audience of students gathered. Feeling emboldened, I invited them to join in the next dance I'd selected – the Nottingham Swing, described as a 'longways progressive' dance. It looked pretty simple on paper. I got them to join hands in rings of four from the end of the lines nearest to the music, assigned them numbers as 'first couple' and 'second couple' and got them to walk through the basic moves. I'm sure I also mentioned that they should keep their same numbers for subsequent times through the dance when they moved up or down the lines to another couple.

Perfect, the first time through with the music! Second time, sort of worked, but I realised I hadn't told the new couples at the end of the line that they were supposed to be inactive for one sequence. The third time through was total chaos, nobody being sure literally which way to turn. No matter, the kids carried on regardless grabbing whoever was nearest to swing or turn and inventing a few moves of their own. Any semblance of a line formation was soon lost in a melee of movement. A few were jiving by the end. Janet barely managed to keep a straight face until I eventually signalled her to stop playing.

"That was great, sir!" said a young girl I recognised from one of my third-year groups, "Can we do it again?"

We were saved by the bell for afternoon registration.

The jungle telegraph must have been working overtime. Next morning John Rhys-Price, recently reinstated and perhaps suitably chastised, greeted me, "Ah, the budding Victor Sylvester in person!"

He put his hand to his face in a theatrical aside, and said, inconsequentially, "Do you know why he wears baggy trousers?"

"That's ballroom!" I said, keen to point out the difference between the TV celebrity's expertise and mine, such as it was.

"Right!" said John and walked away smirking.

***

We gathered in the small ante-room which served as the bar for the main function room half-an-hour before the dancing was scheduled to start. Enough time to set up our gear. But first we had to wait for the speeches to finish.

"Been waffling on for ages," said Jake, indicating with his thumb a portly gent at the top table, presumably the bride's father, who was jabbering away into a microphone. "And there's at least two more speeches to go, I think."

"Is that the mike I'll be using?" I asked.

"Oh, probably," Jake replied.

"And what about the rest of the band?"

"I think they've got another mike we can use."

"In other words, you haven't bothered to check, have you?" I wasn't getting good vibes about the success of the evening.

"Well, I did ask if we could use their P.A.," Jake said peevishly.

"But not what it consisted of?" I persisted.

"Well, not exactly, no. Sorry!"

"Great!" I rolled my eyes. "Janet had better have the second mike, then - if there is one. Huw's bagpipes will cut through any background noise regardless, and Baz will have to thump his drums harder." I looked around.

"Where is your drum kit, Baz?"

"Just brought the snare. Didn't fancy lugging the bass and all the other stuff over the footbridge."

"What about my banjo?" said Jake.

"Same as Baz, play it louder." I said without sympathy. I glanced into the hall. Tubby Dad had started on another page of his wadge of notes. "We've time for a pint," I said, "On you, Jake, as leader of this merry band."

He glared at me but acquiesced without comment. Hopefully he had included drinks in the fee we were charging, since bar prices at Ynysgwyn Manor were grossly inflated.

Fifteen minutes and half a pint later, the same fellow was still in full flight, though it looked as if he'd only got one or two more sheets to go. His captive audience smiled politely from time to time at some anecdote he thought amusing, but you could see a bored, glazed look. Eventually he sat down, to muted applause.

"Nearly three-quarters of an hour," said Jake. "We were supposed to start ten minutes ago!"

A gangling young man was the next to address the guests.

"Jake, what's the protocol if we start late? Do we stop at our original scheduled time, or carry on for two hours regardless?"

"Dunno. Just play it by ear, I guess."

Along with a wing and a prayer.

We were well into our second pint when Baz looked up and said, "Hey, looks as if they are moving."

We grabbed our instruments and eased through the flow of guests, heading in almost equal numbers to the bar or to the loos. The staff were already in action clearing the tables from where they had encroached onto the dance floor in the middle of the room.

I found two mikes, and one mike stand, which I offered to Janet.

The best man, the tall fellow, approached me. "Bride and groom would like to do the first dance, if that's okay with you. A waltz perhaps?"

I glanced at Janet. None of the dances I'd prepared were waltzes. She nodded.

"And then we're all up for it."

The guests drifted back in, looking relieved and refreshed.

The newly-weds took to the floor and shuffled around more or less in time with the slow waltz tune Janet was playing, virtually solo apart from Baz's steady beat. Jake appeared to be struggling with the chords and Huw had given up after a couple of discordant squeaks.

"What key are you in?" he called to Jake, who just shrugged.

I took a deep breath. "Ladies and gentlemen, it's your turn now. Please bring your partners up, join..."

"Peter and Rosie," Jake whispered quickly.

"... Peter and Rosie and take hands in a large circle. It's a very simple dance," I added, more for my own reassurance than theirs.

I walked it through with them. It was mostly going to the middle and back and swinging one's partner. Not that there was a lot of space to swing with fifty or so people crammed into a space smaller than a badminton court. I'd agreed with Janet beforehand some hand signals to start and stop the music - also to speed it up or slow it down if necessary. And away we went.

Surprisingly it went very well and the music sounded great. To me, anyway. Everyone clapped enthusiastically.

"Get your breath back while we play a tune," I said.

Fewer guests took to the floor for the second dance. Even so, the long line of couples filled the space nicely. I shied away from repeating the longways dance I'd tried with the kids, so once again kept it very simple. And once again it was well received. I began to feel more confident

– enough to attempt another circle dance Janet had remembered and described to me.

I was pleased that the walk-through, with a chain-like weaving seven places around the circle actually got everybody to where they should be, having moved on to another partner. Whether the dancers were captivated by the music, forgot how to count, or were just too inebriated to care, I don't know, but I was a little puzzled how it happened that rather than having alternate men and women in the circle, most of the gents had ended up on one side and the ladies on the other. I was wondering how on earth I could re-establish some semblance of order when the best man tapped me on the shoulder.

"Can we make this the last dance?"

Gladly, I thought. "Right, everyone find your original partner!" I called, and, once the Piccadilly in the rush hour moment had passed, "Swing your partner and promenade!" I signalled to Janet with the edge of my hand across my throat to cut the music.

"Thank you, ladies and gentlemen." Tumultuous applause. We took a bow.

As I turned to thank the band, a large hairy bloke in a kilt came up to me. "D'ye ken th' Eightsome Reel, laddie?"

I shook my head, "I'm afraid we've got to make way for the disco," I apologised.

"Och, weel, I'll ha' tae dance it mesel'." He lumbered around the floor with an imaginary partner, and clattered over a table at the end of the room. Pissed as a lord.

I breathed a huge sigh of relief, "How long have we been on?" I asked Jake.

"Twenty-five minutes, half-an-hour tops," he said.

"And that's all they want? "said Huw. "Can't believe it!"

"That's it," said Jake. "And don't worry, I've already been given our money. Another drink? "

"Yeah, but not here," I said. "Let's go where we're

likely to get some change from our fee."

Though it was in the opposite direction to Carrick, we settled for the familiarity of the Castle Inn.

"Wow," said Jake as he extracted banknotes from an envelope, "They've added an extra thirty quid!"

I could get to like this for a hobby.

Chapter 21

One of the reasons I chose chemistry as my specialism for teaching is that it's predictable. You mix substances A and B known to react together, and bingo - you end up with substance C. Always. Although I like to introduce a bit of magic and mystery into my practical demonstrations, particularly to the younger classes and perhaps give them the odd surprise, there's no mystery for me as to what is going to happen.

Except, one afternoon, I was mystified as to why the demonstration was defying expectations. Prior to my registration class trying for themselves some simple investigations into the electrical conductivity of various solutions, I planned to show them how to 'convert' a silver coin into copper, and then a copper coin into silver.

Everything was set up ready: the circuit from the low voltage power supply, a small light bulb to show when the current was flowing, the crocodile clips to hold a strip of copper metal and the ten pence coin. All I needed to do was to pour the copper sulphate solution from one beaker into another, into which the electrodes would be inserted – and switch on the electricity.

I expected the coin to get a red coating almost immediately. But nothing happened. Not even the bulb lit up. I checked the connections, and tried again. Still nothing. The kids were beginning to fidget.

"There seems to be a slight technical hitch," I said. Pretending that it was all part of my plan, I asked them for suggestions as to why it wouldn't work, to gain a bit of time to come up with a valid reason of my own.

"Have you switched on the electricity, sir?" one young lad offered.

"Or perhaps the bulb has blown," suggested another.

By connecting the bulb directly to the power supply I

showed that neither was the correct explanation.

"Sir, you haven't said the magic word abracadabra!"

"Thank you, Fanny." I was surprised she'd remembered the occasion over three years ago when I had used it at her former primary school during my first teaching practice. "Abracadabra!" I said, as I tried again.

I'd definitely lost some - or all - of my old magic. Again nothing seemed to be working. And I hadn't a clue why.

"Okay," I said, "Still some gremlins in the system somewhere. We'll come back to this. In the meantime, we'll get you started on your experiments." I nearly added, 'Perhaps you'll have better luck'.

I was still puzzling over the matter at the end of the day when Sandy came in to clear away the equipment.

"Penny for your thoughts," she said.

"Yeah, really weird, my demonstration didn't work."

"Oh, really? Why's that, Rob?"

"Wish I knew." I pointed to the beaker of blue liquid now sitting on the side bench, "That copper sulphate solution is supposed to conduct electricity but it didn't."

"Oh." She thought for a moment. "Where did you get it?"

"I picked it up from the prep room. You made it for me."

"Ah, perhaps you took the wrong beaker."

"What do you mean? There was only one there!"

"Dennis Bateson had asked me for a beaker of water with some blue dye in for his Physics lesson – something to do with barometers, I think. He must have picked up your copper sulphate solution by mistake."

Well that would certainly explain my problems if all I had was coloured water. And my colleague's experiment would have worked regardless.

"Sorry," said Sandy. "I hadn't got round to labelling it."

"No problem." I breathed a sigh of relief.

***

The next day, bizarre followed weird. Scary too.

"Got a few minutes to spare?" Mark Matthews asked me at the end of morning break.

I nodded. Seems we both had a non-teaching period at the same time. We sauntered towards his classroom, which was on the way to the science block anyway.

"You remember helping out with the residential field trip last Easter?"

I did indeed. So desperate he'd been to find someone to step in at short notice he'd got hold of my phone number at Ty Melin.

"I'm planning a repeat trip to Devon again. Same base, more or less the same programme. I'm wondering whether you'd be willing to take part again?"

"I'm not sure," I said. "I'm..."

I paused. The catcalls of 'Kip, kip, kipper' I'd been aware of as we'd passed by Gerry Kipling's room abruptly ceased. He'd only returned to work the previous day.

A moment's eerie silence then a yell, "No, NO DON'T . . !" followed by a piercing scream.

As we rushed back, a teenage lad staggered out of the door his hand crimson with blood. I went to help him while Mark entered the classroom. I applied pressure to the lad's wrist, to try to staunch the blood oozing from a nasty gash across his palm. I hoped for his sake that no tendons had been severed but no way was he going to get away without stitches. Another youth ran past me, probably despatched by Mark to summon help.

The secretary was already calling for an ambulance when I reached the office. She pointed to the first aid box on the wall. I led the boy over to the small sink to wash his wound and tried to bandage it as best as I could. His face was as white as a sheet and hitherto he hadn't said a word about what had happened.

He grimaced as I applied iodine antiseptic. "Ki... Mr Kipling... he pulled out this knife. I think he was going to gut himself... I tried to stop him. Is he... is he alright?"

"I don't know," I replied gently, "Mr Matthews is with him."

"Oh Christ!" He screwed up his eyes. "We shouldn't have... we didn't mean this to happen... Why... why did he do...?

"I don't know, lad," I said, "The important thing is to get your hand looked at in hospital." I heard the ambulance siren getting closer.

The atmosphere in the staffroom at lunchtime was very subdued. Mark had followed the ambulance to the hospital and was probably still there. I couldn't give any information about the incident other than a student had been cut by a knife. I didn't want to raise any speculation by repeating what he'd said about Gerry Kipling. It was common knowledge, however, that a group of students were being kept in isolation.

Word went round that the Headmaster wished to address all the staff before afternoon lessons.

Moby Dick looked grave and haggard, with none of his usual pomposity. "Ladies and Gentleman," he began, "I regret to inform you that our colleague, Gerald Kipling, attempted to take his own life this morning in front of a class of fifth formers."

Gasps from many of the staff.

"One student, Ewan Rigby, bravely tried to stop him and was injured in the process."

"That's Eric's son!" someone whispered. I looked round. Eric Rigby wasn't present.

"I have just heard from the hospital that Mr Kipling is comfortable, with lacerations to his body less serious than originally thought. And Ewan's hand has only suffered superficial cuts. No permanent damage." Moby bowed his head and paused before continuing. "You may not be aware that Mr Kipling had been diagnosed with lung cancer. However, he wished to continue teaching if possible until the end of this term, and I agreed. That is a decision which I now regret."

Moby Dick had never previously been known to apologise for or regret any of his decisions.

"His students obviously will be very distressed and will be offered counselling. But the police will also want to talk to them, and that will be in the presence of either myself or the Senior Mistress." He paused again, giving the impression he was weighing up the consequences of making another decision. "When you return to your registration groups, they are to stay with you until further notice instead of going to their usual lessons. School will finish early today, as soon as I am satisfied that no children will be at risk by arriving home before their normal time."

Terry Osborne, the head of Religious Education, raised his hand, "What about the children who come in by school bus?"

"I am contacting the coach company to see if they can provide transport earlier." Moby looked round the staffroom. "Any more questions?"

"What should we tell our groups?" I asked. The kids would be buzzing with speculation about a major change to their normal schedule. And many would have heard the sirens from the ambulance.

Moby thought for a moment. "Thank you, Mr Kiddecott. It's probably best to say as little as possible, though I appreciate you and Mr Matthews are very much aware of what happened. Let us just say that there has been an incident and while it is being investigated we feel it is in their best interests to be sent home early." He grimaced. "They are going to hear about it anyway before long."

For a brief moment I almost felt sorry for him.

Give him his due, Moby handled the Gerry Kipling incident very well. Next morning in assembly he presented to the students a well-considered summary of what had happened to disrupt their normal working day. "You may have heard," he began, "that Mr Kipling had to be taken to hospital yesterday. His health has been of great concern for some time and he had only just returned to his post. Unfortunately the stress proved too much and he suffered a traumatic breakdown in the classroom. A boy who tried to help him received injuries which also required hospital treatment. Mr Kipling is unlikely to ever return to teaching, and I am sure you would like him to know that our thoughts and best wishes are with him and his family at this difficult time."

***

Yet another incident convinced me that the unexpected seemed to be the norm in this eventful week. Though trivial in itself, I was quite taken aback by an extreme reaction from a colleague whom I'd hitherto regarded as quite liberal in his opinions.

The previous evening, at morris practice, Jake had stressed the need for the new members of Carpiog to get some experience at dancing out in public prior to our projected visit to France. He'd probably envisaged a caper or two around Tencastle but Janet, surprisingly, had suggested making a day of it in Carrick. Personally, I wasn't so sure I wanted the inevitable exposure of my hobby to the students at Sir Wilfred Robert's School, but if it didn't worry Janet, well...

Jake had jumped at the idea, and proposed Saturday week as the date, to general agreement. How they were going to get to Carrick was up to him to arrange. The consolation was that Janet and I wouldn't have to travel.

In view of the short time scale, Janet and I cobbled

together a poster that same evening, leaving out precise details of venues yet to be decided in favour of 'around the town'. I'd run off a few copies on the staffroom photocopier, and, on the spur of the moment, I'd pinned one to the notice board in the staffroom and another to the general notice board by the school office.

"What on earth are you doing with my poster?" I asked. Terry Osborne was in the process of removing my poster in the staffroom. I could see he'd already got the other one tucked underneath his arm.

"Oh, yours, is it?" He turned to me. He didn't look happy. "I find it most offensive that you are advertising pagan activities. It's against all our Christian values."

I stared at him, gaping. I was flabbergasted. I hadn't ever put him down as a fundamentalist kind of bible basher. With difficulty I controlled my growing anger.

"Do you know anything about the history of morris dancing?" I said.

"It's pagan."

"Then why would the Dean of Hackney be a keen exponent of it?" Something I'd only just found out myself from Baz when he was chatting about his father's involvement with morris.

"I don't believe it." Terry looked flushed.

"Check it out for yourself. And you might also be interested to know that one of the oldest morris sides in the country was started by a vicar." Another gem from Baz.

"But its origins," he insisted, "They're pre-Christian!"

"Perhaps," I said. "No-one really knows for certain." I was on more dodgy ground, relying on some comments Jake had made a couple of years ago when Carpiog Morris was launched, "But it was well supported by the church back in the fifteenth century and has mostly been so since."

Before Terry replied I pressed home a point or two.

"Anyway, morris dancing wouldn't be the only pagan custom taken over by the church."

"What do you mean?" Terry bridled.

"Christmas. It's not when Jesus was actually born, is it? A convenient pagan midwinter festival to Christianise." Frankly I didn't really care now whether I upset him or not. "Besides which, you've no right to remove my posters." I held out my hand for them, which, with bad grace he passed over.

"Thank you," I said, and then to smooth the waters I added, "I'm sorry, Terry, if you felt your beliefs were being undermined, but I would have appreciated you speaking to me before taking matters into your own hands."

"Okay, Rob. No hard feelings."

I was glad he backed down. I'd always got on well with him previously.

Chapter 22

We waited for the train at St David's Station, Exeter, just across the road from the Jolly Porter pub where Janet and I had spent the previous evening at the folk club. Familiar territory for her, being close to the University campus where she'd done her degree, but less so for me as I hadn't hitherto been into the folk scene in my home county. She'd readily accepted my invitation to stay overnight at my parents' farm - separate rooms, of course. Even if my mother had made any assumptions about our relationship, propriety was taken for granted.

We were waiting for Jake and Baz - and our former housemate and dancer, Dan Chater, who had been persuaded to join us on our trip to Brittany. Full of confidence from our successful dance-out in Carrick, the rest of Carpiog Morris were, hopefully, en route for Plymouth on board the best coach Powell's Pleasure Tours could offer, along with most of Tencastle's town councillors, their partners, and a few other dignitaries. The display in Carrick had inspired our new members and given them confidence to represent Tencastle abroad.

"Looks as if the train may be a few minutes late," said Janet, looking at the arrivals notice board.

"Hope it's no longer," I said. "I've only paid for half-an-hour on the meter," Not for Fi but for my father's Land Rover that I'd borrowed. No way would my little Fiat cope with five people and their gear for the journey to Plymouth to meet up with the coach party.

The train from Waterloo arrived ten minutes behind schedule. Jake and co. weren't among the passengers. My poor record at meeting railway passengers took another hit.

"Do you think they might have caught a Paddington train instead?" Janet asked.

I shook my head. "Jake was very specific. It was probably cheaper." But it gave me an idea. "We need to head up into the town," I said.

"Why?"

"It's possible he got off at Exeter Central."

Sure enough, just after we passed the clock tower into Queen Street we saw Jake walking towards us. I pulled into a parking bay.

"Just you, is it?" I said, puzzled.

"Er, no, I left Baz at the station just in case you turned up." He gestured with his thumb over his shoulder. "You didn't tell me there were two stations!" he complained. "Only found out from the clerk in the ticket office when you didn't show up. He gave me directions."

"Sorry," I said. It hadn't even entered my mind. I assumed everyone knew that St David's was the main station for Exeter.

We drove along the short distance to Exeter Central to pick up Baz.

" I was expecting Dan to be with you," I said to Jake.

"He was. As far as Salisbury."

"I don't understand."

"He went to the next carriage to find the loo as ours was out of order."

"So?"

"The train split in two at Salisbury. His half went off to Portsmouth. Our half carried on to Exeter."

I couldn't believe it! "But... he couldn't have spent that much time in the bog, surely?"

"Well, you're not supposed to flush the loo in a station, are you? He must have waited until the train moved off again."

"So what's happened to him? Janet asked.

"God knows." Jake shrugged, "Nothing we could do about it. We couldn't exactly pull the emergency cord and ask the driver to go back and fetch him when he was probably half way to Pompey anyway!"

"Does he know where we're going in Brittany?" I had a vague hope that Dan might find some way of making his way there.

"Yes, but I can't see him swimming the Channel and hitching all the way across Northern France."

Rather than create possible check-in problems at the ferry terminal with our arrival not coinciding with that of the coach, the five (now reduced to four) of us had booked in as foot passengers. The service had only been set up a couple of years ago - ostensibly to give the Brittany farmers direct access to the U.K. market for their onions, cauliflowers and other produce. This season was the first for vehicles.

We spotted the coach in the holding area awaiting embarkation. We were on board first. Jake sought out an area reasonably close to the bar and spread our coats and bags over several seats to 'reserve' them for the rest of the party. Or rather the dancers. The toffs could fend for themselves.

Min found us first. Big hugs all round of course, by which time Huw, Harry, Holly and Posy had also found us. Only Sean and April hadn't been able to make the trip. A thin bespectacled youth with bad acne hovered around on the edge of the group.

"Come and join us, Jestyn," said Harry. And then to us, "Jestyn's our roving reporter for the Tene Messenger. My father wasn't able to come."

I was surprised that the Editor hadn't managed to get invited to the jollies, but then he and Barbara Bowen-Martin, the architect of the exchange, didn't exactly see eye to eye politically or personally.

"Th... thank you," Jestyn stuttered. "Mr. Dickens has asked me to do a fea... feature for the paper, from f... first hand ob... ober... observations."

God, he'd have to work on his interviewing skills!

"Don't look too closely!" said Min, a mischievous grin on her face.

"Right," said Jake, "Let's get organised. First priority beer."

Duly ordered and quaffed, even if it was French lager.

"Anyone for a session?" Jake asked.

"I dunno, our fellow travellers might not appreciate it. They look pretty crashed out." Not surprising as it was already late in the evening.

"Out on deck?"

"I'll hold the seats while you go and look," I offered magnanimously. Janet nodded in agreement.

"No sense of adventure, some people," said Jake, and wandered off, followed by Huw and Min. Jestyn also tagged along, looking rather green now that the ship was subject to the swell of the Channel rather than the calmer waters of Plymouth Sound.

Our civic dignitaries would have booked cabins for their overnight journey. We had to make do with catnapping as best we could in the bar. Even the reclining seats cost extra.

I'm not sure how long I'd been kipping before being roused by the return of Jake and co.

"It's perishing out there," he declared, slumping into a vacant seat. "Managed to find somewhere out of the wind for a while until the ship changed direction."

The ship seemed to have slowed down. Some crew members with torches were making their way out on deck, while another in smart uniform conferred with an elderly woman who seemed very agitated.

"I definitely heard a wailing and screeching out there!" I overheard her say. "Someone was in pain, I'm telling you!"

I glanced at Huw. "Be a good idea if you kept those bagpipes out of sight," I said.

After a few minutes the search party returned. One of

them shook his head at the officer, who gently led the woman away.

I was still suffering from the lack of sleep next morning when we boarded the coach. Apart from Jake, all the other dancers looked in a similar dozy state. I couldn't tell you much about the scenery of Northern Brittany for I soon drifted off, with Janet resting her head on my shoulder.

Some time later - actually it had been barely an hour - I awoke to find the coach had stopped. We were in the middle of a large town. A huge double-decker viaduct dominated the view.

"Where are we, Rob?" Janet asked, also rousing from her slumbers.

"No idea."

Jake had been conferring with Barbara Bowen-Martin and the coach driver. He edged his way back down the aisle. "Right, everyone off," he said, "We've got the afternoon to ourselves. Coach will pick us up here at five o'clock."

"Where's here?" I asked.

"We're in Morlaix." It could have been Timbuctoo for all that meant to me. "You can leave your sleeping bags and stuff, but bring your kit. We might do some dancing."

We shuffled off the coach and stood at the edge of a large square, waiting for some direction from Jake. The rest of the passengers clearly had some plan in mind for they had already dispersed in small groups.

"Christ, I'm desperate for the loo," said Min, hopping around from foot to foot.

Nothing that remotely resembled public toilets caught our sight. "Café?" Baz suggested, pointing across the road to where several tables were set outside on the pavement.

"Yeah, and we can get something to eat as well," said Holly. "I'm starving."

"Snails on toast suit you?" her brother suggested. Holly wrinkled her nose. Jestyn looked queasy.

We settled ourselves amongst the tables while Min dived inside to find the convenience. She returned almost immediately and spoke urgently to her fiancé.

"Problem?" asked Jake.

"She can't find a loo with a seat," Huw whispered.

"That's not unusual in France," said Jake. Though how he knew I didn't ask. He turned to Min, "You just have to squat and take aim."

"You're not serious?" Rarely had I seen Min look so serious.

"'Fraid so. When in Rome, you know…"

"I thought the Romans invented flushing loos… oh never mind!" Min rushed back into the café.

"Anyone up for a dance or two?" Jake asked while we waited for Min.

General nods of agreement.

"Okay, let's start in the square over there. Might collect a few francs for a beer."

"Is it legal, Jake?" Baz asked.

"What?"

"Dancing and collecting. French might be picky about such things."

"Dunno. Any problem we'll stop." Jake looked around. "By the way, who's got the sticks?"

Blank looks. "Thought you'd got them," said Harry.

"Oh bugger! They're still on the coach!" Jake tapped his forehead in frustration. But not for long.

"Anyone fancy a stroll up into town?"

No-one seemed keen, not knowing what Jake had in mind. Including me, but I was used to his ingenuity in a crisis.

We left the rest of the group at the café, with strict instructions from Jake to stay put. Unnecessarily, I thought. I attempted to get some clue from Jake as to his intentions but he just put a finger to his brow, and said nothing. He looked from side to side across the street at the various shops and bars, and eventually dived into some kind of multi-themed shop that was not quite a department store nor supermarket. Amongst the home hardware section he found what he was looking for - three broom handles, one with broom still attached. As he gathered them he whispered, "What's French for 'saw'?"

"J'ai vu?" I offered.

"No, you pillock, a saw for sawing!"

I shrugged my shoulders.

At the checkout Jake resorted to sign language. The assistant got the message and returned with two items, a tenon saw and a pruning saw. Jake selected the former, and promptly set about cutting the broomstick into three roughly equal lengths. The assistant looked on open-mouthed, while a colleague shook her head and indicated with her finger that the customer had got a screw loose.

Job completed, Jake swept up the sawdust with the severed broom head, which he handed to me while he paid the bill. When the assistant tried to ring up the saw as well, he waved his hands to show he didn't want to buy it. She shrugged, and took his money.

"Talk about a rip-off, those broomsticks," he said when we were back in the street.

"Perhaps they charged you for the hire of the saw," I suggested.

Back at the café, we rejoined our group. Plus one.

"Where the hell did you spring from, Dan?" I said, amazed. "I thought you were still enjoying the comforts of British Rail."

"I flew here."

"Sprout wings did you?"

"Sort of." He took a swig of beer. "I'd resigned myself to missing the trip. When I eventually got back home I met a colleague in the pub, and, well, we got talking."

"Go on."

"He's an amateur pilot. Got his own little two-seater plane which he keeps at Shoreham airfield. He was planning to fly over this morning to his holiday pad near Morlaix. He gave me a lift."

"Well, we're very pleased to see you," said Jake. "You've already met the rest of the gang."

We performed a few dances, with 'gentle' stick clashing, demanded by Jake who rabbited on about how much the sticks had cost him. A few passers-by and a gendarme regarded us with mild curiosity. Our collecting hat gathered some assorted shrapnel which amounted to no more than four francs in all. Not enough for a round of beers. I suggested putting it towards the sticks.

At five o'clockish - definitely more ish than five - the coach reappeared. Evidently the main Tencastle twinning party members had been on a shopping spree somewhere, as every available space and lap was overflowing with bags and parcels.

"Where now?" asked Janet.

"Dunno," I said. "Jake?"

"Just a couple of miles or so out of town, I think. Village or suburb, I'm not sure. We're indoor camping in a hall but the rest are staying with families."

"What's the programme for the rest of the weekend?" I asked. Seems we were doing a quite a lot of fending for ourselves.

"Well, tomorrow's the main event. Mayoral reception in the morning, probably a bit of dancing. Procession and display with us and a local group in Morlaix after lunch then back here for a nosh and a Fest Noz, whatever that is."

"And Sunday?"

"Not sure. Some sightseeing I think before we head back to the ferry."

Village it was. We were definitely beyond the urban sprawl but on the coast. Several families were waiting with their cars to greet their visitors, and while our civic representatives climbed into the various cars, one of the locals led us a short way up a side road to our accommodation. The hall had seen better days; a wooden structure, badly in need of a lick of paint.

Jake poked his head inside. "Is this it? Just the one room?" Jake asked our guide, "We are a mixed group."

The guide shrugged, "Morrees - les hommes, n'est-ce pas?"

Anyone could see that our party wasn't all homme-ogenous, as Jake pointed out. The guide shrugged again - I guessed he was the monkey not the organ-grinder.

Closer examination of the premises revealed another shortfall in facilities. One outside loo – fortunately conventional design - with a wash basin and cold water tap. No showers. The only other washing facilities were the twin sinks in the kitchen at the far end of the hall, with hot water from a coin-operated boiler. A small pile of coins had been left beside it. An old refrigerator held cartons of milk, butter, orange juice, eggs, and a selection of cheeses and cold meats, while on the work surface were several French sticks and fruit.

Jake, as usual, quickly took charge. "Right, looks as though we'll have to rough it for a couple of nights. Min, Posy, Janet and Holly, if you set up your beds on one side, we'll take the other. Perhaps we'll be able to rig up something to give you some privacy."

"What about washing?" asked Janet.

Jake thought for a moment. "How about the four of you use the outside loo, with a pan of hot water, and we'll use the kitchen? Most of the time we can just go round the back of the hall for our calls of nature."

Setting up our individual indoor camping pitches occupied us for half-an-hour or so, hampered by Jake's attempt to construct a screen out of some old tarpaulin and rope he'd found stuffed in a cupboard. Which left most of us spluttering and sneezing with all the dust, not to mention a malodorous whiff of fish.

"Jake, for Christ's sake, take the darn thing down," I said in frustration, "It stinks to high heaven."

"Besides which," said Min who'd stretched out on her airbed, "I can see everything you're up to beneath the screen."

"Suppose we'll just have to close our eyes then," said Dan. "And you, too, Min," he added.

"Spoilsport!"

The girls found a few strategically placed chairs with clothes draped over them achieved some degree of segregation of sleeping quarters.

I wasn't the only one whose stomach was beginning to rumble. It was several hours since we'd had lunch at the café. "Do you reckon the food in the kitchen is for breakfast or supper?" Posy asked.

No-one seemed prepared to make a decision.

"One point, if I may," said Baz, "There's no booze here. And in this backwater I doubt if there's anywhere you can get a breakfast."

"That's two points." Dan always had a reputation for being pedantic.

"So you're saying, let's go out on the town tonight, find a bar and hopefully food," I said.

Baz nodded.

"All agreed?" said Jake.

Jestyn put his hand up like a nervous schoolboy. "If you... you don't m... mind, I'd ra... rather stay here."

Wimp.

"Okay, just don't scoff all the food."

"Another thought," Harry said, "We don't know where the bar is, assuming that there actually is one..."

"No self-respecting French village would be without

one," said Baz.

"Right," Harry continued, "Well instead of us all traipsing round looking for it, why don't three or four of us spread out in different directions and report back here, say, in half-an-hour?"

"Good idea," said Jake.

Janet and I wandered down towards the waterside where a narrow jetty ran out above the sandy shore to the river. We stood hand-in-hand gazing at the rather attractive view upstream towards the conurbation of Morlaix.

"Food?" Janet reminded me of the purpose of our walk. So far we hadn't come across any watering hole let alone a restaurant. We continued along the beach road for a short distance and spied – or rather heard – what was obviously the meeting place for all the local youth. They looked at us indifferently as we made our way through to the bar. There was no sign of a menu anywhere but a couple of uncollected used plates gave us hope. Time for my schoolboy French.

"Avez vous quelquechose à manger?" The barman looked puzzled. It might have been my accent or the pop music blaring out from the juke box. "Un repas?" I tried again.

"Ah, je comprends." He pointed to a table and indicated that we should take a seat.

I need to convey that there were more than two hungry people. "Nous sommes douze personnes," I said.

More puzzlement. "Douces personnes?

Sweet fairy ann, I didn't think my accent was that bad "Douze," I repeated and flashed up all digits on both hands plus two more, to make my point.

Amazement or horror, I'm not sure which, from the barman. "Un moment, monsieur et madame!"

He dived into a back room, and emerged again a minute later. "Potage et du pain, c'est tout," he spread his hands in apology.

"Merci. Nous retournons - un demi heure." Hopefully.

We were the only ones to have struck lucky. Soup and bread might not have been quite the banquet we'd had in mind but it was better than nothing!

The village youth certainly took more notice on our return, particularly as Jake had persuaded us to go in kit, and 'perhaps do some dancing'. One young lass fingered my raggy jacket that formed part of my morris costume, and looked quizzically into my eyes. "Anglais," I said, though I don't think she was any the wiser at my explanation.

We emerged from the cafe half an hour or so later, surprisingly well satiated on yards of French bread and bowlfuls of soup, actually more like a meat and vegetable stew. The youths were still there, smoking and drinking. While our strange attire only aroused curiosity, a blast from Huw's bagpipes really gained their attention. We thrashed away at a couple of stick dances, and, encouraged by their loud cheers and applause, Jake invited the locals to take part, which, to my surprise, they did with great enthusiasm. Their level of English was on a par with our proficiency in French - well below par, one might say - but music has no language barriers. When they realised our Welsh connections, we were accepted as long-lost Celtic cousins to the Breton culture. Janet and Huw played along with a young lad who'd produced an extremely strident wind instrument which was quite capable of drowning out any wrong notes we played. Drink flowed freely - we certainly weren't asked to pay for any of it. By midnight I'd long lost track of what and how much booze I'd actually consumed. It was even later when we staggered back to our lodgings. I was grateful for Janet's supporting arm around my waist.

***

"Oh what a beautiful morning, oh what a..."

"F'christ's sake, shut up, Jake!" Dan groaned from his sleeping bag, "My head's thumping."

I really don't know how Jake managed to appear so bright and breezy and sober. He'd probably downed as much assorted alcohol as the rest of us.

"Wake up, everybody," he cried, unsympathetically. "Coach'll be here shortly."

"Wassatime then?" came a grunt from the girls' side of the room.

"Nine-ish"

"Can someone please turn off the light?" Baz this time.

"Sun arise, bring in the morning!" Jake sang loudly. A balled-up sock flew past him and caught Jestyn on the nose as he eased himself upwards - and promptly flopped back down again.

"Anyone fancy breakfast?" Jake asked, undeterred.

"Yeah, a bowl of aspirins!" Dan called.

"And a gallon of black coffee." Min I think.

The next hour saw a gradual transformation of sleep-walking zombies into more or less respectable morris dancers ready to face the day's activities. All except Jestyn, who, despite several attempts to rouse him, remained firmly cocooned in his sleeping bag, until Holly and Harry grabbed the bottom end and dragged it from him.

"Come on, you've got work to do for the Messenger!" said Holly.

"Useless pillock," Jake whispered to her, "Don't know why your dad bothered to send him."

"Yeah, I guess he might have to rely on us for a newspaper piece," said Harry.

We needn't have rushed. We were all ready and waiting outside the hall at least twenty minutes before the coach arrived. Apart from the driver, no-one else was on board.

"All totally pissed from last night, d'you reckon?" I said.

Jake shrugged.

Barely five minutes into the journey, the coach pulled into the square of a larger village, where the official Tencastle party were already milling about chatting, presumably, to their hosts. Jake went to find out the plan of action from Barbara Bowen-Martin. Meanwhile we persuaded an unkempt and unwashed Jestyn to take refuge inside Ewegenie, our mascot - which also meant we had another dancer available.

"Right, three dances, then into the town hall for official welcome and refreshments," said Jake.

"What am I supposed to do?" Jestyn bleated.

"Just amble around and look sheepish," Harry told him.

The French hosts greeted our display with enthusiastic applause, though the Tencastle crowd seemed to regard it more as a delay in getting to the booze. At least our performance was over quite quickly. Not so the speeches from the local Mayor and Barbara Bowen-Martin. Fortunately we'd gathered at the rear of the room next to the table piled with assorted finger food, and sneaked the odd morsel. Until Jake was almost caught when a reference to 'our own unique traditional morris team' by Ms. B-M caused the whole assembly to turn and look as us.

"Hankies are clogged up with cream cheese," Jake muttered as he extracted a gooey mess from his pocket once we were no longer the centre of attention.

Formalities over, we each grabbed a plate of food before the hordes descended and sidled over to the drinks table. The glass of wine we'd all been offered on arrival had quickly disappeared and it seemed that refills were self-service.

"Great stuff, this," said Min, hiccupping. "Must take

some back for our wedding."

"Doubt if there will be any left the rate you're going!" said Huw.

"Yeah, go easy, we're supposed to dance again this afternoon," said Jake.

"What, here?" asked Dan.

"No, in Morlaix. We're dancing in a procession."

"But we don't do a processional dance," I pointed out.

"No problem. We'll think of something."

Far from being just a low-key event, the whole town had turned out for the procession, which included several local dance groups, the ladies all resplendent in elaborate lace headgear. And we were given pride of place, at the front, behind the civic dignitaries. We'd no idea how far we were expected to process. We stuffed Jestyn into the sheep's head again, to bring up our rear.

For the first hundred yards things went more or less to Jake's extemporised plan - stepping forward in two lines and then clashing whenever he called "sticking!" But the massed band of strident bombards from the following Breton group virtually drowned out the music of Huw and Janet.

"Sticking!" yelled Jake.

The four of us at the front obeyed. Baz, leading the rear four, hadn't heard the call, and continued forward, taking avoiding action with those of us stationary. And when we started to move on, Baz realised his error and stopped to clash sticks. So it continued, ad hoc, for nearly a mile, into the main square where we had gathered the day before.

"That was brilliant, Baz," said Jake, "Where did you get that idea from?"

"Dunno, just happened," he said modestly.

Having done our show dance for the crowd, we were about to head for the café while the local groups performed.

"What's Jestyn up to?" Janet asked, pointing to the other side of the square.

Still disguised as Ewegenie he was scurrying around trying to avoid the two collies snapping at his heels.

"Being rounded up, I guess," I said.

At which point, while looking behind him, he tripped headlong over a kerb and careered into a bollard. And lay still. Nobody seemed to notice. They were all watching the dancing.

"Oh hell!" said Jake.

We rushed over to help. Ewegenie had absorbed most of the impact with the bollard, and one of her papier maché ears had broken off. Jestyn was unconscious but Posy, who'd been designated our first-aider, found a steady pulse.

"We need to get him to hospital," she said, "He may be concussed."

I went over to a gendarme standing on the edge of the crowd and drew his attention to the accident. He took a quick look at Jestyn's prone figure and gabbled into his radio. Within a couple of minutes we heard sirens and an ambulance quickly arrived.

"Shouldn't one of us go with him?" said Janet.

"I don't think there's much we could do," Jake replied. "If we know to which hospital he's being taken we can ask one of our hosts to ring and find out his situation." He turned to Harry, "Do you know his surname?"

"Um, it's Davies, I think. Yes, Jestyn Davies. I'll give them my father's phone number in case they need to get in touch with his family."

"Yeah, good idea."

It wasn't until the coach returned an hour or so later to collect the party that we were able to tell our hosts what had happened. The Mayor promised to ring the hospital as soon as he got back to the town hall, and asked one of us to be with him for a first-hand report. Harry and Holly volunteered, out of some sort of loyalty to their father's employee.

"Manic," Harry said, when they eventually joined us at the barbecue that had been laid on for our party. "Mayor's prattling away on one phone to the hospital when the other phone in his office rings. My Dad, it was. Evidently the hospital had been in touch with him but hadn't been prepared to release details as he wasn't family. Anyhow, there's Dad trying to find out what's happening, me relaying his questions to the Mayor who's passing them on to the hospital, and then back to me, as far as his English could cope with medical technicalities, and then me trying to convey the message to Dad. Seems 'tetanie' doesn't mean 'tetanus' which is what I thought they meant."

"So what is wrong with Jestyn?" I asked.

"As far as I can gather, he's regained consciousness but they are keeping him in overnight for observation. Ankle's badly sprained, possibly broken. They are going to do an X-ray tomorrow."

Although Jestyn wasn't actually one of us, we felt a sort of responsibility for him, as he'd been acting as our mascot at the time. It put rather a damper for us on the evening's festivities, which continued with a Fest Noz- the Breton equivalent of a barn dance. Loud wailing, hypnotic music on bombards and hurdy-gurdy, and dances which all seemed to consist of shuffling round, trance-like in a circle with linked hands that were supposed to gyrate to a particular pattern.

***

Even Jake was more subdued the following morning. We did our best to get through the rest of the food that had been left for us. We were due to catch the afternoon ferry back to Plymouth after a visit to a farm. It was actually a cider press and distillery I discovered later.

We'd gathered up Jestyn's gear, expecting him either to be on the coach or otherwise to collect him at the hospital. But the Mayor's news rather altered our plans. He explained that because the doctor suspected a broken ankle, he would be staying one more night in hospital, and would then require someone to accompany him back to the U.K.

After blank looks all round I could see only one practical solution.

"Look, I've got a car in Plymouth. I'm willing to stay over if someone can give me a bed for the night. And get us to Roscoff for tomorrow's ferry.

"I would be delighted to help you, monsieur," said the Mayor.

"Okay, the rest of you can get the coach back to Tencastle - and Dan, you can get a train from Plymouth - unless you sprout wings again."

He shook his head.

"Rob, I'd rather stay over with you," said Janet. "Would you mind?"

Mind? I could have taken her in my arms and kissed her there and then. "Of course not," I said discreetly.

She turned to the Mayor, "Would that put you to great inconvenience?"

"No, no, my pleasure."

We bade farewell to our coach party. Rather than mooch around our hamlet we took up the Mayor's invitation to go with him to Morlaix where he had business during the day.

"Can't believe we've got this place to ourselves for the day," said Janet.

"Yes indeed. Thanks very much for staying."

"Well, I didn't fancy getting stranded in Tencastle, and I didn't really want to impose on Jake to run me all the way to Carrick."

"And I thought it was my charms that kept you," I said teasingly.

"That too," she chuckled, and took my arm.

***

"You enjoy Morlaix, oui?" said the Mayor, when he picked us up at the agreed time and place.

"Very much," said Janet, and I nodded. Though very few shops were open on the Sunday, the town offered a good selection of cafés and bars which we sampled in between walking through the old town and along the waterside towards the large viaduct and back.

Fortunately his English was pretty good, and he chatted very amiably about the history of Morlaix all the way back to his house. His wife, who'd prepared a huge meal for us, wasn't quite so fluent but between us we managed to convey a reasonably good account of what morris dancing was all about.

"Votre chambre!" he said, several glasses of wine later, "You are tired, yes?"

We both missed the grammatical point in translation. One room. One double bed. As he closed the door, we looked at each other - and laughed.

"I'll take the floor," I offered.

"No you won't!" Janet insisted.

"But..."

"And I'm not sleeping on the floor either."

"But..."

"Rob, you've always behaved with respect to me since you moved in to my flat, never made any improper advances and I really appreciate that. We have a double bed - I'm happy to share it with you. Unless you'd rather sleep on the floor."

"Janet, I... I don't know what to say. You... you're so... so..." I took her in my arms, and rested my head on her shoulder, happier than I could imagine.

"Rob, one thing," she said more seriously, "Don't push the limits too far... okay?"

"Okay, promise." I knew what she meant.

She was still in my arms when I awoke the next morning.

***

If Jestyn was rather a pathetic looking individual before, hospitalisation had done nothing to improve his image. He looked pale and utterly dejected, flopped out in the bedside chair with his heavily bandaged ankle stretched out in front of him. Fortunately, the X-ray shad shown that it was not broken He'd mentioned to me that he couldn't speak French, and he would have been like a fish out of water in the alien environment of a foreign hospital.

"Rob!" he perked up. "What are you doing here? I thought you'd all gone home."

"The others have gone. Janet and I offered to stay over and take you back."

"Oh thank god!" He heaved a great sigh of relief, "Haven't seen anyone apart from nurses and doctors since I woke up in here. Thought you'd all just left me." His brow creased. "But how will we get back to Tencastle?"

"I've a car at Plymouth. The Mayor will drive us to Roscoff, as soon as you are ready."

Janet helped him out of the chair and gave him the pair of crutches propped against the bed. "Can you manage?" she asked.

"Yeah, I'll be okay. And thanks."

We took his arm anyway as he stumped along the corridor to the lift.

The Mayor had made all the necessary travel

alterations with Brittany Ferries on our behalf. My mild concerns about having to make small talk for hours or endure long periods of silence were unfounded. Jestyn was surprisingly chatty, with no trace of the stutter which I suppose had been largely due to nervousness. He was a local lad who enjoyed writing and had ambitions to make a name for himself as a journalist. He agreed with our suggestion that he might like to direct his writing talents in another direction which didn't require so much direct contact with the general public. He also said he'd really enjoyed being involved with Carpiog Morris, despite his accident, and he'd like to join us, if we would have him. Well, what a turn up for the book!

It was well into the evening by the time we arrived at Plymouth, with another hour's drive to my parents' farm to collect Fi. The prospect of several more hours on the road didn't appeal to me, even though Janet offered to share the driving. I hadn't realised hitherto that she even held a driving licence. I rang ahead to ask my mother if she would mind making up another bed for our extra passenger. I thought it prudent to leave out any suggestion that I would be prepared to share a room with Janet if necessary.

My mother fussed over Jestyn, just as she had done a few days earlier when I had introduced her to Janet for the first time. Even got him smiling.

Next morning we were in no particular hurry to leave, and took our time over the huge breakfast my mother had provided. Since we had all day at our disposal we made a leisurely journey back to Tencastle, stopping off for a pie and a pint in the Forest of Dean. We headed back to Carrick after dropping Jestyn off at the house he still shared with his parents.

"What a wonderful weekend," Janet murmured as she rested her head against my shoulder on the sofa.

"Mmm," I said. "Your room or mine?"

She punched me playfully on the chest, "Single beds, silly!"

Nevertheless it was another hour or so before we retired to our separate rooms.

Chapter 23

I had only just entered the back room of the Castle when Min planted a kiss on my cheek, dropping a sheaf of envelopes on the floor as her arms wrapped around me.

"Rob, will you give me away!"

"What?" I was confused. She wasn't mine to give.

"I would have asked Jake but Huw's already claimed him."

"Min, can we start at the beginning? What is it exactly you want me to do?"

"Our wedding. Jake's going to be Huw's best man. I need someone to hold my arm as I walk up the aisle."

"You're not intending to arrive drunk are you?"

"Pillock!" She thumped my chest. "You know that I've got no parents nor any family that I'd want to invite. Can you be my honorary father for the day, to escort me?"

Knock me down with a feather! "I'd be delighted."

She gave me another kiss, rummaged to gather up the envelopes, and thrust one in my hand. "Official invite." She looked round, "No Janet?"

"She's tied up with a musical production at school this evening," I said.

True to his word, Jestyn had turned up at the Carpiog practice. A most entertaining article about our trip to Brittany had appeared under his name in the local paper though I suspect he'd had considerable help from Holly and Harry. Surprisingly, too, he was pretty quick on the uptake with the couple of dances Jake got him to try. And helped, too, by Posy with whom there seemed to be a mutual attraction.

"Min's got a few words to say," Jake announced when we took a break from dancing and had refilled our glasses.

"Thanks, Jake," she said. "You've all got an invite to our wedding at the end of July. I hope all past members of

Carpiog will also be there. It will be at Huw's parents' farm in Pembrokeshire. We'll have a big marquee and camping in a field. And there will be lots and lots of dancing and barrels of beer and singing... "

"Sounds great," said April. She'd missed out on the French trip and had yet to experience Carpiog on tour.

"Show of hands for all those likely to go?" Jake suggested.

No dissenters at all.

"I remember when my dad used to dance at weddings," said Baz. "They'd do a dance called 'Haste To The Wedding' followed by another called 'Getting Upstairs' and then 'Pram Pushing', though I think that was a nickname.

"Can we do them?" said Min enthusiastically.

"Expecting already, are you?" I said, earning another thump.

"If Baz can get hold of the details we can give them a try," said Jake. "As long as Min dances in her wedding dress."

"You bet!" she said.

After practice, while some were swapping yarns over another pint, Jake asked if he could have quiet word with me.

"I'd like your advice, Rob."

That was the last thing I expected him to say. "About being best man? Don't lose the ring and make sure the groom turns up sober."

"No, not the wedding. I've been thinking about next year."

"Next year?" I said, puzzled.

"Well, obviously I need to get a job. Question is, do I stay around this area or go somewhere else? I'm not keen to move back to London." He paused. "I've really enjoyed the four years here in Tencastle but many of my friends from the morris will be finishing this year. You're still nearby but Min and Huw are likely to be in Pembrokeshire, Harry and Holly may well go their own way. Don't know even if Carpiog with continue. I don't really want to be seen as a dinosaur clinging on to past memories."

A flashing image in my mind of lumbering black dinosaurus jacobi in morris bells.

"Well, it really depends on what jobs come up around here, Jake. You may not have any choice but to look elsewhere."

"Ah well, that's what I wanted to ask you about. Your school is advertising for a temporary games teacher."

"It is?" It was news to me. Mind you I hadn't noticed John Rhys-Price around in the past few days.

"I've more or less finished my duties as Union President - you know Rhiannon will be my successor?"

"Yes, I had heard." Rhiannon Legge-Upton, or Annie, as I'd known her, had run Jake a very close second in the election the previous year. A good-looking very focussed lass with the gift of the gab and oodles of charm. Which I'd nearly succumbed to when she tried to get inside information from me as Jake's campaign manager to possibly use against him.

"Well, I could spare a couple of days, possibly three, doing some supply teaching. Get me back in the frame of mind, as it were."

"So what advice do you want from me?" I still couldn't really see where my input would be relevant.

"Just wondered how you'd feel about my being on the staff."

"Why should I have any objections? I'd be pleased to see you."

"It's almost certain that there would be a full-time post available in the autumn and I'd probably stand a good chance of getting it if I helped them out this term."

"Yes, I can see that." I was still wondering when Jake

was going to come to the point.

"I wouldn't want to commute. I was wondering whether to ask Janet whether her downstairs flat might be available. I wanted to ask you what you thought about it first. I understand you've moved back upstairs."

"I was actually only downstairs for a few nights when I was expecting Dilly to visit."

"Right," He looked at me quizzically, "about you and Janet... you know?"

"Sleeping together?"

"Er, yes, though it's not really any of my business."

"We still have separate rooms." Which I thought neatly avoided answering the question directly.

"Okay, so what do you think?"

"It's up to Janet, really, but I don't have any problem with you asking her. Might be prudent though to wait until you've actually got the job." Since my brief occupation of the downstairs flat it had remained empty. Janet's parents were probably under the impression that I was still the tenant.

***

Janet wasn't aware of any reason for John Rhys-Price's absence. But Terry Osborne, his housemate, filled me in.

"Been suspended," he said. "He made a rather obscene reference to Moby Dick to a group of sixth formers just as the Headmaster unexpectedly entered the room."

"Ouch," I said. But given John's record of indiscreet comments it didn't come as a surprise. And of course there was his night in the cells after the fracas at the inaugural meeting of the folk club. We'd not had any problems since.

I put Janet in the picture later that day, and mentioned Jake's interest in the temporary post.

"Great," she said. "Does he want somewhere to stay?"

"Not for now," I said cautiously,. "He'll probably travel in on the days he's working, and no doubt he'll have Union commitments in the evening."

"And morris."

"That too."

***

"Is it my imagination, or did I see your old banger in the car park?" my head of department asked me at the end of the afternoon when we were in the prep room sorting out our requirements for the next day with Sandy.

"Not dreaming, Nick. I sold it to my former housemate."

Nick and Sandy looked at me, puzzled.

"He was here for an interview. To stand in for John while he is… er… indisposed."

"Is he the black chap?" said Nick. "I'm sure I've seen him somewhere before."

"Quite possibly. He played at the PTA Barn Dance with Janet and me, and he was with the morris dancers in Carrick a few weeks ago."

"Right." Nick looked thoughtful. "I wonder if he might get any… er… adverse reaction from some of our older students. It's a bit out of their experience where they've never been used to seeing anything other than white faces, even among their teachers."

"I don't think you need to worry on that score, Nick. He's well capable of holding his own and defusing any potential aggro. He'll soon have them eating out of his hand like tame puppies." Though I was confident that Jake wouldn't be fazed by any deliberate or unintentional racial comments, I did wonder whether some of our young toerags would try it on.

***

It seemed quite strange seeing Jake dressed respectably instead of his usual jeans and sweater. Formal attire was rarely required of a Union President except, perhaps, when he moved in official circles to which I was not privy. Over the past few months I'd got used to wearing a jacket and tie. At least we weren't required to wear an academic gown and mortar board, although by convention the former was used by whoever was on playground duty, whether they were a graduate or not. Kind of official guard duty uniform, I suppose.

Moby Dick was on fine form. "Ladies and Gentlemen, allow me to introduce Mr Jacob Moses who will be covering two days a week this term for Mr Rhys-Price in his... ah... absence."

Jake rose and took a bow.

"The rest of the physical education lessons will be taken by Mr Pedro da Seliva who will be joining us later this week."

Someone else of probable non-Celtic origin might take some attention away from Jake's ethnicity, I thought. My attention slowly drifted back to Moby who was still in full flow.

"... activity week in which our young people will have the opportunity to experience some extra-curricular activity to broaden their horizons and give them a sense of adventure."

It sounded like some bullshit rationale he'd picked up on one of the many seminars he attended.

Janet enlightened me during the lunch break. "His idea is that in the last couple of weeks of the summer term, after all the exams have finished, the tutors of each year group should organise an activity to broaden the horizons..."

"Yes, I got that bit. What do we have to do?"

"Organise something, I suppose." Janet was also a form tutor for our first year intake.

"Will we be given any budget for it?"

"Um, the impression I got was no expense spared as long as the parents are paying."

"Sounds like Moby's style," I said.

Jake joined us.

"How did it go then?" Janet asked.

"No problem. Took one group for a cross-country run."

"Really? You don't know the area that well," I said.

"Apparently it's the standard route that all the kids know. Including passing the sweet shop that a couple of the little rascals tried to sneak into. Down to the river and along through the woods to a boating lake and back. Kids kept looking at me expectantly - like I was going to start swinging through the trees like Tarzan."

Which reminded me of Jake's embarrassing incident there last year involving a bursting bladder and a party of twitchers. "That lake where you…"

"So what are you going to do for the Head's activity initiative?" Jake quickly changed the subject.

Janet and I looked at each other. I shrugged, "No idea." I certainly didn't fancy climbing, caving or sailing for which some other groups would almost certainly opt.

"Survival," Jake said.

"Ours?" I wondered what Jake had in mind. I doubted it would be to my liking.

"There's a centre that's just opened up near Tencastle," he said. "Where you can build your own shelter, forage for food."

"Sounds fun," said Janet.

"Hmm." I didn't share her enthusiasm.

"Want me to find out more?" Jake asked.

"Why not?" said Janet. "Unless you've any better ideas, Rob."

I hadn't.

***

I recognised the handwriting. I hadn't heard from Dilly since we'd last met. I was reluctant to open the letter. Though I was still very fond of Dilly, I really didn't want the dilemma of trying to handle two relationships simultaneously. Janet and I had become closer to each other over the previous couple of months, particularly since our trip to Brittany.

Dear Rob,

I'm sorry I haven't been in touch with you for a while. You will be pleased to know that I am feeling very much better, and that there is no threat from cancer. If I keep strictly to my diet I can live a pretty normal life. I've been back at work for some time. The staff there have been very supportive.
 I would still very much like to visit you in Carrick. But I've a favour to ask.

Oh bugger! I turned the page of the notelet.

 I now have a steady boyfriend. He's a junior doctor at the hospital. Would it be possible for us both to stay? I can't really remember what you told me about the rooms in Janet's house. If not, perhaps you could recommend some bed and breakfast place - not too expensive, though. I'm thinking of sometime during Whitsun half-term, if possible,
 I can't thank you enough for being so understanding and considerate to me when we last met. Your support was so important to me in helping get my life back together.

Love,
Dilly.

Phew!

I showed Janet the letter.

"Bet you're relieved," she said.

"Why do say that?"

"Oh come on, Rob, you were very nervous about a conflict of interests last time she wanted to visit, weren't you?"

I nodded. I still hadn't told her the full story.

"You won't have the dilemma of dividing your affections between Dilly and me."

I nodded again. "I'm really happy for Dilly, though."

"Yes, me too."

"So shall I tell her it's okay for them to stay?"

"Ye...es. We could sort out something downstairs."

Downstairs was still empty, mostly, though Jake had undertaken to do some painting and decorating, in lieu of rent for the occasional overnighter, and in preparation for his possible occupation if his appointment became full-time in the autumn. Fortunately Janet hadn't experienced Jake's decorating skills first hand.

"Is there a problem?" I said, noticing her hesitation.

"Well, I was going to ask you..."

"Yes?" I had no idea what was on her mind.

"I'm thinking of visiting my parents again at half-term, and wondered whether you'd like to come with me."

I didn't need to think twice. "I'd be very happy to, Janet. You've already met my folks."

"It wouldn't be for the whole week, so it should be possible for Dilly to visit and for us to get away."

"Brilliant! You're a star!" I kissed her.

***

Jake obviously didn't find the information that Baz had passed to him about the new dances for Min's wedding at all helpful.

"It's all in code, Baz!"

"No, it's from the new Morris Ring book." said Baz.

"Doesn't ring any bells for me," Jake complained. "Here, what do make of it, Rob?"

Some pages from a ring-bound book had been photocopied. Whilst the musical notation for the tunes was clear, the instructions for the dance didn't make a lot of sense, since the author had made extensive use of abbreviations, meaningless without a reference key.

"They're Cotswold, not Border dances," said Baz, trying to be helpful.

"They look very complicated to me," said Jake. He thought for a moment. "If Janet and Huw can play the tunes we could make up our own dances to fit."

"Is that allowed?" I asked.

"Dunno," said Jake. "Tell you what, I'll have a word with Gron and see if he can translate."

No doubt Jake would be scribbling frantically all night to put some ideas down on paper. We only had another three practices before the end of the college year. When we all gathered together for Min and Huw's wedding we would obviously need a reminder of the dances anyway - not least for past members who would be unfamiliar with the mostly subtle changes Jake had introduced during the current year.

Over another pint after practice Jake asked, apropos of nothing, "Have you met my other half?"

"No, didn't know you were hitched," I said. "Who is she?"

"No, you pillock! My other half at school. You know, the chap who's covering the rest of the games lessons." He paused. "Saliva or something, he's called."

"Ah yes!" I said, "Pedro da Seliva. Wiry little Spaniard, very Mediterranean looking. Apparently he's been signed by Swansea Town as their new midfielder for next season and he's just filling in this term. Seems a decent sort of bloke."

"Right," said Jake, thoughtfully. "But the boys at Carrick play rugby in the winter, not football, don't they?"

"Uh huh," I agreed. "Should improve your chances of a permanent post."

"He's already got a nickname, though," Janet chuckled, "I overheard some boys calling him 'Dribble'."

***

The arrangements for Dilly's visit weren't straightforward. In the first place, she wrote again, apologetically, asking if the downstairs had two beds in separate rooms rather than a double bed. Her boyfriend's parents were very strict about these things, she wrote, being committed Christians, and all that. Personally I didn't think it was any business of the parents. As a trained doctor he was old enough to make his own decisions. Anyway, Janet had neither double bed nor two bedrooms downstairs, just two single beds in the same room.

"He can always sleep on the sofa, I suppose." she said. "And I'm not going to have you and him downstairs and myself and Dilly up here. Or vice versa."

As a result, Dilly phoned to say they had decided to take bed and breakfast in Tencastle, but perhaps we could meet up for a meal.

"Stephen, that's her boyfriend, drives, it seems, so I've invited them here." Janet said, holding the phone to her chest. "Is that okay with you?"

"Yes, fine," I said, and then added, "You'd better ask her what food she can eat and what she's allergic to."

"Good thinking."

We settled on the Tuesday evening, which actually gave us a bit more flexibility to travel up to Janet's parents. I was keen to take her to the Friday night folk club in Brighton which I'd visited when I'd been that way for a job interview a year ago. She hadn't been there before.

Precisely on the dot of seven o'clock, the time we had agreed, the doorbell rang. We both went down to welcome our visitors.

"Dilly, good to see you!" I said. "Come in!"

She stepped in, gave Janet a hug and peck on the cheek, then did the same with me. Her boyfriend frowned in apparent disapproval at our innocent intimacy. He was about my height, but slightly built with a rather sharp, weasely face, dark hair and dark eyebrows which almost met above his nose. Particularly when he frowned.

"Janet," he said formally, "I'm Stephen. Pleased to meet you." Not that he sounded too sincere about it. "And Robert." he said, offering me his hand.

Which I took. "Most people call me Rob," I said.

"I'm not really happy with diminutives," he said, "I believe people should be addressed by their christened name."

Oh god! I wonder what he'd make of Min. She'd probably give a pretty strong retort if he addressed her as Wilhelmina. I was tempted to call him Steve just to see how he'd react, but I didn't want to spoil the evening before it had begun.

"Come on upstairs," Janet invited them.

"Can I get you a drink?" I asked Dilly when they were both seated. "Beer? Wine?"

"Dilys is not allowed to drink," Stephen interrupted. "And I'll have a tonic water, if you've got one."

"Oh yes, you're driving," I said.

"I don't drink alcohol," he stated. Why was I not surprised?

I found a half bottle of supermarket tonic water in the larder. I hoped it hadn't lost all its sparkle.

As I sipped my glass of Merlot I couldn't help but noticing that Dilly had lost some of her sparkle. That captivating twinkle in her eyes was missing and there was only a hint of her lovely smile. Of course, it might have been the worry of her medical condition but I had my suspicions that Stephen may have also been a negative influence.

Conversation was somewhat stilted. Generalities about her teaching job, the drive down, where they were staying in Tencastle and so on. It was a welcome break when Janet announced that supper was served.

"May I ask what it is?" said Stephen looking suspiciously at the casserole dish.

"Dilly told us in some detail what she was allowed in her diet, and Janet has followed that to the letter," I said, probably more curtly that I intended.

"I see," he said. And then quizzed Janet about every ingredient she had used.

Remarkably she kept an even temper. Dilly was looking rather embarrassed by her boyfriend's behaviour.

Between courses I asked Dilly casually, "How are you getting along now healthwise?"

"I hardly think that's a topic for conversation over dinner," Stephen butted in.

"I wasn't asking you." I'd just about had enough of the pillock. "I'm sure Dilly is quite capable of answering for herself, if she so wishes."

His face turned quite red, and I wondered whether he was really going to lose his rag. I turned to Dilly, to encourage her to answer.

"I'm getting along fine now, thank you," she said politely.

Janet brought out the sweet. To my amusement Janet served it to Stephen with a sheet listing every single item down to the last pip - and a teaspoonful of salt."

"Salt!" Stephen was aghast. "She's not allowed salt! And in a dessert!"

I caught a glimpse of the Dilly I knew as she grinned

and suppressed a chuckle.

"Just the most meagre pinch," said Janet, "I'm sure you won't notice it." I doubt if he would even realise he'd been the object of a subtle joke.

Even though Dilly did begin to relax and start chatting without looking to Stephen for approval, I was relieved when, soon after coffee - decaffeinated of course - Stephen announced that they needed to leave. "It's an hour's drive," he said. Which I knew well.

While Janet had gone downstairs with Stephen to get his coat, 'and show him the flat', Dilly spoke to me quietly, "I'm so sorry, Rob. Stephen is not very good with strangers."

"The main thing is, Dilly, are you happy?"

"He's been very good to me, very kind and supporting." She looked at me wistfully. "But sometimes I wonder..."

"Yes?"

"Oh never mind." She put her arms round me and kissed me fully on the lips. "I wonder... if things had worked out differently. But you've got Janet... I really like her."

We held each other close without speaking. Until Stephen called to say he was waiting to leave.

"I'll always love you, Rob... even though we didn't... we can't..." She was near to tears.

"And you'll always be in my heart, Dilly. I mean that."

One more kiss and she was gone.

"Strange bloke," said Janet when she joined me on the sofa.

"Mmm, anally retentive control freak." I put my arms round her.

"You know, I do wonder about Dilly."

"What do you wonder?"

"Well, I think she'd be better off with someone more, um..."

"Cheerful?"

"Yes, and easy going, like you."

"So do you think I should offer myself to her, then? Would you mind?" I said teasingly.

"That's not what I meant, you dumbo!"

Chapter 24

The coach dropped us off where the track led into the forest, past the sign advertising Woodland Adventures. While the rest of the year group had opted for a less challenging visit to the Tallyllyn railway, Janet, Jake and myself were in charge of a couple of dozen intrepid first year pupils who would have to build their own shelter and cook their own food.

After trudging half a mile or so up the track we came to a large, level clearing in the woods. A stocky long-bearded chap of indeterminate age emerged from a low thatched hut and greeted us. "Welcome! Dump your rucksacks over there," he boomed, pointing to a rickety old trestle table, one of several. "Gather round."

"Your task here is to build yourself a den from natural materials, and then later, to prepare and cook yourself a meal. You should be prepared to spend the night in the den, so it will need to protect you against rain and wind. You could construct several small shelters for three or four people but I suggest that you work together to make one large den for the boys and another for the girls."

The children looked around, disconcerted. There were no obvious materials available for any construction.

"Don't worry, you'll find everything you need," he said.

"Sir," said Fanny, Sandy's daughter. "Will the teachers be making their own shelter too?"

"Well now," our host said seriously, "we would expect you to show due respect to the elders of this tribe, and make them the best house to stay in."

"That's not fair!" another girl protested.

Jake smiled. "He's only joking. We'll be mucking in as well, won't we?" He winked at Janet and me. Before he could get any hands-on experience, however, Jake was led away to discuss - well, whatever needed discussing.

Apart from gathering names and money from the kids for the trip, Janet and I had left all other details to Jake.

I took charge. "Right, five minutes to decide whether you are going to go for two big structures or several smaller ones."

The youngsters got down to business surprisingly well, far better than some adult groups would have done in similar circumstances, I thought. A babble of chatter, lots of hands going up. And Fanny and her friend seemed to have taken on the role of co-ordinators for the girls.

Jake returned. "It's like a primitive society's builder's yard over there." He pointed to where the track disappeared behind some bushes. "Take a look."

Sure enough, there were piles of brushwood and stakes, blocks of hardened clay, a mound of grass turf, rocks and stones of various sizes, hemp rope, raffia string, and dried reeds. I was a bit doubtful about the authenticity of what appeared to be a stack of buffalo hides that proved on closer inspection to be brown tarpaulin sheets. And for the more educated Neanderthal, there was a set of d.i.y. architect's plans for various types of structure.

"Are we going for a twosome or threesome bivouac?" said Janet.

"Who would be in the single unit then, you or Jake?"

Janet laughed and punched my arm playfully.

When we returned, the girls were lying on the ground with their feet towards the centre of a circle. All except Fanny who was pacing round. placing a small stone at their heads

"New party game, Jake?" I asked.

"No, she's measuring how big the den needs to be."

Great initiative, I thought. The boys, who had been watching in puzzlement, caught on to the idea, but, to be different, laid down side by side in a long line.

For the next couple of hours, the clearing was a hive of

activity as the boys and girls entered into fierce competition to see who could complete their den first. The three of us supervised in order to nip in the bud any potentially dangerous procedure.

The girls made a promising start, hammering pointed stakes with crude rock mallets into the ground at intervals marked by the circle of stones, then filling in the gaps with a weave of bendy saplings. But they were scratching their heads about how to construct a roof.

Fanny approached me, almost in tears. "Sir, can you help us, please? We don't know how to put a roof on our den."

"Okay, let's have a look," I said. Janet wandered over with me. Jake had disappeared somewhere with a spade in hand.

"How are you going to get inside?" Janet asked, having walked around the outside of the girls' construction.

"We… er," Fanny wrinkled her brow, "Oh… um…" She started sobbing.

"Don't worry, lass, that's quite easily sorted," I said. "Now, about the roof. What's the distance between opposite walls?"

"Er," Fanny paced out some steps.

"That looks about three yards," I said. "What's the longest sapling or pole you've got?"

"Just over half that length."

"Okay, now, think! You can span a distance at least from the side to the centre. Any ideas?"

Fanny thought deeply. "Well…" she said eventually.

"Yes?"

"We could put something in the middle to support the roof."

"Well done! And, Fanny, don't forget to make a door!"

"Yes sir. Thank you." She scurried off, with new enthusiasm.

The boys had gone for a Nissen hut design, with flexible saplings anchored to the ground between large stones and turfs then tied to a central beam – a long wooden pole supported at each end by a stake to which it was lashed by rope.

No foraging for lunch, thank goodness. We'd been told to bring a packed lunch. The wild side would come later.

"Please sir," said one young lass, fidgeting as she stood before us, "I need to... I need the loo."

"Ah," said Jake, "I forgot. We should have done that first."

"Done what?" she said.

"Dig the latrines." Jake reached for his spade propped up against a tree.

"Sir?" she looked as if she was going to burst into tears. "I need to pee!"

"'S'okay lass, if you just go down that track, you'll find some toilet cabins."

"That was cruel," I said, as the girl hurried off down the track. I was used to Jake's sense of humour but I doubt if the girl appreciated it.

"Sorry."

"Seriously though, Jake, we are surely not expecting these youngsters to spend a night in their ramshackle huts and wander off into the woods to go to the loo?" said Janet. "I wouldn't be happy if I were their mother."

Jake had been a bit vague as to exactly what facilities were available but had urged us to trust him.

"You're absolutely right. We'll be in a proper cabin. It's basic, but with proper beds and ablutions. It will focus their minds if they believe a comfortable night's sleep depends on their own work."

"Incidentally, what were you up to with the spade?" I said. "I presume you weren't digging a latrine."

"Buried treasure."

"Searching for?"

"No, hiding. Tomorrow morning's treasure hunt. I've hidden a box of sweets and chocolates."

"Assuming the squirrels don't get there first," said Janet.

"Don't worry, they're in a sealed tin."

Our bearded host - or Glyn, as he had introduced himself to Jake - reappeared mid-afternoon, just as the children were putting the finishing touches to their dens. He was impressed, as were Jake, Janet and I, with the way the youngsters had put their hearts and souls into the task.

"Well done, girls and boys. Very well done!"

They all beamed at his words of praise.

"Right," Glyn continued, "We need to check that your huts are big enough for you. Also, since there are scattered showers forecast for this afternoon, it might be a good idea to take shelter now."

I looked up at the clear blue sky, puzzled.

The children scrambled into their respective dwellings, with lots of giggling, which slowly gave way to a muffled chatter.

I noticed a hose-pipe lying in the long grass just behind where Glyn was standing. He disappeared briefly behind a tree, presumably to reach a standpipe, since water started trickling from the hose.

"Scattered shower," he whispered to us. "Don't worry, it's only a light drizzle." He pointed the nozzle towards the newly-occupied huts and directed a fine spray over each roof in turn for about thirty seconds.

No reaction from the girls' shelter but from the boys, a sudden cry, "Hell, I'm getting dripped on. Move over!"

"No room, you pillock, sit down!"

"Me too, I'm getting wet!" came another anguished wail.

After a clamour of agitated voices and the sounds of a general kerfuffle, one body came crashing backwards through the flimsy straw wall.

"Now look what you've done, you idiot!" someone shouted as the lads emerged one by one into the bright sunshine, to the amusement of the girls who'd left their hut to see what all the fuss was about.

"It was raining, I tell you!" cried the ejectee, picking himself up from the ground.

"Rubbish!" said another. "Does it look like it's been raining?" Any drops of water that had fallen on the ground had already evaporated.

"But he said..." the unfortunate boy pointed towards Glyn, then shrugged his shoulders, realising no-one was going to believe him.

Fanny put her hand on the reeds overlapping the wall of her hut, rubbed her fingers together and looked suspiciously at us adults. She didn't say anything but I'm sure she suspected foul play.

Glyn called for the group's attention and gave them a briefing on how to make the roof reasonably watertight. "I was a bit premature with the weather forecast," he said, "but rain is expected overnight."

The boys started talking in obvious consternation.

"Don't worry, though. You won't have to sleep out here. We have some comfortable beds in our bunkhouse – and proper facilities, so you won't have to crawl around in the woods at night to use the loo." Glyn paused to let the good news sink in. "Now to your next task. Unless you want to go hungry, you'll need to forage for your supper."

He handed out some printed sheets and several plastic bags.

"Now, on this sheet are a number of edible things which can be found in these woods. See how many you can collect. But," he emphasised, "YOU MUST NOT TASTE THEM. Do not put any of them into your mouth or try to eat them."

"Why not, sir?" one girl asked.

"Because there are things which look very similar but are deadly poisonous. I will need to see what you have collected to make sure you will survive."

I thought I heard a few sharp intakes of breath.

"I suggest you split up into groups of three or four. At no time are you to wander off alone, and you are not to go beyond any fences at the boundary of this woodland. And when you hear this," he blew a shrill blast on the whistle attached to a lanyard around his neck, "come back to this clearing immediately." Glyn turned to us, "Best if the three of you go on patrol to make sure they follow instructions."

"Ugh," I heard Fanny say, "No way I'm going to eat creepy-crawlies."

"Or stinging nettles!" said her friend, Daisy Colville.

I took a glance at Glyn's sheet. Grubs, snails, fungi, berries, leaves – not exactly an enticing menu for a barbecue.

The children, despite some initial reservations, again tackled their challenge enthusiastically. For the next hour I could hear giggles, shouts, excited chatter and occasional groans of disgust all over the forest. Until the shriek of Glyn's whistle called us back to base – very clearly signposted by arrows liberally sited along paths and at each junction. Even so I was relieved that a head count still tallied with our party complement.

"You sod!" yelled Daisy, as a gangling lad dropped a slug down the back of her blouse. She whipped round and lashed out with a stinging nettle grasped in her hand, inspirationally gloved in a plastic bag.

"Yeow!" cried the lad as the leaf brushed his cheek.

"Serves you right," Janet said without sympathy.

Daisy wriggled and managed to dislodge the mollusc by pulling out her blouse from the top of her jeans. Fanny stopped her from trying to push the poor creature down the front of the lad's trousers.

"No need, he's already got one," she said.

I heard Janet suppress a chuckle with a fit of coughing.

Glyn was speaking to the group again. "I'm afraid you haven't gathered quite enough for a banquet," he said, "but, if one was really desperate all of these could be eaten. There's a lot of protein in bugs, and boiled nettles are a bit like spinach."

Several wrinkled noses, particularly among the girls.

"Just as well then that I caught plenty of these little creatures earlier in the day. Only see them at the break of day, so you have to be quick. They're really quite meaty once you top and tail them and take the legs off." He held up a wooden skewer upon which an elongated greyish-brown object was impaled.

"Looks suspiciously like a pork banger," Jake whispered.

"Free range, obviously," I replied.

I wondered whether Glyn would fool any of the kids into thinking there were dozens of little furry sausage dogs scurrying through the undergrowth. Probably a few, I thought, seeing the look of awe on some innocent faces.

"Now you'll need to cook them over a camp fire," said Glyn. "How will you do that?"

Hands went up. "Put them in a frying pan, sir," said one boy.

"Will this do?" Glyn produced a metal dustbin lid. Much shaking of heads.

"Use a prong?" another lad suggested.

"Like this?" Glyn held up the skewer again. "Problem?"

"It will burn, sir." said Fanny.

"Correct. Any more ideas?"

"We could wrap the... er... meat in damp leaves and put them in the ashes," Daisy offered.

"Good, good, that might work," said Glyn. "In fact, I've already got some potatoes wrapped in foil to bake that way." He paused. "Tell you what, if your teachers show you the bunkhouse and get you settled into your dormitories, I'll get the camp fire going."

Despite being described as basic, the two-storey wooden bunkhouse, well-screened from the den construction area, was modern and surprisingly well-equipped. I'd certainly been in far more basic youth hostels. The ground floor was taken up by a kitchen, toilets, and a large dining room-cum-lounge which could also be used as a classroom, while on the first floor were two fourteen-bunk dormitories, each with their own toilets and showers. Between them at the top of the central staircase were situated two twin-bunk rooms and another bathroom for the party leaders.

Three of us between two rooms. "I think it would be prudent for Jake and me to share," I said to Janet. "We don't want to start tongues wagging if the kids start suspecting that you and I are sleeping together. In the same room I mean," I added hastily, for Jake's benefit.

"Okay with me," she said.

Back outside, Glyn had been busy. In another clearing, tables and benches were arranged in a large semi-circle around an open camp fire over which various pans and kettles dangled from a Heath-Robinson array of metal supports. The table was laid out with metal plates and cutlery, plastic beakers, jugs of various cordials and wooden bowls of green salad.

"Right, dinner is served," Glyn announced. "Bring your plate and line up."

Extracted from the ashes with enormous metal tongs and stripped of its foil wrapping, a large baked potato, sliced across and dolloped with butter, was served to each hungry child - and us, of course.

"Help yourself to the meat and onions," he said. "Everything you are eating has come from this forest and the nearby farm," Glyn declared. "Apple juice, mixed berry cordial – all natural. No added chemicals!"

"Sir, are we really eating wild sausages?" asked one girl, innocently.

"Now that would be telling, wouldn't it?" said Glyn with a twinkle in his eye. "Perhaps tomorrow I can show you. Early rise for those who want to have milk with their breakfast. See you then!" Glyn took his leave. He obviously wasn't resident on site as such.

The youngsters had pretty much cottoned on to the fact that much of what Glyn said needed to be taken with a pinch of salt, and seemed unperturbed by the possibility of a hands-on udder experience. Nevertheless, it gave Jake the opportunity to remind them that they would be turning in to their beds in an hour or so. "But who's for a sing-song round the camp fire first?" he asked. Not that they had any choice.

I'd guessed what Jake had in mind when, earlier, he'd found a rather battered guitar on the wall of the bunkhouse dining room, and passed it to me. Being rather more appealing than Jake's original suggestion which had been to get the kids morris dancing, I got its remaining five strings roughly in tune. Without Janet's help, though, I would have had no idea what songs they might have come across that also were part of my repertoire. Apparently she still used 'BBC Singing Together' booklets in her first-year music lessons, so 'No John No', suitably bowdlerised from the version performed in our folk club, 'The Mermaid' and the odd shanty rang out round the camp fire, more or less – probably less - to my guitar accompaniment.

"Please sir," Fanny asked, during a pause for breath, "can you do David Essex?"

Short answer from me would have been 'no' but Jake launched into 'Rock On', with all the body movements while miming guitar playing. I didn't have to pretend to mime - I had no idea what key he'd pitched it in. Tentative plucking on the strings failed to find a suitable match.

Huge applause.

It was still light after we'd packed the children off to bed, made sure they'd cleaned their teeth, and impressed upon them that, apart from a toilet trip, they were not to stray from their dormitory until reveille.

"Fancy a beer?" said Jake.

"We can't leave the kids, even if we knew where to find the nearest pub," I pointed out.

"Boy scout," he said. "Be prepared." He fished out three bottles of brown ale from his rucksack.

We drank from the bottle, squatting round the embers of the camp fire and chatting until dusk was well-advanced. We felt the odd spatter of rain from the darkening sky and a strengthening breeze.

The door of the bunkhouse did not yield. The handle turned but the door would not open. I noticed a Yale lock.

"I thought we left this door open," I said.

"We did," agreed Janet, "Must have blown shut."

"Got the key, Jake?" I asked.

"Shit, no. Didn't think we'd need it. It's hanging up in the kitchen."

"So what do you suggest?"

"Knock on the door?"

"We gave the kids strict instructions to stay in their dormitories, remember?" I said.

"And they'd probably be scared stiff if they heard someone knocking," Janet added.

"Well, we could use the dens," Jake suggested, "At least, let's get into some shelter."

It was beginning to rain more steadily. We hurried back down the track and crawled into the girls' roundhouse. The boys' hut we knew was not waterproof and there was still a gaping hole in the side.

No room to stand up, or really to lie down. Our height, even that of Janet, exceeded the girls by several inches at least. We sat, huddled together. It was going to be a long, uncomfortable night. And we soon found that our shelter was no match for persistent precipitation.

"Janet, have you got a hairpin?" Jake asked.

"Yes, but..."

"I've an idea. I'll try to pick the lock. We can't really stay here. We'll be soaked by the morning."

We picked our way back to the bunkhouse in the darkness along a now quite slippery and muddy path. The slight overlap of the roof gave a little shelter, and a green emergency light provided just enough illumination for Jake to locate the lock and fiddle around with the hairpin. I wasn't too hopeful of success but after about ten minutes juggling around and a few whispered imprecations, the lock yielded.

"Eureka!" he called.

But before he could step inside, the door blew shut again, catching his wrist. He yelped and dropped the hairpin.

"OH BUG..." I waved a finger to remind him that there were young children sleeping within earshot.

Jake scrabbled around on his hands and knees trying to find the pin. Janet knelt down to help him.

"Back in a mo," I said. I made my way to the rear of the bunkhouse, to see if I could find an open window.

"What the... !" Picklock Holmes exclaimed, as I opened the front door. He was just about to set to work again with the hairpin.

"Back door was open," I said. "Front door probably got caught in the draught."

No early call from Glyn to milk the cows, thank goodness. When I wandered downstairs next morning, before the children were up and about, a buxom middle-aged woman was bustling about laying the tables for breakfast.

"Hi, I'm Molly," she said cheerfully.

"Rob," I said, extending my hand. Pointlessly, since

she'd got a large jug in each hand. "No Glyn this morning?"

"He's busy on the farm. He's my husband."

"Can I give you a hand?"

"Almost done, but yes, if you'd like to take these."

I took the two jugs brimming with milk, no doubt freshly from the farm, and placed them on a long serving table, where already there were bowls of cereal, fresh fruit, warm freshly-baked rolls, hard-boiled eggs, plates of sliced ham and cheese together with a dish of golden butter, pots of honey and home-made jam.

An hour later the table resembled Mother Hubbard's cupboard. The children were more effective than a plague of locusts at devouring everything edible in their path.

Our coach wasn't due to pick us up until midday. Time for more adventurous activities before a tour around Glyn and Molly's farm.

"I want you to imagine you are pirates," said Jake to the assembled children.

Pirates? In the middle of rural Wales? Janet and I exchanged wry glances. But if Jake didn't recognise the incongruity I doubt that the youngsters did either.

"You'll be searching for treasure buried by that famous pirate, Blackbeard. I have some maps here on which you'll find the location of various clues. Split up into groups of four - and remember what you were told yesterday, no wandering off alone or straying beyond the boundary fences. Good hunting!"

The children dashed off in various directions, guided more by enthusiasm than reference to the map, I suspected.

"Christ, Jake," I said, "You and Glyn are two of a kind for laying on the bullshit."

"What do you mean?" he said, innocently.

"Well, for a start, Bluebeard must have been seriously off course and up the creek if he buried treasure here. He was a pirate in the Caribbean."

"Really? Oh well, just using a bit of poetic licence."

Janet rolled her eyes.

We didn't have much to do apart from watching the groups rush excitedly from one part of the forest to another for the best part of an hour. Until a huge cheer went up and a quartet of rather muddy and sweaty lads appeared triumphantly bearing a wooden chest which they set down in front of us. The other groups gathered around closely to see what riches had been found. The lid was flung back to reveal the bounty – or the little chocolate bounty bars that filled the box!

"Enough for everyone to share," said Jake, disappointing, perhaps, the box's finders who were preparing to stuff their pockets with their spoil.

Later, as we relaxed on the coach back to Carrick, we reflected on the adventure experience that Jake had organised for the children.

"Brilliant, Jake," said Janet. "You certainly seem to have the knack of coming up with something out of the ordinary."

"That's the understatement of the year," I said. "Still, it will have given you a lot of kudos with the kids for when you start full-time in September."

The other first-year excursion hadn't been quite as lacking in challenge as I'd expected. At the furthest and most inaccessible point from anywhere, the Tallyllyn train had suffered a derailment. No damage was done to the rolling stock or to the passengers but it took nearly three hours to get the journey back on track, so to speak.

Chapter 25

With the confirmation of his appointment as full-time games teacher at Sir Wilfred Roberts school from September and the house at Penybont finally reclaimed by Benji's god squad colleagues, Jake had moved, prematurely, into Janet's downstairs flat.

Janet's parents had been very happy with the arrangement, though I'm not sure whether she had left them to assume that both Jake and I would be living downstairs. Mind you, during my visit at the Whitsun break they had seemed quite broad-minded, and had welcomed me to their house, a modest semi quite close to a large park. It had been very pleasant to visit Shoreham-by-Sea in more relaxing circumstances than previously when I was stranded there on my way to an interview by bizarre failings of public transport. Janet took me to see the school in the nearby town of Steyning where I might have ended up teaching. In that event, I suppose it would have been within the bounds of possibility that we would still have met each other. She had also been keen for me to see the main church in the centre of town, "where I was confirmed," she'd said, and the quaint old flintstone church near the rickety wooden toll bridge that had once carried the main road. We'd taken a trip to the folk club in Brighton on the Friday, but I'd followed her wishes of going to a barn dance at the church hall in Shoreham on the Saturday evening rather than heading off to another folk club we'd been told about in Lewes. At least we had been able to leave Fi at Janet's parents. During the interval I had persuaded Janet to slip out of the dry ceilidh for a quick drink. I prudently avoided the oddly named Marlipins pub where I'd had an unfortunate encounter with the landlady's daughter a year earlier.

Having Jake on hand actually made discussion about the forthcoming wedding much easier. Huw had left the logistics of getting invited guests to the wedding in the hands of his best man, Jake. Or rather, those guests - probably the majority - that weren't part of his extended family. Jake was actually good with logistics, even if the logic wasn't apparent to anyone else. Though several of us were still in Carrick or Tencastle, several members of Carpiog Morris had, like Huw and Min themselves, departed for home territory as soon as the college year came to an end. Former members of Carpiog, now scattered across the country, would also be travelling down to Pembrokeshire by various means.

"So who have we got coming?" I asked.

"Well, from hereabouts, obviously you, Janet and myself. There's Harry and Holly and Jestyn - and also, probably Posy. She's staying down with Jestyn." He paused, apparently checking mentally whether he'd omitted anyone. "Oh, Benji's also been invited."

"Gron?" I asked, referring to our mentor who'd taught us dances when we started last year.

"No, he's declined," said Jake, "but it's quite likely Dilly and her boyfriend... er..."

"Stephen."

"Yes, Dilly and Stephen will probably come via Tencastle. I offered them a lift when they were here a few weeks ago."

"You did?" It was the first I knew about it. "I didn't think that Min and Huw knew Dilly that well."

"They went along to a Carpiog evening when you and Janet were away."

"So, that's potentially nine people, plus camping gear and so on, in two small cars?" I remembered

Jessica being pretty loaded up with a roof rack on top when just Jake and I travelled to Huw's place a couple of years ago.

"I'm going to hire a minibus. We can pick others up from the station or whatever in Haverfordwest, and it will also be handy for us all to travel together around the area."

"Who else has confirmed?"

"Sean. He'll get the ferry from Rosslare to Fishguard. April - she's quite close, from Newport. Baz, of course, and most of the old gang. There's only one I haven't be able to contact.

That still gave us a pretty good representation of Carpiog Morris, past and present. It would be good to see Sophie Brasier and Kissy Kesteven again. Min had asked them to be bridesmaids. I'd taken a fancy to both of them at various times, not that it ever led to anything. And also Rud, aka Brian Cheeke, who had been a whiz at collecting money and very keen to exercise fertility rites on any willing female. Dan had been with us, of course, on our French trip. I'd been in touch, sporadically, with Dicky Swift, my former neighbour in the all-male student hostel in Tencastle. He'd taken up a teaching post in Swindon.

We left Carrick more or less on time. Eric Dickens had offered to bring the twins, Harry and Holly, over from Tencastle, and also gave Jestyn and Posy a lift. Which saved us travelling nearly thirty miles in the opposite direction and back. We had to wait a few minutes for the bus to deliver Benji. Dilly had rung up a week earlier to say that she and Stephen wouldn't be coming after all. No doubt he'd forbidden her to socialise with those involved in his perception of heathen rituals.

The plan was to get to Huw's family farm by midday, set up camp and have a bite to eat before Jake collected the various railway travellers in the afternoon.

"Oh bugger," said Jake, just after we'd exited a roundabout somewhere beyond Carmarthen. A few hundred yards ahead, brake lights were coming on. I realised I hadn't seen any traffic coming the other way recently.

We cruised to a halt behind a line of stationary vehicles that stretched as far as we could see. A coach pulled up behind us. Ten minutes later, and with no movement at all, people were getting out of their cars and peering into the distance in the forlorn hope of identifying the cause of the hold up.

"Janet," said Jake, "Can you get your fiddle out?"

"Why?"

"Well, if we're stuck here we may as well try to earn some beer money. We've got a captive audience."

Though we hadn't got our full kit easily accessible, our raggies sufficed to identify ourselves as morris dancers.

"Benji, can you pass the hat round?" said Jake.

"But..."

"Think of it as passing the collection plate round in church."

Some travellers, clearly frustrated by the delay, ignored us, but we soon had an attentive audience. Particularly the German tourists in the coach behind us who swelled our coffers considerably and clapped in appreciation. Just as we were about to begin our sixth dance, Benji called out, "They're moving again!"

Everybody scrambled back into their vehicles, and after another couple of minutes we began to move, slowly. We crawled at a snail's pace, stop, start. It took us half-an-hour to travel a couple of miles.

"Junction ahead," said Jake. "I'm going to turn off. See if we can find another route."

The signpost indicated a couple of Llan-unpronounceables to the left. Jake turned into a minor road, barely wide enough for two vehicles to pass.

"I'll let you navigate," said Jake, generously.

"Got a map?"

"Er, not sure."

No map was found in the minibus.

"You'll have to use dead reckoning," Jestyn suggested, unhelpfully, from the rear seat.

"Yeah," said Jake, "we need to keep heading west."

That was all very well in principle but not so easy when the road twisted and turned every which way. But at least the sun was shining, so we did know the general direction in which we should be going. After perhaps another twenty minutes or so wiggling around ever narrower lanes and taking pot luck at the numerous unmarked junctions, we eventually approached a halt sign that suggested we might get back on track.

"Yes!" cried Jake, "Haverfordwest left."

The road was very busy. Nose to tail traffic but at least it was moving at a speed which would let us get out of second gear. The coach driver with the German tourists very kindly let us out of the side road. Further on, two wrecked cars occupied a lay-by.

With a delay of nearly two hours a leisurely lunch was clearly off the menu. Jake had just enough time to drop off persons and paraphernalia at the camp site before heading back to the station. Was it my imagination or did I glimpse Dilly standing by a marquee? But it was only a back view so I thought no more about it.

"Rob, I'd like you to come with me," said Jake.

"Okay." I shrugged. I couldn't think why he'd need a chaperone.

On route, he explained. "I'll drop you off in town, so you can buy three bras and six nappies, cloth not disposable."

"What?"

"Six... "

"Yes, yes, I heard! Why, for Christ's sake?"

"Ah, surprise!"

I groaned. "Wouldn't it have made more sense for Janet to buy them?"

"Didn't want the girls to know."

"Hmff!" Further explanation - if, indeed, it had been forthcoming, was curtailed by our arrival in Haverfordwest.

"See you later, by the bridge at the bottom of the main street," said Jake, as I clambered out.

"What time?"

"Oh, an hour should be plenty."

Jake and his schemes! I doubted whether the town was big enough to have one of those amorphous department stores where I could 'accidentally' creep into the lingerie department. I wondered whether bras actually counted as lingerie. Was there a Mothercare shop? Would they even cater for the mother's clothing as well as the baby's needs?

I wandered up and down the two main shopping streets.

Boots! Yes, they'd probably sell nappies.

"I'd like six nappies, please," I asked the young female assistant.

"We only sell them in packs of five," she said.

"Um, okay. Two packs then." And as I was paying, I asked, discretely, "Can you tell me where I can buy a bra?"

She looked at me oddly. "For your wife, is it?"

"Yes, yes," I replied, trying to hide my blushes.

"Turn left out of here, and just go straight across the next road. You'll find the shop. It's called Women's Own."

"Thank you," I gabbled, and hurried away. I glanced back briefly to see the lass talking to her colleague, point in my direction and shake her head.

Women's Own was a short way along a street I hadn't hitherto explored. There was no mistaking its purpose. The window was full of slim mannequins scantily dressed in sexy underwear and see-through dresses. A bell rang as I entered the shop.

Deep breath. I approached the counter. From behind a curtained partition appeared a shapely young woman with ivory skin every bit as perfect as her mannequins in the window. It must have cost a fortune at her hairdresser's to set her mass of copper red hair into such intricate waves and curls. Her matching dress barely covered her ample cleavage.

"Yes sir?" she said.

The objects of my desire were all too clearly displayed before me but even so I found my voice with difficulty. "I want to buy three bras," I croaked.

"What size?" she asked without batting an eyelid.

"E ..." Jake hadn't specified and I hadn't asked. "My wife... she didn't say."

"I see." She looked at the packs of nappies under my arm. "Is she nursing?"

"No, she's a teacher."

She pursed her lips briefly in frustration. "Is she breast-feeding your baby?"

"What? No... I'm sorry... I mean... yes," I stammered, as my mind made the fictional connection.

"Right." I'm sure she thought she was dealing with an imbecile or a pervert. "Now we just need to get the right size."

Large, medium, or small? God, how was I supposed to know whether Jake had big or small boobs in mind? I made a decision on the basis of what you see is what you get. "Very similar to you," I said.

She actually smiled briefly. "Very well, sir. Plain or fancy?"

"Plain and simple will do." I was anxious to get the transaction settled. "Oh, and could you wrap them, please?"

She gave me a carrier bag with the shop's name and logo boldly displayed. I stuffed it under my arm and acquired another plain bag from a nearby mini-market, together with a pack of sandwiches. I hadn't had any lunch.

I barely had time to finish them before Jake pulled up.

"Got them okay?" he said.

"Uh huh," I said and thrust the bag into his arms. Under other circumstances he would have had a lot more than chapter and verse from me. I scrambled into the back of the minibus.

"Rob! Great to see you again!" Sophie gave me a hug.

"You too," I said, "and Kissy. You're both looking gorgeous." I noticed the ring on Kissy's finger. "You're engaged?"

"Yes. You met my fiancé briefly in the Chinese restaurant last summer. You were with Liz, weren't you?"

"Uh huh," I acknowledged. My wild aspirations had actually been for Kissy and I to have a date but bizarre circumstances had brought myself and Liz Burke, a pleasant but lonely fellow student. together on her birthday. "Congratulations! Have you named the day?"

"Not yet. We're working to save up money for a house first."

I said 'Hi' to Sean and April, and shook hands with Dicky and Dan. We all chatted as old friends do all the way back to the camp site, where Huw and Min were there to greet us with hugs and kisses. I was surprised to see he had shaved off his beard.

They'd been busy setting up the camp. Two large army-issue tents were available to sleep those of each sex who had not brought their own canvas. I'd taken up Janet's invitation to share her small hiking tent, while Jestyn and Posy had evidently made similar arrangements. Holly and Harry claimed the third small tent. And Dilly was definitely among the party.

Um.

"Hi Rob," she said. But she didn't seek to embrace me.

"Hi, Dilly, what a surprise!" Which truly it was. "How did you get here? You told me you weren't coming."

"That was what Stephen wanted. I got fed up of him

telling me what I could and couldn't do. I decided I really wanted to get out and have some fun. And I did enjoy the practice evening with Carpiog."

I wasn't sure whether I was intended to feature in her fun. She picked up some concern in my expression. "Don't worry, Rob," she said, "I've had a long chat with Janet. I'm not going to come between you two." She paused. "You - and strangely, Stephen too - have restored a lot of my self-confidence, and I'm keen to get on with my life. You'll always be a part of it - as a dear friend."

Min led us into a small marquee where tables and chairs had been set up. "Make yourself at home, and help yourself to food and drink." At the far end a generator powered a fridge and hot water urn. Calor gas supplied a small stove. On a long table were packets of cereals, fruit and rolls, and for us recently arrived hungry travellers the ample remains of a buffet of sandwiches and pasties. And a barrel of beer.

"Bit more civilised than our previous visit," Kissy said to me. "Proper toilet block with washbasins and showers. I thought we might have to put up with those disgusting earth closet loos and cold water."

"Jake did provide hot water showers," I said.

"Yeah, from a watering can in a toilet tent!"

Jake called all the company together. "Now we're all here," he began.

"Isn't Rud supposed to be coming?" I interjected.

"Travelling down first thing tomorrow, apparently," said Jake. "You'll want to know what the programme is for the weekend."

Nods of agreement - or anticipation.

"This evening we'll split up. We lads will take Huw down into Little Haven for his stag night. Also sort out a couple of things for tomorrow." He winked at me. I suspected my unusual purchases might feature in that sorting. "Min and the girls will do their own thing. Got to keep the two lovebirds apart until the proper time, haven't we?"

Huw and Min held each other more closely.

"Tomorrow morning, we'll all dance down at the pubs in Little Haven, then make our way to the church for the wedding ceremony."

Dicky put his hand up. "Are we dancing at the church as well?"

"'Fraid not," Huw answered, "If you've seen the church, there's absolutely no room inside or out, and the road is very narrow."

"But we will form a guard of honour with our sticks when the newlyweds come out of the church," said Jake. "And we will dance at the reception. That will be at a barn at Huw's parents' farm. It's very close."

"Not here, then?" I asked. I'd assumed that was the main purpose of the marquee.

"Too small," said Huw. "This is for you all to chill out. Not enough room to seat everybody and certainly not enough space for the ceilidh."

"Any questions?" said Jake. "Yes, Sophie?"

"What about Sunday? Anything planned?"

"Aspirins at breakfast, probably. Then, really, it's just wind down. Depends what time people need to be away. Survivors' pub lunch, I guess."

"What time do we set out this evening?" Dan asked,

"Gather here at, say, six o'clock." Jake looked at his watch. "That gives you a couple of hours free to do whatever you want. Go for a walk, go for a swim perhaps – the beach is about ten or fifteen minutes' walk."

I sought out Janet. "Thanks very much for putting the tent up. I would have helped you."

"No problem. You weren't expecting to see Dilly here, were you?"

"I certainly wasn't." I agreed. "She told me she'd had a chat with you."

"Yes, very interesting, poor lass. She has left Stephen, thank goodness. She hitched her way to Haverfordwest."

"Really?"

"And she told me about the real reason for wanting to visit you back in the Spring and what happened when you met up in Aberystwyth. I had no idea."

"It didn't seem appropriate to go into all the details," I said lamely.

"Rob, you really are such a gentleman. You could have taken advantage of her. I wouldn't have known. Suspected perhaps. But she's adamant that she sees you as a good friend not a partner."

"Yes, she said as much to me, just now."

"I'm glad for all our sakes," said Janet. "By the way, what did Jake want you for?"

"You don't really want to know now. You'll find out tomorrow. Promise!"

A smaller minibus, complete with female chauffeur, arrived soon after six o'clock to transport the ladies to wherever they were planning to go. Though Jake was all for leaving our minibus and walking down the hill to the seaside village, Jestyn offered to drive. "I don't drink," he said. The thought of a stiff climb back up to the campsite removed the only mild objection from Jake that Jestyn might not be covered by the insurance.

First port of call was the Castle Inn, right next to the sandy beach in the small cove. Early evening it was still quiet, since the day trippers had already gone home and the holidaymakers were no doubt sitting down to dinner at their guest houses. Jake had a word with the landlord and led us into the back room.

"Couple of dances I'd like you to try out," he said. "Put on a surprise show tomorrow at the ceilidh. Not a word to Min, though, Huw. Or from the rest of you!" For a side whose repertoire hitherto had only involved stick dances, having to coordinate arm movements with non-rigid items in our hands didn't come naturally. Even more so when pairs of dancers were physically linked together by one such item. Fortunately Jake had kept the figures and foot movements within our previous experience, and, after an hour or so and a couple of pints, we were reasonably confident, if not proficient.

"Where on earth did you get those dances from?" wheezed Dicky, obviously out of condition from lack of dancing since he'd left college.

"Had a long chat with Gron, and we went through his black book, as he called it. Plus a few ideas of my own."

I could guess which bits weren't in Gron's black book.

"Next pub," said Jake. "Need to sort some details there."

"No more dances, I hope," said Harry. "My brain hurts."

"Not to mention our legs!" said Dan.

We traipsed round the corner to the rather quaint St Brides Inn. Just a pint there, since any hopes Jake had for getting a session going was rather dashed by the loud chatter from the goodly number of people in the pub.

It was still daylight when we emerged, though the sun was getting low out across the bay, reflecting off the calm waters in the cove.

"I've been thinking," said Dicky. "You remember when we were down here last, we went skinny-dipping in the dark."

"Bit too public here," I said.

"No, we could go up to that place we were at before. Nobody else there."

Jake turned to Huw, "What do you think?"

"Well, it's not that far up to Nolton Haven, if Jestyn's happy to drive. We could miss out the Swan here and have a pint in the Mariners instead."

"Okay with me," said Jestyn, "But you'll have to tell me the way. I don't know these roads at all."

By the time we'd meandered slowly along the minor roads to the hamlet of Nolton Haven, it was already dusk.

"Seems we've been beaten to it," said Jake as we pulled into the car park. A familiar minibus was already parked there. Nevertheless we climbed out of our vehicle.

"Couldn't we..."

"I don't think it would be appropriate, Dan," said Huw. Across the beach we could see several people bathing in the sea. It was too far and too dark to see any detail but we could hear their female voices. "I suggest we head back to the pub at Broad Haven - or there's still beer at the camp site."

Reluctantly, we concurred. But as we opened the van doors we heard a raucous male voice. "Hey, fellas, come and get an eyeful of this! Looks like a load of naked girls in the water."

Three youths staggered out of the pub to join their companion on the shingle at the top of the beach. We could hear their lewd comments.

Huw was off like a shot, followed by the rest of us. I grabbed a couple of morris sticks. The loudmouths began to move towards the sand. We outflanked them and stood in a line in front of them.

"What the f***?" yelled the lout who'd first noticed the girls.

"No further, lads," said Huw, grimly.

"Jealous are you?" sneered the same bloke. "Tell you what, we'll leave some totty for you."

"They are our friends," said Huw, "Now back off."

"Oh yeah?" He made to dash past us. Dicky stuck out his leg and sent him sprawling.

"You f***" he snarled, "I'll..."

"You'll go back up to the road and get lost!" Huw said forcefully.

"And if we don't?"

"Do you really want to find out?" said Huw. We began

to move towards the four pissheads. I passed one stick to Jestyn and grabbed mine firmly. I hoped it would not be necessary to use it.

"Aw, leave it, Griff," one of the other guys said. "Not worth the hassle."

Griff glared at us then turned to follow his companions, still swearing and cursing. They began to trudge up the hill, in the opposite direction to the way we'd come.

I breathed a sigh of relief. Resisting the temptation for my eyes to linger, I glanced just briefly towards the shore line, where the girls were crouching down so that the water covered their nakedness. Except Min, who rushed up to Huw, sea water dripping from her body, and clung tightly to him.

"Back to the bus, lads," said Jake. "Let's respect the ladies' privacy."

We'd lost the enthusiasm for a pub crawl and headed straight - or as straight as the roads permitted - back to the camp site, dropping Huw off at his parents' house on the way. "My last night at home as a single man," he said wryly. And he also needed to get out of his damp clothes.

We'd downed probably half the barrel by the time the girls turned up with a distinct whiff of curry in the air.

"Starving, we were," said Min. "Just been into town for a takeaway."

It was quite some time later that we all began to feel drowsy and, aware of a full day to come, I wriggled into my sleeping bag, close to Janet's.

"Thank you, Sir Galahad, for coming to our rescue," she murmured, and kissed me goodnight.

Bleary-eyed sleepwalkers scantily though modestly clad probably best described those of us shuffling round the marquee next morning in search of a caffeine fix. All except Jake, of course, who always seemed to appear bright and breezy no matter how much alcohol he'd consumed the night before.

"Minibus leaving at ten-thirty sharp. Full kit. Room for all of you unless you want to walk." Grunts of acknowledgement greeted Jake's announcement.

"What would you like me to do?" Benji asked "I've never really been into the dancing."

"Would you be happy to take charge of Ewegenie?" Jake suggested. "You don't have to dance, just wander around."

He shrugged, "Okay, I suppose." He didn't sound over-enthusiastic. He'd probably been hoping he'd have a role in the church service.

"He could always pretend he's the Lamb of God," I whispered to Janet.

Never before had Carpiog Morris had such an impressive turnout, with more than a dozen dancers plus musicians. In view of the formal proceedings later we'd dispensed completely with any face paint. It wouldn't have been right for Min to risk smearing blacking over her wedding dress, nor for any of us principal characters in the ceremony to face a similar embarrassment when we togged up later.

We worked pretty much through our whole repertoire, apart from Jake's new dances, in front of the Castle Inn, gathering an appreciative, though transient audience. The display wasn't perfect by any means, since those past members had to rake their memories and one or two new recruits hadn't really got the movements in their head anyway. Nevertheless I doubt if anyone unfamiliar with border morris would have noticed, since we managed to avoid dancers colliding. Just a few interesting variations on the proper notations.

Jake's original intention had been for us to dance at each of the three pubs. We decided to give the Swan a miss when we saw the very restricted space and uneven surface between the entrance to The Swan and the harbour wall - actually 'harbour' would be exaggerating, since there was just a slipway to a sandy beach.

Our performance in the street outside the St. Bride's Inn was much more confident, boosted by a pint and re-awakened brain cells. Strange, though, how a quiet road suddenly becomes a major thoroughfare as soon as one starts a lengthy dance. Fortunately the motorists were patient and allowed us to finish without blasting their horns. With the prospect of a slap-up meal later in the afternoon we hadn't really made any plans for lunch, but it would have been churlish to refuse the landlord's donation of bowls of chips.

"Take your time finishing your drinks," Jake said. "Some of us have to get changed."

The landlord had agreed to let Jake, Huw and me use a room at the pub to change into our best suits, while Min, Sophie and Kissy returned to the Castle, where a similar arrangement had been made. I wasn't sure how the four of us were supposed to get to the church when Jake prepared to leave with the rest of the gang, still in morris kit, and a bundle of raggies and bells from those of us now more formally attired.

"Your transport will be here shortly," he said. "Don't worry."

After a few minutes standing incongruously outside the Castle looking as if we'd been left in the lurch, a pony and trap appeared, both bedecked with white and pink flowery garlands. The driver, Huw's cousin I was later told, was dressed for the part, with a shiny black topper. He dismounted to help us clamber aboard.

Just as he jerked the reins to set off, we heard a frantic voice, "Hey, Rob, wait! Wait for me!"

I looked back as Rud, looking, well, very ruddy-cheeked and out of breath, rushed up to us from the direction of the St Bride's pub.

"Oh thank God," he gasped, as we hauled him up into

the carriage.

"What happened?" I said.

"Got a taxi from the station. Couldn't remember the name of the church but I told him to take me to the one in Little Haven."

"So what was the problem?"

"Dunno. He dropped me off at the top of the hill back there and shot off. Little church in the middle of bugger all, all locked up and no-one there. Didn't know what to do, so I started walking - bloody miles it seemed - down here. And then I saw you."

The coachman, who'd heard the exchange, turned and said, "I think I know what happened. Little Haven is split between two parishes, divided by the stream. He took you to St Mary's. The wedding is at All Saints, just up this road."

We'd begun to climb the steep hill out of the village. I looked at my watch. We still had twenty minutes before the scheduled 2.30 pm start of the wedding service. Plenty of time, though it would be slow going. To lighten the load Rud and I offered to walk but the coachman assured us that the pony would cope.

But there was no way a pony and trap was going to get past a car coming the other way. The middle-aged woman driver in the Ford Escort had to slam the brakes on, and luckily managed to stop about ten yards in front of us. She was sitting there waving her hands and showing no inclination to reverse.

"I'll have a word with her," I offered.

She was not happy. "You've no business being on the road!" she ranted. "You'll have to go back!"

"We have every right to use this road, madam," I said. "Please reverse back to the junction." Which I could see about fifty yards or so behind her.

"I am not reversing!" she insisted.

"Well, you're certainly not going forward. It is not

possible for us to go backwards and we do not have enough space to turn."

"I'm not used to reversing."

"You have passed your test, I presume?"

"Don't be impertinent, young man, of course I have!"

"Then you will know how to reverse." I was beginning to lose patience with the silly woman. "Look, as you can see, we have the bride and bridesmaids for a wedding which is due to start..." I looked at my watch again, "... in five minutes time. You wouldn't want to ruin their day, would you?"

"Hmmph! Oh very well." She ground the gears into reverse, and, revving furiously while slipping the clutch, zigzagged wildly for a short distance before stopping again. I detected an acrid smell and was worried that she'd burn out the clutch before she got to the junction.

She was sitting holding her head in her hands. Oh God!

"Would you like me to back the car up for you?" I offered. "I am used to driving along narrow lanes like this." I added.

"I think that might be best," she conceded.

I took her place in the driving seat, and with Rud acting as an advanced look-out for other approaching traffic I carefully eased the car back up to the junction.

"I think, Rud, it would be a good idea for you to keep ahead of us. We don't want another such delay."

As it happened, it was well past the appointed hour when the organist struck up the music for our entry. Jake scurried back to his place beside Huw.

Carpiog Morris occupied the pews on one side of the aisle, with Huw's extended family on the other. Several other people, presumably friends of the family, were seated in the lower-roofed gallery to one side. It felt really strange walking up the aisle as an honorary father to a girl only a year or two younger than me. But I felt very proud to be given the honour. The officiating clergyman also thought it a little strange, I think, as I saw him wrinkle his brow as we approached. It was difficult to keep a dry eye as Wilhelmina Smith and Huw Parry-Evans exchanged their betrothal vows and rings.

The congregation - or at least one side - raised the roof with 'Lord of The Dance' while the register was signed and witnessed.

Huw and Min emerged into the bright sunshine and an arch of morris sticks carried by Carpiog members perching on the grassy banks on either side of the narrow sunken pathway. Min made sure that they all got a kiss - the dancers kneeling down and Min stretching up on tiptoe. Most of the party spilled out into the road to give the photographer enough space to take all the traditional photos. He may have even managed to get the coast at Broad Haven into the wider-angle shots.

The pony and trap pulled out of a driveway opposite the church gate, followed by a decorated tractor and flat wagon to carry the dancers and any other able-bodied person to the reception. Jake used the minibus, which he'd parked next to a couple of other private cars in the field adjacent to the church to transport the older and less mobile guests.

Huw's parents had gone to town by transforming a humble barn into a banqueting hall fit for a king - the concrete floor scrupulously cleaned to leave no trace whatsoever of its former bovine occupants, and the wooden slatted walls draped with white finery. Like an elongated capital E, three tables stretched down the barn at right angles to the top table, all covered with immaculate white table cloths. Vases of fresh roses sat between the place settings for the feast.

And what a feast! A local seafood starter, home-reared beef, roasted to perfection and served with all the trimmings, strawberry pavlova, cheese and biscuits, and the wine flowed freely. Plenty of Dutch courage to prepare myself for the speech I was expected to make, but I also needed to remain sober enough to deliver it.

Though there was probably some sort of protocol for the order of speeches, Jake, Huw and I had tossed for it. I drew the first straw. I promised to keep it short.

"Ladies and Gentlemen," I began, "It is customary for the bride's father to address the wedding guests. You will no doubt have realised that I am not Min's father." I paused for the titters of laughter. "The fact is that Min lost her parents many years ago. She doesn't have any family at all with whom she is still in contact. Carpiog Morris and her friends from college are her adopted family. And now she is so fortunate to be the newest member of the Parry-Evans family."

Cheers and applause.

"One advantage, of course, in asking me to give her away and be, in effect, her honorary father for the day, is that I can't embarrass her by telling stories of all the mischief she no doubt got up to as a little girl. And I'm not going to embarrass her by recalling the mischief she got up to at College."

More chuckles.

"Just you dare," she whispered. I didn't think she'd appreciate Huw or the world knowing about the time she'd stripped naked before me and then promptly fallen asleep in a drunken stupor after I'd given her a lift back to her college rooms following a morris party. I'd behaved honourably and not taken advantage of the situation.

"What I can say is that from the first time she turned up at morris practice searching for fertility rites, she's been a right inspiration to us all, with her cheerfulness, enthusiasm and love of life. The fertile ground for the love between Huw and Min to grow came in no small part, I believe, from the kindliness and affection shown by Huw's parents when they cared for her after her horrific accident two years ago. I am sure I speak for all of us when I say we are so proud and happy to be here today to celebrate your wedding. Ladies and gentlemen, please raise your glasses in a toast to Min and Huw as we wish them the very best of happiness in their future life together."

After the clapping, I sat down. I felt I could relax now and enjoy the rest of the day.

Huw was next up, thanking everyone for their good wishes and generosity, thanking his parents, and his best man, myself, and bridesmaids, thanking the caterers, and in advance, the ceilidh band. And ending by thanking Min for agreeing to be his wife.

Jake's main task was to read the telegrams, from various friends and relatives who had been unable to attend the wedding. "One here from Cher and Gus," he announced, "Short and sweet, 'Our best wishes.'"

"Christ!" Min whispered, "they're my cousins! Wonder how the hell they got to hear about it?"

"Announcements in the paper?" I suggested.

"But they live up north, nowhere near here."

I shrugged, "Who knows? Chance encounter, perhaps. I shouldn't worry."

"I won't. Thanks... Dad," she giggled.

The band arrived as we finished our coffee and the tables were being cleared away. Tom's Twmpath had kindly offered to play just for expenses in appreciation for us coming to the rescue at the PTA barn dance, and perhaps some guilt on Tom the caller's part on letting us down at short notice at the booking - our one and only so far - of the Accidentals. Though his broken leg, the cause of his withdrawal, had healed, he was still limping. They set up on a wagon at the far end of the barn. A few hay bales had been placed in front of the rustic stage.

The ceilidh was soon in full swing and despite discarding jacket, waistcoat and tie at the earliest opportunity I was soon sweating like a pig. I caught one dance with Dilly, though it seemed as if Dan had hitched up with her for the evening. Sitting on a hay bale, Rud had his arms around April. Huw and Min flopped down next to Janet and me at the end of a particularly energetic dance.

"Are you staying till the end?" I asked.

"Why wouldn't we?" said Min.

"Well, I wondered if you would be heading off on honeymoon,"

"And miss all this fun? Not likely!"

"We're staying at the farm tonight," said Huw, "And we'll be off tomorrow morning."

"And, no, we're not telling your where!" said Min.

Jake was waving furiously at me. "Gotta go," I said. "Oh, and I think he needs you as well, Huw,"

"Get your raggies and bells on, Rob, we're just about to do our new dances."

Huw retrieved his bagpipes, and after a few squawks and squeaks as he filled the leather bag, he launched into the tune we were told was called 'Getting Upstairs'. Six of us formed up in two lines of three, and as Jake called, "this time" we raised our inside arms to show a bra held between each pair, and started stepping. A few gasps of astonishment but mostly guffaws of laughter and then steady clapping in time with the music as we moved side by side and back to back in pairs and attempted a 'dip and dive' figure with pairs going over and under the suspended bras. It worked well the first time – and again, but on the third attempt someone tried to go over while his partner went under and the bras got irretrievably knotted together. The music grunted to a halt as Huw found it impossible to blow and laugh at the same time.

"And now the consequence of 'Getting Upstairs', Jake announced, "The men of Carpiog Morris give you... Pram Pushing!"

The set reformed with a couple of substitutes. Bearing huge white terry-towelling nappies, the dancers thrust them forward and waved them around at head height in a selection of figures that bore a vague resemblance to one of our stick dances.

After the applause had died down, Tom was preparing to start the next ceilidh dance when Janet came on with her accordion.

"Hold on a moment," she said. "The ladies of Carpiog Morris have also got a new dance. We call it 'Min's Delight'."

Led by Min, still in her wedding dress but with bells strapped around her legs, the girls processed on with make-believe bagpipes consisting of a balloon under their left arm and a short stick as the chanter. They danced first in columns then in a large circle around Huw, beating the balloons above their heads, finally bursting them all together in an explosive finish.

"Brilliant," I said to Janet when she came over to me after the performance. "Your brainwave?"

"More or less, though it was Min who came up with the bagpipe balloon idea."

"Your tune, though?" I hadn't heard it before.

"No, it's a Manx tune I learned, called 'Mona's Delight'. Near enough."

Some of the older guests began to leave during the evening but we kept going until, approaching midnight, Tom called all those remaining up for the last big circle dance.

No way Jake - or anyone else - was sober enough to drive either minibus or wagon, so it was Shanks's pony for us campers. But earlier that day someone had had the foresight to prepare a couple of flaming torches out of splintered morris sticks to light our way the few hundred yards along the lane to the camping field.

"Just don't get any idea about practising stick chucking," I said to Jake who led the procession.

Jake suggested we could finish off the beer in the

marquee but we were all pretty much knackered and made for our respective tents.

Lying close to each other in our sleeping bags, Janet said softly, "That was such a lovely day, Rob. Wish we could do it all over again."

"Perhaps we can," I said.

"What do you mean?" she murmured.

"If you were to marry me."

She put her arms round me. "You lovely man, I thought you were never going to ask."

Mr. & Mrs. Arthur Milward
kindly invite you to celebrate the

Wedding

of their daughter   Janet Louise
to   Robert Edward Kiddecott
at
St. Mary de Haura Church
Shoreham-by-Sea
2.00 pm
Saturday 10th April 1976

and to the reception at St Mary's Hall

AUTHOR'S NOTES

After my first novel, A Matter of Degree, was published in 2011, a number of readers asked if I was working on a sequel, as they wanted to know what happened next. I hadn't really considered the idea hitherto but I decided that there was indeed the potential for a follow-up. A Matter of Degree had an obvious start and finish point, covering the three years of the degree course of the principal character, but how far to follow his subsequent career was a decision over which I deliberated for some time. One year seemed to be the most appropriate. This novel is therefore rather shorter than its predecessor. It is once again set during the mid-1970s in the fictional towns of Tencastle and Carrick Major, in central Wales. Tencastle is on the heart of Wales railway line and the setting for a teacher training college attached to the University of Wales. Most other locations mentioned are real.

While a few of the incidents described in this book are loosely based on some personal experiences, the novel is entirely fiction, and no reference to any person living or deceased is intended.

Carpiog Morris (the name means 'ragged', in reference to the raggy jackets of their costume) would have been one of the very first mixed Border morris sides in the country. Reference is made to the Ring book - this is A Handbook of Morris Dancing, by Lionel Bacon, published by the Morris Ring in 1974. The Morris Ring is the original national organization for morris teams (or 'sides') and until recently was restricted to teams with exclusively male members. The Rev. Kenneth Loveless, Area Dean of Hackney until his retirement in 1976, was elected Squire of the Morris Ring in 1980. The other two national morris organizations are The Morris Federation and Open Morris.

The first ferry crossing between Plymouth and Roscoff was in 1973. I was a member of a combined party of Plymouth Morris Men and Exeter Morris Men that travelled to Brittany the following year. The unicorn and dragon mentioned as mascots for morris sides belong to Westminster Morris Men and Chanctonbury Ring Morris Men (my first morris side!) respectively. When I joined them they used to practice close to where I lived in Shoreham-by-Sea.

There was a thriving weekly traditional folk song club at the Jolly Porter pub, near to St David's station, Exeter, during the sixties and seventies. Some of the resident singers from that time are still running a monthly session on the outskirts of the city. The Railway Hotel at Crediton, which used to host a folk club, was converted very many years ago into private accommodation.

The pubs mentioned in Little Haven, Nolton Haven and Shoreham-by-Sea are real. The church described in the wedding is situated in Walton West but whilst its outline on the front cover is quite realistic, some artistic license has been taken in location.

I would like to thank my friends, Susie Golightly for her constructive comments on the narrative as the novel developed, and Mecki Testroet for proof reading of the first draft of the complete novel. Many thanks also to Jeremy Child and Barbara Brown for further detailed proof reading, and to Annette Shilling for the cover illustrations.

Colin Andrews
February 2018

Colin took early retirement from teaching in 1995. He lives with his wife, Sonja, in mid-Devon. He is a folksinger, a barn dance caller and musician, and an active member of Winkleigh Morris and Exeter Morris Men. Further details on his website: www.bonnygreen.co.uk

OTHER BOOKS BY COLIN ANDREWS

SHATTERED PRETENSIONS (Matador, 2015) Two very different stories in which the actions of a young teacher have devastating consequences. In **'Fragile'**, a headmaster standing as a parliamentary candidate is reluctant to answer questions about his wife's mysterious disappearance many years earlier. The main story, **'Out Of This World'**, focuses on the tensions generated among teenage students participating in an extended role-play exercise.

WHO GIVES A HOOT (New Generation, 2014) A collection of short stories and poems, some set to music, which offer a wry and mostly amusing view of aspects of modern life.

A MATTER OF DEGREE (Matador, 2011). The precursor to 'One Degree Over' follows the comical and dramatic exploits of Robert Kiddecott and Jacob Moses through the three years to graduation at fictional teacher training college in Mid-Wales during the early seventies.

SHEPHERD OF THE DOWNS (1979, 1987, 2006) Non fiction. The life and songs of Sussex shepherd, Michael Blann, whose hand-written notebook of songs is in Worthing Museum. The first two editions were published by Worthing Museum. The third edition also includes a CD.

A direct link to Colin's fiction titles is www.colinandrewsauthor.co.uk, while full information and ordering details for all of Colin's publications and recordings can be found on his main website: www.bonnygreen.co.uk.